Praise for *Jane Is Trying*

'I LOVED *Jane Is Trying*. It ha
wit and turn of phrase I fell in
forming'

T0286376

Jane Is Trying is Isy Suttie's first novel but her voice has the easy, warm confidence of someone who's been at the lark for yonks; slyly funny, gently incisive, compassionate yes but with just enough wicked accuracy about the process of growing up and getting things wrong to make it painfully true'   Stuart Maconie

'Big-hearted, stacked with empathy, and properly splutter-coffee funny. A book so full of love that there ought to be a huggable version of it. Isy goes from warm-hearted to outrageous so deftly that I think she might have special powers. WHAT a book. How many times can I say 'brilliant'?'   Jason Hazeley

'A hilarious and touching story about going backwards in order to move forwards, imbued with Isy Suttie's unique voice and outlook on our stressful, ridiculous world'
                                      James Acaster

'Sharp, tender, darkly funny and so well observed'
                                      Daisy Buchanan

'Gripping, laugh out loud funny and heart-warming. Suttie has created a charming world of oddballs (and their even odder parents) I miss them all already!'   Sara Pascoe

'This is a very entertaining book but it's a lot more than a comic novel. It has real heart and humanity and goes deep into the anxieties of pregnancy, relationships, home, and (in Jane's case) pretty much every other aspect of life'
Mark Watson

'A phenomenally funny, thoughtful and, at times, pulverising novel'
Mike Wozniak

'Isy Suttie writes with a warmth and wit that makes me want to move to the Peak District and open a bookshop'
Josh Widdicombe

'Suttie brightens the page with her eccentric characters and wonderful observations of small-town life . . . will have you scoffing with laughter'
Stylist

'Some of Jane's musings are so relatable you'll catch yourself laughing out loud, slightly alarmed by the accuracy . . . Suttie portrays the more honest aspects of what are usually regarded as the best parts of life – family, relationships, friends, career – with the perfect concoction of warmth and grit'
i Newspaper

'Suttie has a keen eye for supplementary detail, which makes her story seem all the more real, and an ear for a nice turn of phrase, which makes it delightful to read'
Chortle

'Funny and so relatable, this is a winning debut'   *Heat*

Also by Isy Suttie

The Actual One

JANE IS TRYING

Isy Suttie

WEIDENFELD & NICOLSON

First published in Great Britain in 2021 by Weidenfeld & Nicolson
This paperback edition published in Great Britain in 2022
by Weidenfeld & Nicolson,
an imprint of The Orion Publishing Group Ltd
Carmelite House, 50 Victoria Embankment
London EC4Y 0DZ

An Hachette UK Company

1 3 5 7 9 10 8 6 4 2

A CIP catalogue record for this book is
available from the British Library.

ISBN (Mass Market Paperback) 978 1 4746 0107 8
ISBN (eBook) 978 1 4746 0000 2
ISBN (Audio) 978 1 4091 7096 9

Typeset by Input Data Services Ltd, Somerset

Printed in Great Britain by Clays Ltd, Elcograf S.p.A.

www.weidenfeldandnicolson.co.uk
www.orionbooks.co.uk

For Caroline and Hannah

Summer

Chapter One

'God, sorry, Stuart,' I gasped, bursting through the door, a half-eaten chicken drumstick gripped between my teeth.

I'd taken to gauging Stuart's mood from whereabouts his glasses were perched on his nose – something that had served me well so far. Today they were pushed right up past the bridge, his eyelashes brushing the insides of the lenses. This meant he was energised, jumpy.

'Mum took her keys to evensong,' I said. 'And they might be in bed when I get back – Mum and Dad, not the keys – so I had to wait for her to run down from church and give them to me.' Stuart looked blank. 'So I don't wake them up later,' I added. I knew Mum was secretly glad to have nipped home. Going to church in the evening always felt a bit wrong, she said, like eating pizza for breakfast. 'I'll get some cut at some point,' I said, chucking the chicken drumstick in the bin behind the counter.

Stuart jerked his head down sharply so that his glasses jumped onto the end of his nose. This was a new move, and I didn't know what it meant. 'Well, here you are now,' he said, hauling himself out from behind the counter. He looked at my mouth and shoulders rather than my eyes, which meant he was warming up. He was going to forgive me. I wasn't going to lose my job for being half an hour late.

I'd only worked three shifts in the bookshop, but already, being with Stuart was like putting on an old pair of slippers. There might be a bit of Lego stuck inside one, but you knew any discomfort was easily resolved. His sulks floated on top of him like petrol in a puddle.

'OK,' he said, 'one of us needs to go across to the pub for wine, and extra chairs, and punters maybe? No, no, no, not punters. We're not that desperate.' He trudged across the shop floor. 'You go? No, I'll go. You'll hurt your back with the chairs. Well, you might. I might. It doesn't matter. I'll carry them in stacks of four. We might only need four. Two. None. No one'll come. It's too warm out.' He opened the door. 'She'll be here in a minute. She only drinks Pinot Noir, apparently. Not even tea. These bloody poets.'

I watched him cross the narrow road to the pub opposite, The Rainbow's End. I hoped punters were going to come, for his sake. My window display was perfect, written in my best calligraphy: *Fenella Burch. Foodie and Wordie Poetry Reading and Book Signing. Tuesday night, 7 p.m.* I'd even made a fried egg and saucepan out of tissue paper.

Squinting at the screen so I couldn't see what it said, I placed my mobile onto the counter, face down. *It doesn't matter if he's texted or not*, I said to myself. *Breathe in for six, out for eight.* My eyes were so swollen from crying I'd had to apply two layers of make-up. Patting my fingers to my face, I could already feel the cracks forming in the powder as I glanced around.

The room I was in – the main bit of the bookshop – contained fiction. A rickety staircase led to the upper floor, which consisted of tiny rooms full of books on everything from origami to local history, plus the customer toilet – complete with a working bath, which books were normally stacked in – and our kitchen. I wasn't too enamoured with the hygiene implications of the bath being used as a storage unit, but I wasn't in a position to complain. Stuart lived in a little cottage behind the shop but spent most of his waking hours in the shop itself. He was fastidious about books being in the right place, which was lucky, because we had so many of them. They were packed into the wooden shelves, crammed into display stands, piled in boxes labelled *Valentine's present for someone you loved six years ago* and *Buy one of these books for your parents and you'll get more in their will than your brother.*

Stuart and I had conducted the 'interview' right here at the counter, with me standing awkwardly, like a customer. Dad had stayed in the corner with his back to us, like he was in an odd remake of *The Blair Witch Project*, leafing through books and tapping his foot out of time to the Debussy in his head. I kept wondering when the interview element was going to start, and afterwards realised that it had just happened. All I'd said to secure my new job was that the only book I'd read in the last three years was Sharon Osbourne's autobiography, and that I loved sniffing the centres of second-hand books. And one of these was a lie – I hadn't actually finished Sharon's book yet.

'Mum said the vicar looked a bit annoyed when she got up and left to give me the keys,' I said, when Stuart returned with the stools from the pub. 'Can't blame him,

I suppose. She *was* in the middle of playing "Guide Me, O Thou Great Redeemer".'

'Well, that vicar's a spy, I reckon,' Stuart said. 'We think he's just concentrating on his sudoku, but he's taking it all in. He knows when his disciples are having their windows cleaned, what kind of mortgages they've got.'

'Not like God needs to know all that,' I replied.

'Maybe he does,' sang Stuart. 'I am weak but thou art mighty, dah dah dah dah something hand.'

This was often how conversations with Stuart ended: him saying, '. . . Maybe *something something*,' and then there was a feeling that you just had to shut up. Adding anything else was like when someone buys a sambuca no one wants at the end of the night.

'I've never been to a book launch,' I confessed. My only experience of launching books had occurred on the last day of A-level exams, when my best friend Megan and I had lobbed all our schoolbooks into the river, screeching and clutching one another as *Tricolores* and Jane Austens sailed over our heads into the thrashing water. 'So long, Foley!' we'd screamed that day. 'We're out of here, you losers!'

'It's not a *launch*,' said Stuart, sellotaping a balloon to a shelf. 'That was in Sheffield. It's just a reading. She'll read some poems, you'll ask some questions, she'll sign some books. Then pub. Pub, pub, pub.'

Me ask some questions? 'Hey, listen,' I said. 'What's this? You're the book guy. I can't ask the questions.' I felt barely able to get through the evening as it was.

'The last time *I* asked some questions at a book launch,' he replied, winding Sellotape slowly round his finger, 'Foley Joe ended up raiding the stage with his guitar, then

I got so pissed they found me trying to lick the grey off the pavement. So maybe' – he pushed his glasses right up onto his nose – '*you* should ask some questions.' He mumbled something about getting his money's worth from me, and although his eyes sparkled with mirth, I realised I didn't have a choice in the matter.

'I'll just revise her stuff,' I muttered, grabbing a copy of Fenella's book from the display pile and rushing behind the counter. It wasn't like I hadn't had ample time to read it: we sometimes had two customers an hour. How would the knowledge of Sharon Osbourne's never-ending feud with Dannii Minogue serve me now? I thought frantically about Mum or Dad taking my place. But Mum would be finishing the service, and Dad was still at the office. Within two weeks of arriving back in Foley, I had reverted back to thinking my parents could solve all my problems. My hands shook as I opened the book. I closed it again.

Come on, I told myself. *You can do this in a heartbeat. You're Jane Wildgoose.* I'd stood up and pitched hundreds of times in front of blank faces glued to phones, often having not slept the night before. I'd improvised workshops about the art of advertising copywriting. I'd challenged – and convinced – clients over the best way to communicate that a cake is moist without saying the word 'moist'. What was I possibly scared of about a book event in my tiny hometown, which I only visited a couple of times a year anyway? No, I could do this.

I opened the book more firmly this time. *When Foodie and Wordie Meet/Mate: A Seductive Poem for Every Item in Your Kitchen by Fenella Burch.*

Courgette

Smooth as cream
A cuisinier's dream
Taut and green
Did I see you in a dream?
As field becomes fallow
Courgette begets marrow
Mash, roast or fry
Then I'll kiss you till you cry.

I skimmed through the quotes on the back of the jacket: *Surely a must-have lingual ingredient in every future feminist's kitchen – Time Out.* What? *As risqué and relevant as ever, Fenella's poetry is best consumed raw – The Poetry Guide.* What the fuck? *Relevant – Poetry Train Magazine.* Always suspicious, those one-word quotations. And two *relevants*. I mean, everything was relevant, wasn't it? Even *ir*relevant things were originally relevant. *I* should be a poet. This was all going to be fine. I felt my shoulders relax. Poets were airy people, gracious, and light as gossamer, overjoyed that normal people were taking an interest in them. I flicked to another page.

Anchovies

No
Thankchovies.

Did you pretend not to like anchovies so you could make up the word 'thankchovies'? I wrote on the back of some till-roll paper. I scribbled it out. Better to keep it broad.

Why do you write? I scrawled. *Do you get all your ideas while you're eating? Is it true there's no rhyme for orange?*

*

Cakes and Ladders

I used to bake you cake, my love, I used to bake
    you cake
Then I saw you were a snake, my love! I saw
    you were a snake!
I threw you in a lake, my love, I threw you in a
    lake
And now I stand and eat my cake
While you get scoffed up by a hake
And though I pause to call you fake
I do not miss a single chance to bake for Jake
    he's late I ache for you for him for us for
    them

And now
My
Cakes
Go
STALE.

Fenella slammed the book down onto her knee, glaring at
her audience as if goading them to challenge the fact that
her cakes go stale, perspiration glistening on her forehead.
She'd been sweating since she arrived. She and Clare, a solemn woman she introduced as her 'manager', had crashed
through the door at five to eight, their breathing ragged
and their hats wet with drizzle, a distinct aura of 'hot wet
dog' about them.

Muttering about delayed trains and events in the middle

of nowhere, she'd immediately begun to aggressively shed endless coverings of chiffon and velvet, like a pass-the-parcel that would never be finished. The excited audience had gazed at her, whispering. Tiny trinkets had emerged with the removal of each layer. A Fox's mint rolled onto the floor, followed by a screwed-up tissue, a tube of lip balm, two biros, a sanitary towel, a box of paracetamol, a single raisin.

As I'd taken a final petrified glance at my questions, I'd spied a woman with a string of tinsel around her neck (it was July, but it had been raining earlier, so it could possibly have been acting as a scarf) peruse the floor and lazily pocket the lip balm like she was choosing a prize at a tombola.

This woman comprised a twentieth of the crowd, which was mostly made up of people I had already come to regard as regulars, clutching plastic cups of lukewarm white wine and looking towards Fenella with excruciating apprehension. 'No photos till the end!' Clare had breathed into their bemused faces.

Foley Joe stood next to Stuart beside the counter, jumping from foot to foot and stroking his palm in a circular motion. 'Round and round the garden,' he mumbled to himself.

There were a few strangers who must have been fans of Fenella's from out of town – one was wearing a home-made appliqué T-shirt, which said: *If you can stand the heat . . . get Fenella in the kitchen.* A boy of fifteen or so sat in the front row with a notepad and pen on his lap. A reviewer? Bring it on.

'Wow,' I breathed from the seat next to Fenella, her first

poem complete, the word 'stale' fresh on her lips, painted that nineties shade of beetle blood. 'That was powerful.' She nodded once but didn't respond verbally. 'Powerful indeed,' I said. Still nothing. I could hear my blood pumping in my ears. Time for my first question. 'So, Fenella, why do you write?'

She looked at a woman in the front row. 'Wow,' she drawled. 'Hear that, love? Never had that one before.' She turned to me at last. 'So, human,' she said, 'why do you talk?'

I glanced at Stuart. He nodded as if to say, 'Keep going.' 'Just make sure there's no silences,' had been his last words to me as he'd patted me on the shoulder before introducing us.

'Why do I talk?' I said. She nodded, her eyes dancing. 'Well, I guess the other options are sign language – which I don't know – or writing everything down. When I was thirteen, I got glandular fever and couldn't talk, so I made signs that said "yes", "no" and "*Neighbours*". But generally I think if you *can* talk, you *should*. Speech is an instinctive thing . . .' At this point, Stuart moved his finger across his neck, guillotine style. 'Even in executions, at the . . . the lowest point of life . . .' I continued – was this what he meant? – '. . . speech . . . is important. A prisoner might shriek, "No! I'm innocent!" as they're about to die, or, "I didn't want ketchup with my last meal!" It'd take ages to write all that down, so . . .' I looked to the people in front of me for help: a mixture of puzzled faces met my gaze.

Foley Joe shrieked, 'Cut! Cut!'

Fenella was grinning from ear to ear. 'Who are your favourite three authors and why?' she said. 'Fenella feels like asking a few questions tonight.' She turned to the room. 'All I do is go to these events, and – I mean, I love the *Play School*-style window display and the *one* balloon, Stuart' – he smiled sheepishly – 'but I sell about three books afterwards, and all I get asked is, why do you write? How do you write? Do you think poetry can survive in the modern world? – and all this shit.'

'Fenella—' said Clare from the back.

Fenella turned to me again. 'Favourite three authors, and why. Go.'

My mind raced. 'Jane Austen,' I said, 'cos, erm, she changed the face of fiction.' *That sounded good*, I thought. My mind was completely blank, though, and I couldn't think of a single other author. Susan . . . Kennedy? Wasn't she a character from *Neighbours*? Who'd written *Tricolore*? My eyes darted frantically round the room until I spotted a book I recognised. 'Max Porter,' I said. I hadn't read any of his books, but I knew they were well regarded. 'He's changed the face of grief.' I was on a roll with this 'changed the face' business. 'And Sharon Osbourne,' I said. 'She's just changed her face.'

I was very chuffed with this impromptu joke, but there was no reaction from Fenella. 'I don't think I want to ask you anything else, human,' she said.

'Well,' I said, heart hammering, 'it's all food for thought.' I inwardly congratulated myself on this pun, considering. Surely that would have been a better title for her book, in fact. Best continue on this tack. Talk about the text. I had to pretend I liked her poetry, or my job was probably on the line. I felt sick. 'You write a lot about cake,' I said. 'I like cake, too.' This wasn't a question. 'Who here likes cake?' I asked pleadingly. A muted cheer rose from the audience. The tinsel woman unscrewed the lip balm and began slathering it on. 'I know, Fenella,' I said, making my voice as level as possible, 'you can look at my list of questions and choose which ones you want to answer.'

She perused the scrap of till roll leisurely, screwed it up and threw it in the air, then turned to me. 'I don't even know your name,' she said. 'And' – she put up her hand to cut me off – 'it doesn't matter. Your questions are shit. Your reserve questions were about my favourite pet and whether I prefer being indoors or outdoors.' People chuckled.

I looked at Stuart as his head folded down towards his hands. In fact, no one would meet my eye. Only Foley Joe was grinning, leaping from side to side, ready for the next bit.

'I mean, they're like . . .' Fenella stood up, her eyes glittering. 'They're like –

> Why? What? How? Who?
> Without direction, without any true'

She stood up and started to gesticulate, dewdrops of spittle launching from her mouth.

> 'You sit in the bookshop like Anne of Green
>   Gable
> But the only thing you've read is the bus time-
>   table.'

Everyone in the room cheered and the 'reviewer' put down his pen. With relief, I saw he'd in fact been beavering away at a drawing entitled *Daenerys from Game of Thrones*, who resembled a cross between a lion and Dean Gaffney.

Locked into a rhythm now, Fenella continued. I felt colour rise up my throat, sharp and warm.

> 'You want to know what it's like to write
> > poetry,
> But the best you can do is,'

She mimicked a little girl's voice.

> *"Does* tree *rhyme with* me?"
> It lives in the heart, in the brain, in the soul,'

She squatted beside me, her face close to mine, grinning.

> 'It is the moment that your team scores a goal,
> But you've got to give in, you've got to let go,
> 'Stead of counting out your money like Ol'
> > Queen Cole!'

Everyone whooped and clapped along, entranced.

> 'It's not just you, it's them, it's him,'

She pointed at Stuart, whose biggest crime, to my knowledge, was feigning innocence when there were no biscuits left – but he didn't seem to mind. In fact, he was hanging onto her every word.

She beat a rhythm on the back of her chair.

> 'It's the estate agents, it's the politician's grin,
> If you let art into your heart, for a start,
> You'd be happier, and sadder, you'd buzz, you'd
> > smart,
> But, moreover, you'd be you, but you squared,
> > or you cubed,

You feeling every moment, you ready and
    lubed,
You'd drink, you'd dance, you'd scream, you'd
    mange,
And you'd be able to rhyme with the notorious
    l'orange!'

She stood panting, her broad shoulders stooped, her head craned slightly forward towards the crowd's wild applause. A tiny halo of greying hair topped her head. She rocked slightly, as if more words might tumble out at any given time. Like food poisoning, when you never really know if it's over.

Chapter Two

The sky was a flamingo pink, the sun on its way to setting, as I left the pub and bookshop behind me to walk down the hill to my parents' house.

There was no doubt that the evening had been a roaring success. Everyone in the bookshop had bought Fenella's book – even Foley Joe, who'd 'paid' with a battered astronomy book from the bottom of his bag and three cigarettes, to her delight. People had come in off the street to see what all the cheering was about during Fenella's improvised rant, and they'd bought copies, too. One woman wanted five of them to post to ex-boyfriends anonymously, which Fenella had adored, writing: *Eat shit! Fenella xx* on the inside cover. Afterwards, everyone had decamped to the pub.

'You off, duck? That were great,' Foley Joe had said, nabbing a sausage roll off Stuart's plate and taking a big bite. 'No one else would have sat there and taken that shit. You were in cahoots with her anyway, though, weren't you, duck?'

'No,' I said, 'I've never met her before, and I hope I never do again.'

He'd tapped the side of his nose like I hadn't denied a thing.

'Would thee like to buy any puppets, Fenella?' I heard him say as I opened the door to leave. 'I've got dogs, cats and Prince Charleses.'

Foley Joe's congratulations – and Stuart's, for that matter – had done nothing to assuage the unsettled feeling inside me. The truth was that things hadn't been a success *because* of me, it was *despite* me. This hadn't stopped me from milking the temporary goodwill in the air by asking Stuart for some more hours. He'd responded by giving me an extra fiver for doing the Q&A, which I'd gone through the motions of refusing, while simultaneously stuffing it into my pocket.

Why couldn't I have stayed for a drink with them all, singing along with whoever picked up the guitar tonight as more sausage rolls and shots materialised?

Why couldn't I just trust that everything was going to be OK, with my new, simple life in Foley? I was in one of the most picturesque areas of Britain. I could walk every where, with hills, caves and a river seconds from my door. This was the kind of life that *The Times* wrote articles about Londoners coveting.

I didn't have any real money worries – I'd always be bailed out by Mum and Dad, who were hardly going to start charging me rent. All my meals were cooked for me. The worst thing that could happen to me now was that they might forget to buy extra bread.

And yet I couldn't relax, not for one minute. I didn't dare look at my phone, I found it hard to sleep and some days I could barely eat. All because of what had happened.

It wasn't a long way to my parents' from the pub, but it was enough to remind me I wasn't in London. Everything was shut apart from the chippy and a late-night convenience store I passed before crossing the road into the park. In South London, I could leave my flat at 9 p.m. and get a flat white if I so desired. Here, they'd think I was talking about a breed of dog.

I crossed the tennis courts, wended my way round the rusty old bandstand where I'd once watched Ally Cain and Lee Taylor snog for two hours non-stop while we all threw pens and compasses at them. What were Ally Cain and Lee Taylor doing right now? Probably having a 'cheeky drink' – ugh – having put their respective kids to bed. They would definitely have stayed in Foley, going to the same pubs in the same order on Saturday nights, still guffawing about the time in biology when I'd fainted at the sight of a dissected frog. Who was I to judge, though? They probably weren't sleeping back in their childhood bedrooms at their parents' house.

I looked at the hills beyond the park, my eye following rectangles and rhombuses of green and yellow upwards as the buildings grew sparser. Before long, my eyes found the slated roof of The Arch. It didn't need to do anything to catch my eye – I would have been able to point it out on a map blindfolded. Even from this distance it looked more decrepit than I remembered, but it had been well on its way there when we used to go in as teenagers. Looking at it still made my heart beat a bit faster. The jumble of bedrooms upstairs where we'd peeled off strips of wallpaper to spell out the letters of our names, the empty optics on the bar where Megan had placed her own bottle of absinthe,

the bottom of the main staircase where Olly had covered himself in old wires, screaming, 'I'm a very wiry person!' while we all collapsed into helpless, stoned hysterics. It was a time capsule of everything that I'd been and wanted to be, up until my eighteenth birthday.

As I exited the park, next to the part of the river where Megan and I had chucked all our textbooks, I looked at my phone for the first time that evening. Nothing from Jonathan. *Good*, I thought. *That's good.* If I could just get in and upstairs without Mum and Dad asking me yet again if I was all right, then do all my checking without anyone interrupting, I had a chance of sleeping more than a few hours.

Walking up the drive, a few unfamiliar cars lay parked at slightly odd angles on the gravel, as if dropped from above by a giant in a hurry. The bell-ringers.

'Jane!' Mum said, getting up from the sofa as I opened the back door. 'Erm – book, no, film!' she shrieked back towards the small group scattered around the living room as she padded towards me. 'David keeps doing the sign for book right in front of his face, so it looks like he's doing film, the silly man!' she laughed, tucking my hair behind my ears. '*You* might read books like that, David! We're not all blind yet! How was the poetry reading, darling? It's such a gorgeous evening – did anyone come?'

'Fine,' I said.

'Well, it's Jane!' boomed David, the ringing master, towering between the piano and the pouf, mid-mime. I was surprised to see that Mum had allowed him to leave his shoes on.

19

How to respond was unclear. 'Hellooo,' I said, elongating the word to try and make it serve as a greeting for everyone in the room. At a glance, there were about six or seven of them, including Mum and Dad, and David, who I'd known since I was a youngster, stealing sips of communion wine and dressing up to play the Holy Ghost in the nativity play, yelling, 'Your money or your myrrh!' as the Wise Men approached the stable.

I recognised some of the others, in the way you might recognise an old doorknob in a house you haven't lived in or thought about for years. A man with enormous milky earlobes, which waggled independently of his head as he spoke; a woman who used to wear the same zigzag turquoise jumper every Sunday with a penny-shaped rip in the sleeve. She perched on the edge of the sofa, a spoonful of cream and meringue en route to her smiling mouth. 'Jane, hello!' she said, then crunched into the meringue.

'Hello,' I said again. How many times did I have to say hello? 'I'm quite tired, so—'

'You know everyone, don't you?' asked Mum, looking about. 'Oh, no, you don't!' She pointed at a tall, slim woman in her mid-fifties with darting, beady eyes and spiky blonde hair, three heavy coin pendants around her neck. 'That's Monica, that is.' Mum giggled, then a silence. She liked doing this: creating social disquiet, then metaphorically deserting the room.

I smiled at Monica with my lips in a line, not opening my mouth. I sometimes did this as a prelude to a proper smile, when I was trying to gauge what I was going to get from the other person.

She opened her mouth to reveal large slabs of teeth the colour and shape of Scrabble letters. 'I'm Monica, I am,' she said.

'And I'm Jane, I am,' I replied. Everyone laughed quietly. Ah, it was good to be home, in these small ways.

'Monica's staying in Foley for a bit, just like you are,' said Mum.

'She's from *Cornwall*,' said David. He said this in an exaggerated West Country accent, and everyone laughed, including me. This was something I would never have laughed at in London. How much had the bar already been lowered?

'That's nice,' I said to Monica.

'Ugh!' groaned Mum. 'What does that mean? Say something specific.'

'OK, Mum,' I said. This was a dance Mum and I did every single day of our lives. 'Then, why are you here, Monica?' Automatic platitude, shame, deliberate petulance.

'Our church is linked with yours,' said Monica, holding her hands wide. 'I'm seeing what Foley brings me.'

'That's nice,' I said, just to annoy Mum. Now it felt rude to go straight upstairs. 'How long have you guys been playing charades?' I asked them. I felt somehow that this was an offensive question, something one shouldn't ask adults, then remembered that I was thirty-eight.

'Ooh, too long,' replied Mum. 'We were supposed to finish hours ago, but we're all enjoying it too much!' There was a smell of room-temperature dairy in the air.

'We're practising for the charades competition,' said zig-zag jumper. 'Tibshelf have held the trophy since the beginning of time, so this year we're going to up our game.'

'We're getting to know each other's styles within the group,' said Mum.

'Oh right,' I said. 'Isn't that cheating?'

'Oh, Jane!' said David's wife, Lynette, from the corner, who had the longest neck I'd ever seen. 'Don't say that!' A vein in her neck throbbed.

'I was only joking,' I said. 'I'd be practising, too, if I were you.' What was I saying? 'I meant if I was anyone,' I added.

'Fancy coming along, to keep score?' asked David. 'It's not for a few months.'

I laughed. 'Oh, I'll be long gone by then,' I said.

I made a move for the stairs, then it came, the question I was dreading, just as I thought I'd got away.

'No Jonathan with you?' David boomed.

'No,' I blurted, stepping on the end of David's line like a bad actor. 'He's got to work.'

Mum was beaming at everyone. She obviously hadn't told them the full story, which filled me with grateful surprise.

I glanced at Dad on the piano stool, hunched forward with his elbows on his knees, gazing into the centre of the room as if at a mildly pleasing apparition only he could see. I knew he wished Mum had just stuck to playing the organ, rather than adding on bell-ringing, fête-organising and church-newsletter-editing. I couldn't really imagine him throwing himself into charades. At fancy-dress parties he went in a suit, as an accountant.

He was an accountant.

He smiled lopsidedly at me. I smiled back, doing a thumbs-up in my pocket I hoped he could sense. I wanted to tell him about the Q&A, to get into the nooks and crannies of it, the awkwardness. But only Dad. At the moment, Mum was so eager for everything to be OK that she grasped any whiff of good news and whipped it away, breathing unearned life into it and hanging it like bunting. Dad, however, listened, considered, spoke slowly, laughed easily and generously. He said things like, 'Is there a desperate need?' and, 'Let's all zoom out for a moment.'

'Well, just give us all enough notice to ring at your wedding,' said David. I quickly covered my left hand. 'And I expect your Mum'll be hopping straight from the belfry to the organ seat on the big day, won't you, Nora?'

'Plenty of time to plan the wedding,' said Mum. 'They've not even had time for an engagement party yet, they both work so hard!'

I gazed around my bedroom: peeling yin and yang stickers on the bookshelf, woodlice fossilised beneath decades-old copies of *My Guy* magazine under the bed. My old A-level artwork sat in plastic boxes on top of the wardrobe, and I could see actual notches in the actual bedpost.

I thought of my – our – bedroom in London, a million worlds away from this one. Two identical laptops always skew-whiff on the desk at the end of our bed; our balcony, which snaked around the flat; our silent washing machine; our ironic *Buffy* duvet set; the way our fridge door squeaked like a crying baby when you opened or closed it. I thought of how I'd absent-mindedly wind Jonathan's hair around my finger when I was formulating an idea or when things got too much. Of how he'd always know where my keys were when I was panicking that I'd left them in the outside of the door, ready to be stolen; of when he knew before I even spoke whether it was a sugar-in-tea day or a good day. A sugar-in-tea day was when things just got too much, and the thoughts hurtling through my head seemed like they would never stop.

I felt a lump in my throat like a stuck paracetamol. I walked to the mirror and looked at my wan reflection. I felt an urge to punch the glass. *Breathe in for six, out for eight. Don't look at your phone.*

The only person who could have stopped me from going over and over in my head how it had possibly, then almost definitely, then catastrophically gone wrong between us was Jonathan himself.

I stepped away from the mirror and closed the door on the muffled hubbub downstairs. I'd do my rounds once they'd all gone: check the gas hob and the door and the window locks.

Why couldn't I just go down now, to sit with them? I could join in charades, pour myself some wine, tell them the truth. But, instead, I sat bolt upright on the rug, heart racing and sweat breaking out on my palms, not even knowing how I was going to brush my teeth that night without him. How had it all gone so wrong?

Chapter Three

The realisation that there was something wrong between Jonathan and me had snuck up on me insidiously, like the flu. Back in April, we'd been sitting at our kitchen table eating chilli, both of us looking at our phones, and I realised that this was now what we did whenever we ate together – that we hadn't had a decent conversation for a long time. One of us always got our phone out, and the other would follow suit seconds later, relieved.

I mean, we were always on our phones for work. We both understood this necessity, especially as we were creative partners. But this was different him-being-on-his-phone. This was him being locked in the bathroom with his phone for ages and ages, and telling me, 'It was just my brother with a joke,' when I asked who he was texting. This was not the way he usually spoke.

I put it down to overwork. He was tired. We were both tired. We needed space away from each other. We'd been working non-stop for months on radio scripts for a big supermarket who demanded that the words 'fresh' and 'vibrant' appear in every other line, and who sat in on every voiceover session, breathing over our shoulders, changing the price of apples at the eleventh hour.

Throughout all this I was still peeing on ovulation sticks most mornings, because my periods were so irregular I never really knew when I should be ovulating, and we were having clusters of quiet, hurried sex at odd times – clusterfucks, if you will – before one of us had to return to the office or to a laptop. We'd be lucky if we kissed. Kissing wasn't necessary. We just needed to extract the nectar, so to speak, as quickly and efficiently as possible.

'There's a smiley face this morning!' I'd shout from the bathroom, holding the plastic stick aloft. 'We have to have sex today and tomorrow.'

'Shit!' he'd reply. 'We've got the edit tonight.'

'OK,' I'd say, my mind skittering through our diaries. 'What about this afternoon? Toilets at work?'

As time went on, I couldn't believe I'd ever thought of sex as a luxury, a joy, a thing that celebrated my body and his, something to while away an afternoon.

We'd often discuss work as we systematically removed our own clothing and laid down side by side. We'd taken to 'getting ourselves ready' before conjoining at the last crucial step, as that made everything quicker. There was never any time to be wasted – our boss usually wanted script amendments or pitch ideas urgently.

Once, aware of how sad it had all become, I tried to talk about something different. 'Andrew Marr's got a new show on the BBC,' I said as I pulled my knickers down. It took eight minutes for him to regain his erection, and he was late for a conference call.

Another time, he ordered an Uber to take him to the office when he figured we were six minutes away from completion, and we watched the little car icon stutter its way towards us on the screen as we raced against it like we were in a bizarre game show. 'Thank God for the roadworks on the high street!' we laughed as the car icon stopped dead, and we allowed ourselves a rare kiss of victory.

He'd always sworn he wouldn't be able to do it if his parents could hear. The spare room was right next to ours and the walls were thin. We had a smiley face once when they were staying. Sadie and Bryan never left the flat without us. We tried the bathroom, claiming to be brushing our teeth together. Strands from the bath mat kept going up my bum, and trying to do it in a dry bath hurt our shoulders and knees. This was the only time we were so stressed about it that I thought he might be physically incapable of doing it.

'Get out,' he said in the end, pushing me into the hall in my dressing gown. 'I'll sort it.' He locked the door and did it on his own, into the only thing he could find, the big Sports Direct mug we used for our toothbrushes. We exchanged places wordlessly and I slung the lukewarm liquid up – grits of toothpaste and all – into my reproductive system, that mysterious abyss; a thing I found as hard to understand as war. Afterwards, I lay on my back with my legs up against the wall like the old wives' tales said to, marvelling at how quickly he'd managed it, then momentarily worrying, with a cold, hollow stab, if he'd thought about me or someone else. I crossed the fingers of both hands like I always did, resting them on my belly. I straightened my legs against the wall and moved them in wide sweeping motions like I was making a snow angel until his mum knocked on the door and asked if I'd fallen down the plughole.

I started to get obsessed, like my mind was not my own – not that it's ever really felt like my own. I could see myself hurtling down the old familiar road, letting it invade more and more of my time, and I was powerless to stop it. *Chances of getting pregnant in late thirties*, I'd google on my phone, again and again, until all the websites would be purple because I'd already clicked on them multiple times. Some sites would be so gentle about it that it almost made me cry. *Maybe it'll be harder for you than ten years ago*, they'd say in a bright, playful font. *But that's no reason not to try! Plenty of women have no problems! Be kind to yourself and make love every two to three days!* Fat chance.

As my forkful of chilli had hung suspended in front of my mouth that April evening, while I watched him on his phone yet again, I'd realised that all the things I would usually relay to him had started to burst out of me unprompted. I'd tell tired hairdressers about the chipped vase I'd had delivered from a department store, how I couldn't be bothered to return it so was going to turn the chip to the wall: with flowers in, you'd never tell. I'd find myself gabbling to Mum on the phone about whether I should move dentists because mine was so expensive now, but they had hazelnut hot chocolate in reception and special glasses so you could watch *Breakfast at Tiffany's* during thousand-pound root canals.

The only subject we still made time to talk about was the wedding, clinging to this anchor like it was the only thing that mattered in the long run. Arguments about which elderly relatives should come – or would even remember having come – would stretch into the night, as would to-and-fros about whether to allow babies there, when we so desperately wanted one ourselves.

We'd eaten our chilli and looked in silence at our phone screens. I'd gazed at baby cardigan knitting patterns I knew I would never knit – firstly because we would never have a baby and secondly because I can't knit – and tried not to bite the skin off my fingers as I scanned more and more articles about my chances of getting pregnant and the risks it carried. I lived in my head, and all the stuff in my head started to get worse as the gulf grew between us, and for the first time, Jonathan wasn't damming the flow.

Chapter Four

Now that I'd left him, all Jonathan was trying to do was start a conversation, ironically. He kept repeating this whenever he made contact, like a malfunctioning robot that had swallowed a self-help book. 'I'm just trying to start a conversation,' he typed in texts and emails, spluttering it at the end of phone messages. He hadn't given up trying to reach me ever since Dad had driven down to London to pick me up exactly fourteen days before. It was the most backbone and persistence he'd ever shown in our relationship.

I hadn't spoken to him once. Sometimes I listened to his voicemails and sometimes I just deleted them. I especially liked deleting them mid-sentence, like when Graham Norton tips the audience member off the red chair as they're telling their story. He wanted to explain; he wanted to see me; I'd left so many things behind; where was I going to live? I had developed a system for deleting his texts and emails, which involved me squinting my eyes so that all the words became blurry and turned into swimming shoals of black lettering. As I did this, lying in bed at the end of each day, short strings of words would leap out at me. Jane, sweetheart . . . I'm so sorry . . . just let me . . . Sorry. Sorry. Sorry.

Occasionally, depending on how I'd been that day, Mum would answer the landline to him rather than letting it ring off. We knew it was him from the caller ID. I'd watch through the crack in the door as she placed her feet hip-width apart and stilled her body for a few seconds before picking up the receiver. 'Hello, Jonathan,' she'd say, and the back of her head would tremble slightly, her short dark hair just grazing her collar. 'Yes, Jane is here.' It was like a script from a soap. 'No, no, she can't, Jonathan.' Her shoulders would droop slightly in their mohair. Every sentence contained a name, sometimes two. 'Jane can't do that, Jonathan. Yes, we're aware you're just trying to start a conversation, Jonathan, and I think that now is the time to end it.'

Mum often needed a drink after contact from Jonathan – mind you, she often needed a drink after she'd discovered her parsley hadn't grown as much as she'd predicted, or the vicar hadn't mentioned her organ-playing after the service. Slopping white wine into two globe-shaped glasses, she'd conspiratorially whisper, 'Well, I've never liked Jonathan's mother,' as if this was shocking information, like it should maybe even be communicated to the police. 'Underweight. Talked about the past too much. Thin gravy.'

Dad hadn't spoken to Jonathan since I'd arrived back in Foley. He was probably scared of what might happen. Dad never loses his temper, not because it's not in his nature, but because he's done it in the past and no one likes it, least of all him. Dad didn't even speak to Jonathan the night he drove down from Foley to get me, which was the same night I'd established for definite that something had gone on between Jonathan and Rachel. Mum had told me to get a bag packed, and Dad had got in the car immediately, not even taking the cheese-and-Marmite sandwich Mum had hastily made him, which was all for the better, really, because the bread was frozen. She'd said it would defrost in no time 'in the heat of the M1', but Dad and I agreed on the way back that it wouldn't have, as we stopped for a late-night meal at the services. This gave me the feeling of being nine. The moment I bit into my burger, tears flowed down my cheeks, like I was an automaton. Dad put his hand on mine – something he had never done before. 'There's no more packing and planning to be done, pickle,' he said. 'Let it out.'

When I got downstairs the morning after the book event, no one was to be seen and there was a mobile phone in the middle of the table. It was so ancient – an original Nokia 3310 in a thick, extremely dusty plastic case – that it took me a few seconds to realise that it was even a phone. I ignored it and made some toast. I had a few hours before starting at the bookshop, where I hoped to be able to bask in the glory of the Fenella business last night, enough to get away with reading some more of Sharon Osbourne's autobiography.

As I poured the milk into my tea, the ancient phone started to ring. I looked at the display, which said 'HOME'. This felt like an odd game. Had Mum and Dad bought me a new house, and this was an interior designer ringing to ask what kind of radiators I wanted? Yes, please.

'Answer it!' came Mum's shout from the direction of the

piano room. With difficulty, I located the 'answer' button through the plastic cover.

'Hello?'

'Oh, hello, is that Jane?' said Mum's voice in a quavery tone. 'I'm a . . . a ghost!'

'Hi, ghost,' I replied, chewing my toast. 'I'm eating toast, ghost.'

'Woooo! I know everything! Ask me any question!' she said.

'OK, who do you love best out of Jane and Amanda?' I said immediately.

'Ah, the ghost cannot answer that,' came Mum's answer.

'It is me, though, isn't it?' I said. 'I'm the creative one. She's just a number-cruncher. Who wants to live in an apartment in New York when they can scrounge off their parents back home?'

There was a pause.

'This is your new phone,' said the ghost. 'Now, I must go and eat some ectoplasm! Or produce some! I don't know what ectoplasm is! Goodbye!'

'It's David's old one,' said Mum as she walked through into the dining room. So she *had* told the bell-ringers about me and Jonathan. I pictured them all pitying me over their bowls of meringue. 'I didn't tell them, if that's what you're thinking,' she added. 'I just said you needed a new phone, and he sprang to the rescue.'

'I don't, though, do I?' I said.

'You need a number you-know-who can't reach you on,' she replied. 'Then the temptation isn't there. To answer.' She waved her hands rapidly from side to side. 'Clean slate.

Now, where's your laptop? Let's hide it so you can't answer his emails.'

'I didn't bring it,' I said. It was still in my bedroom in London, which proved how temporary I regarded this visit to Foley to be.

I looked at my new phone. The buttons were so stiff it was a wonder you could type anything more than a brief text message. Oh – you couldn't.

'It doesn't go online,' Mum said, gathering some crumbs into a pile on the tablecloth.

'Well, I can't use it then,' I replied. 'I need to send emails on the move.'

She laughed for a long time. 'You're not in *Sex and the City*! You're in Foley!'

I felt awash with rage. Foley being quaint was fine, even desirable, when that was where I was from. Now I was back, it didn't hold quite the same charm. 'I like to be able to have access to the Internet when I'm out,' I said. I sounded like I was compiling the worst dating profile in the world. *I like walks. I like skiing. I like to be able to have access to the Internet when I'm out.*

'Why?' she asked.

Good question. I wouldn't be able to keep checking if Jonathan had tried to contact me. But what about googling symptoms of various diseases I frequently became convinced I had? When I felt the urge to symptom check, it had to happen immediately. Maybe not being able to do it would be good for me.

I sipped my tea and scrolled through the address book. *MUM MOB*, I read. *DAD MOB. HOME* showed my parents' landline. *BOOKSHOP, VET* – 'That must be left over from David's numbers,' Mum said. 'But it never hurts to have the number of a vet' – *GP SURGERY, MONICA.*

'Monica?' I said. 'The woman from last night?'

'She's a counsellor,' said Mum. 'She's been helping Lynette get over her fear of clowns.'

'And how many clowns does seventy-year-old Lynette encounter,' I asked, 'on a yearly basis?'

'Just keep it in there,' said Mum. 'You might want to talk to her one day. About everything. She's impartial.'

EMERGENCY showed 999. This summed up the new chapter of my life: my phone address book didn't reach double figures and one of the numbers was nine nine fucking nine.

Chapter Five

My thirty-eighth birthday in May had heralded further jigsaw pieces that I was frightened to fit into place. The day had begun with Jonathan giving me much, much better presents than usual. It wasn't just the expense; it was the effort and the thought.

On my birthday morning, he produced a home-made cake, which was supposed to have my initials inside it in food colouring, in a sort of cross section, like when you bite into a piece of rock, but he'd done it wrong and the whole of the inside was a mouldy-looking grey-green. I loved this even more than if it had worked, which he must have predicted I would. Maybe he'd never even tried to make the letters in the first place. Then he gave me a bear from the Build-A-Bear shop, which said in a deep, creepy voice, 'I watch you while you're sleeping.' He'd also bought me a silver bracelet with five charms on it, one for each year we'd been together. There was a teapot charm, because it had taken him ages to learn to make tea just the way I like it. A heeled boot for Italy, where we went on our first ever holiday. A 'J' for Jane, and a horseshoe, which meant absolutely nothing to either of us. Last was the charm of a tiny bird hatching from a sapphire-encrusted egg. 'That's a symbol for, you know, when we, you know . . .' he said. As I cried briefly into his shoulder he said softly, as he always did, 'We will, we will, we will.' This was the most physical contact we'd had in a long time, apart from our regular stoic attempts at baby-making which made *The Handmaid's Tale* look like *9½ Weeks*.

After breakfast, he took me on the London Eye and kept his hand on my leg the whole time because of a recent row about lack of bodily contact. His hand sat frozen in place like the grabber from a claw game in an amusement arcade. He took me for afternoon tea, where he asked strangers to take photos of us and made jokes with them about how difficult phone cameras are to operate. He didn't look at his phone once, which highlighted how much he normally did. This effort of abstinence didn't stop his right hand from occasionally flickering forwards in a 'phone shape' to grab at thin air before he remembered his phone wasn't on the table. And all the time, it was like there was an extra skin around him, a slimy film only I could see. Every action was too perfectly executed, his laughs were slightly too loud, his laid-back demeanour too studied. I could feel him distancing himself and moving in too close at the same time.

He was doing what he thought was best, in the circumstances. Because in the same way a murderer changes out of their bloodstained clothing into a dressing gown and Garfield slippers, cheats aren't just cheats – they're actual people, too. They're feeling their way. They're like someone making Cornish pasties from scratch for the first time – they don't know how things are going to turn out either, or if all the effort will be worth it in the end. Rachel was more than a Cornish pasty, though. She was from Wimbledon, for a start, and her filling was lukewarm at best. She was a property developer, so she probably had no filling at all. Just a wasteland inside, single fifty-pound notes cartwheeling past her pitted heart.

But I didn't know Rachel on my birthday. At that point, I just felt seriously freaked out by the effort that had been put into the celebrations by a man who, the previous birthday – and I didn't mind this – had handed me a *Father Ted* DVD from his parents' house and a free badge from a beer festival.

And that effort didn't end in the restaurant as we accepted a third round of cucumber sandwiches. Once we'd got home, after we'd shunned his pre-planned prawn pasta for tinned tomato soup because we were so full from the afternoon tea, he proposed the idea of going down on me for hours. 'Just like the early days,' he said, hunkering down between my thighs and clapping his hands together as if he was about to open a car bonnet.

'Take your T-shirt off,' I muttered, trying to remember how many pillows I liked under my head.

'Just a sip of wine before I start,' he said, having briefly surveyed the area. He leapt off the bed and went downstairs. I opened my book. Why did he need a sip of wine? He wasn't about to give a best man speech. 'I brought one for you!' he said, bounding back in and handing me a large glass of red wine. It was like he was on coke. Not a massive amount, just something to help the world go round. The level where people think they're acting completely normally but they just spent twenty minutes telling someone their system for filing their receipts.

There was something quite unsexy about cunnilingus being part of a 'birthday package'. What was next, midnight paintballing, then on to a carpeted nightclub to claim our free bottle of cava? It was perfectly pleasant, but it just trundled along in the background like the radio while I thought about all the birthdays that had gone before, and pushed away memories of my eighteenth. Could he hear the tomato soup sloshing about in my tummy? I swallowed down its acidic fog and tried to sip my wine casually, but I'd only plumped for the one pillow and ended up pouring most of it onto my neck. Despite his dogged determination to just carry on regardless, the thought of it soaking through onto our memory-foam mattress meant I found myself downstairs alone moments later, feeding the bedclothes into the washing machine and feeling relieved the whole thing was over.

When I went back up, he lay crumpled in half at the waist on the bare mattress, his forehead pressed against it. Thick charcoal hairs licked at his shoulders like they'd been painted on, becoming more and more serious as they moved upwards until they reached the nape of his neck, where they expanded into a mass of curls. I never really liked looking at his shoulder hair. It was something private, like a scar; the price you paid for having that heavenly crown of head hair. The older we got, the more his hair was a talking point. Toddlers wound it around their fingers and sang to it. Old ladies commented that he was very lucky not to have lost his hair, it being so lovely. Jonathan adored it all, letting people stroke it and smell it, bending down so that no one felt left out. His hair was a comfort, a muse, a weapon. It seemed to follow his moods – wiry and tough during a row, soft and calm when he was.

I watched him as he lay face down. He rocked softly from side to side as though to comfort himself, like I'd whipped the tablecloth out from under him. The room still smelt of Shiraz.

Chapter Six

'Sorry about the wait,' said the woman behind the counter.

'Now,' Mum began, 'we're here to—'

'Oh my God! It's Jo Wildgoose, isn't it?' the woman said to me. Her name badge sat wonkily on a Post Office blouse. *Kelly*, it said in black lettering.

'Not Jo, no,' I mumbled. I couldn't quite place her, but instinct said not to engage with her. I looked at the floor.

'Could Jane please redirect her post, Kelly?' Mum said. I was relieved she was doing the job for me. *What should Jane have for lunch, Kelly? Can Jane have a pill that erases her past, Kelly?*

'Jane! That's it!' said Kelly.

I smiled weakly. An intense stare and fluffy brown hair, like a doll from someone else's attic. A delicate spattering of bright orange crisp dust lay across her collar.

'It's me! It's Kelly, from school.' She pointed at her badge. 'Tanya-and-Kelly!'

Of course. Kelly Webster. At school, like many of us, she'd been part of a female double act who were often terribly matched, but they'd become best friends at primary school and were then stuck together like Tweedledum and Tweedledee. In an instant, I recalled their stats. Tanya had been tall and pretty, like a character from *Sweet Valley High*, pissed off at the burden of how easily it all came to her, whereas Kelly had been shorter and more complicated. I remembered Kelly once sitting on a rock while we all ran the cross-country course and colouring her whole leg in with permanent marker – up to the crotch.

'Yeah, you can redirect your post, Jane,' she said. 'You just need ID with your old address on, and—'

'Oh, I haven't got that,' I said.

'Come back when you have, then,' she said. 'I'm here all the time. What you up to these days, babe?'

Say something specific, I could hear Mum thinking, but this was a situation in which it would surely pay to be as ambiguous as possible. 'Oh,' I said. 'Just back here for a bit.'

'Awww,' Kelly said. 'What you doing back?'

'Not a lot,' I replied. 'Just back here for a bit.' Could I say this in answer to every question, ever?

'Where you working then? You went to London, didn't you? Had any kids?'

People in Foley tended to regard London with a mix of suspicion and curiosity, as one might the Loch Ness monster. 'Driving in London's like driving in the Bronx, me duck,' I remember my driving instructor saying, who'd never been to either place. 'No kids,' I told her. Then, 'I'm working at Stuart's bookshop part-time.'

'No, you're not,' said Mum sharply.

Mum was massively overreacting to this whole 'hiding the fact that I work in the bookshop because of gardening leave' business. Having worked for smaller London advertising agencies for years, I'd joined Brave Psyche five years ago, nervous and excited. Within two days I was pulling all-nighters on pitches, and within two months I'd started going out with my creative partner. When I'd told my boss Martha that I was leaving, she was sad for me but sadder for the agency – we were in the middle of so much work, and no one there had ever thought Jonathan and I would split up. They'd even started discussing who should share hotel rooms at the wedding. I'd rung Martha from Foley the morning after Dad had come to pick me up. Mum had written out what I should say in a flow diagram.

'You two are like peas in a pod, though,' Martha had repeated, as if that could undo everything. 'I can't believe it.'

After much toing and froing, during which a coffee spill on a key part of the flow diagram led to me stammering, 'Sorry, but I've loved working for Jonathan's infidelity,' I made it tearfully but firmly clear that it was impossible for me to return. It was agreed that I would be put on 'gardening leave' for three months, where I'd receive full pay on the condition I didn't talk about company business or work elsewhere, after which I was free to do as I pleased. Mum and Dad both felt I should be doing something with myself right now. The benefits of working cash-in-hand at the bookshop – company, money, a distraction for my busy old brain – outweighed the risk that someone in London would discover I was breaking the terms of my employment contract.

I didn't think the team at Brave Psyche would be exactly shitting it to hear I was in danger of divulging Lidl's summer promotions to the likes of Stuart, or Foley Joe, who Mum and I had just glimpsed on the high street atop a giant inflatable hot dog, declaring, 'The Lord be with you, and also with you.'

But no one I knew in Foley had any connection to London anyway, and there was no way Jonathan was going to find out.

'I meant I'm *volunteering* in the bookshop,' I said quietly. I was aware of people fidgeting in the queue behind us, clutching their packages and letters.

'Is that what you were doing in London? The book stuff?' she asked. 'Snazzy!'

Here was a word I hadn't heard since 2001. 'No,' I replied. 'I was . . . I'm . . . a copywriter. I write adverts.' Some people didn't react brilliantly to this, I'd found.

'Wow,' said Kelly. 'I love adverts. My sister likes to turn them down, and then I turn them up again. Well done, babe.'

I felt tears quietly waiting for their turn, suddenly, at the corners of my eyes.

'We should meet up in the park!' she continued. She was oblivious to the customers' rising ire in a way I envied. 'I've got two kids, but they can just watch stuff on my phone and we can catch up. They know my passcode. They won't interrupt us.'

'Yeah,' I said, in a vague way, like someone had asked if I thought it might snow in winter. How could I make all this stop? I wasn't staying in Foley. I mean, I was, but I wasn't *staying*. There was no need to meet up with a girl from school who probably still had blue marker pen all over her legs.

'Are you on Facebook?'

'No,' I said.

'Twitter?'

'No,' I said. 'I'm not really on any of that stuff.' I had been on Facebook, until recently, but I'd deleted my account to stop myself looking at photos of Rachel. Then persuaded Megan to tell me her password, so I could do it from her account.

Mum grinned. 'Tell you what, Kelly, I'll write down Jane's number. It'll be useful for her to have a friend while she's back.'

'Ace,' she said. 'And pop back in when you've got that ID from your old place for the redirection, babe.'

I knew I could never meet up with Kelly in Foley Park, picking our way through crazy golfers and condom wrappers in search of a clear patch of grass upon which to crouch and drink weak tea from the café while her kids squabbled and ate broken glass. Tempting as it sounded.

Chapter Seven

It was at the beginning of July, two months after my try-too-hard thirty-eighth birthday, that the final Rachel clue had occurred, although it would be a while until I could bear to put the pieces together.

I'd just finished my Pilates class when Laura, the teacher to whom I told pathological lies about the amount of exercise and sugar in my life, came to chat at the door. She told me she'd spotted Jonathan in our new local café, The Sphere, last Monday, a day when I'd taken a rare afternoon off to go to Dungeness with Megan.

'How is he?' she said. 'Ask him what the food's like there. And tell him he's welcome back to class whenever he wants.' There was still an indentation in the opposite wall where Jonathan had dramatically crashed while trying to balance on one leg the only time he'd come with me. He wouldn't give up, even as he was about to hit the plaster. *'I was still balancing, wasn't I, Laura?'* he'd said as she'd helped him up. *'I didn't put my foot down, Laura.'* He'd had a headache for the rest of the day. 'His friend left her book behind, on their table,' Laura said. 'I told the owner I'd let you know. They're keeping it for her.'

'Ah, OK,' I mused. 'Just trying to think if it's someone we work with.'

'Don't know,' she said. 'They did look deep in conversation, so I wouldn't be surprised. I didn't say hello for that reason.'

'Just trying to . . .' I paused. 'Did they leave together, then?'

She nodded, stretching her hamstrings.

I knew it wouldn't be anyone we worked with. They'd never come this far south of town. Everything was done in Soho or remotely. He had a brother, no sister. Although adrenaline pumped round my body like I was about to go into a boxing ring, I didn't feel shocked. I felt a strange sense of, not exactly *déjà vu*, but perhaps *maintenant vu* – like I knew everything that was unfolding exactly as it unfolded: a completely redundant superpower.

'Are you sure it was him?' I asked, aware that it was a wholly rhetorical question, but that I had a duty to go through these motions.

'I'm pretty sure,' she said. 'Well, you tell me. He was wearing bowling shoes.'

A fortnight earlier, Jonathan and I had been in the supermarket when we'd both become aware of a cacophony of tutting. We'd turned round to discover that Jonathan had left a trail of golden-brown dog shit from the entrance to the pitta bread, where we were. A shop-floor assistant was ushering people out of the way, desperately calling for a mop. I couldn't watch. 'I'd better get out of here,' Jonathan said. He began to retrace his steps as best he could, leaping from splodge to splodge.

We'd been bickering about whether to invite Megan's son Art to our wedding and were barely aware of our surroundings. Art made *We Need to Talk about Kevin* look like *The Waltons* and there was a daily discussion about how we could get away with not inviting him, but Megan was a bridesmaid, so we were going round in circles. Recently, when we'd all met up, Art had stamped on Jonathan's bare foot, claiming he thought there was a bee on it about to sting him. Later, he'd produced a picture of a monster he'd drawn, which held aloft a severed male head in one hand and a severed cock and balls in the other.

'Take your shoes off, mate!' shouted a man with blond hair and a red beard, like two *Guess Who?* characters merged together. His eyes shone, like he'd been waiting for this moment all his life.

Jonathan took his trainers off and carried one in each hand, scurrying in his bare feet as people moved out of the way in horror, one of them filming it on their phone.

I'd given Jonathan a weak wave, then watched him slowly examine then lace up his shoes on the wall outside, before sending him a text telling him to use a chopstick to get it out from between the grooves. Now that the drama was over, all the fruits and vegetables looked so vivid and inviting. Anything was possible: I could cook something nobody ever cooked, like ratatouille!

I'd arrived home to find one of my grandmother's ceramic chopsticks a living science experiment in the bin, and the free splintery ones you get free with a Chinese takeaway intact in the drawer. His trainers stayed on the balcony, as he wasn't sure he'd got it all out, and he forgot about them for two days of rain while we were working from home, by which time wearing them would have led to trench foot. He was a man of few shoes – he'd bought exactly the same pair of burgundy Adidas trainers for years, keeping them pristine, scouring international eBay sellers when they stopped making them. Rather than re-sort to wellies or shiny wedding shoes, he was forced to opt for the only other option for the following few days: the blue, cream and red striped bowling shoes we'd stolen on one of our early dates, leaving charity-shop flip-flops behind in the pigeonholes as we scarpered out of the bowling alley, clutching each other and giggling, our complicity a springboard for even more physical contact, which, back then, was all we lived and breathed.

The server behind the counter of The Sphere was a tall, lazy-limbed guy in his early twenties who always leant on the side of the coffee machine like a cat in the sun. We nor-mally chatted whenever I went in. That afternoon, as he'd taken his time over making my flat white and I'd wondered if I should have changed out of my Pilates clothes before marching straight there, he told me about how he'd started going for therapy where a woman clicked her fingers and he repeated certain words until he felt they'd lost their power. I wondered if I should go for therapy, too. I'd spent the whole ten-minute walk from Pilates to The Sphere picturing Jonathan and a faceless woman with an athlet-ic body having sex in every room of our flat, laughing to-gether at the framed photo of Dad on the *Coronation Street* set, at my collection of seaside fridge magnets, at my old, frayed underwear.

I'd been about to ask for the therapist's details when he'd told me that in today's session the only word he could think of to say was 'sauerkraut' because he'd just seen a shop selling it outside her clinic. She'd insisted that he'd chosen this word because sauerkraut is fermented, and therefore so were his feelings, so it was going to take more sessions to release them. He had a strong gut, she said, but residual tension in his solar plexus. It was a hundred pounds a session.

As I paid for my coffee, I mentioned casually about Jonathan and 'a friend', about her leaving her book behind.

'Oh, yeah,' he said, reaching behind the counter. 'Looked expensive.' He brought out a hot-pink leather notebook. I flicked through the pages. Totally blank. Inside the front cover, a name was neatly written in black pen. *Rachel Gorston-Greaves.* When I thanked him for looking after it, I told him his solar plexus didn't look that tense at all to me. He was over the moon. My solar plexus, on the other hand, was chomping at the fucking bit. *Rachel Gorston-Greaves.*

Chapter Eight

A few days after my visit to the Post Office, relieved that Kelly hadn't yet texted me about meeting up, I mistakenly answered a call from Jonathan – damn any-key answer – as I was trying to make a quick call to Megan on my 'London phone'.

I was behind the counter at the bookshop, and already distracted because I'd been twenty minutes late due to repeatedly checking that my hairdryer was off and unplugged, something I was only able to resolve by taking a photo of it off and unplugged, which I now had to look at every five minutes to still my swirling insides. I was using my London phone (a) because my new phone, AKA The Brick, was unable to take photos of said hairdryer, or anything else for that matter, and (b) because The Brick was the shittest phone in the history of humankind and had been banished to the windowsill of the bookshop. Mum had tried to make me wear a special belt to put it in, like a bumbag with a plastic pouch for The Brick to slot into, which I'd declined. 'David will be sorry you're not using the belt,' she said. 'You'd better wear it at the charades contest.'

Of course, I wasn't supposed to be in possession of my

London phone, but I knew exactly where Mum had hidden it: in a big box of material where she hid Christmas presents and anything else secret. After she left for the day, I'd get it out of the box, delete Jonathan's emails, text messages and answerphone messages using my squint-eyes-so-can't-see-words method, then enjoy feeling like a semi-normal person with a phone that worked until I had to hurriedly return it before she came back.

'Jane?' said Jonathan's voice when the call connected.

I hadn't said anything at all as yet. I was still trying to work out what had happened in the last two seconds that meant I could now hear his voice in my ear. He seemed as shocked as I was that we were finally talking – or, at least, breathing – to each other.

'Yeah?' I said. 'What?' I darted to the stairs, aiming for the safety of the toilet, then remembered I was supposed to be manning the till, so hovered between the two. The blood had rushed to my ears and I was surprised I could still hear him.

'Jane! I can't believe it,' he garbled. 'Oh, Janey!'

A few metres away, a customer in a muddy gilet swayed from side to side dangling a weighty, expensive-looking book by the cover with one hand and eating an Eccles cake with the other. His smaller companion stood next to him, absent-mindedly kicking a box of postcards wedged into the bottom shelf. Stuart scrutinised their movements from the children's section like a spider would a pair of trapped flies, breathing deeply into his belly, waiting for them to do something worse before he pounced.

All this time, Jonathan stammered maniacally into the

phone, all his words variations on the Jane theme: Jane, Janey, oh Jane, darling Jane.

'What?' I said again, then I quickly added, 'Send me my passport. It's in my knicker drawer.' There – nobody could say I hadn't done it. Now I could get my post redirected, if I could bear to see Kelly again.

'Do you need any of your other stuff? There's still loads here.' He sounded on the edge of tears. 'I want to see you. I'll send your passport, yes, Jane, of course.'

I stayed silent. I hated him knowing I wanted my passport.

'Look, look,' he continued. 'I'm so glad you've answered . . . please. I'm going to cut to the chase. I know you think you know what happened, and I know this is what everyone says, but honestly—'

I banged my fist in frustration on the counter, but luckily Stuart was too absorbed in his prey to notice. The guy's Eccles cake had deposited two currants on the carpet: Stuart had been right to wait.

I couldn't have this conversation. I couldn't hang up, though. Jonathan was never, ever like this. And nor was I. I'd hardly said anything so far. Listening to him squirm and beg was exquisite.

'Oh God, can't we meet? Please? I can even come up today.'

I didn't say anything. Maybe I really would never speak to him again. It wasn't that crazy. People climbed freezing mountains and put all their belongings on eBay – this was nothing.

He took a deep breath as if he'd rehearsed what he was going to say.

'Let me just say quickly – don't hang up, OK – this wasn't to do with you. It's been really hard for both of us all the years we've not been . . . successful at, you know . . . and I was trying to hide how I felt, cos you were such a mess.'

I fought the urge to whack my phone into the side of my face until either it or my brain gave up.

'No, sorry, sorry. Not such a mess. A *bit* of a mess,' he said. 'Your . . . paranoia, your OCD—'

'Not OCD,' I hissed, turning myself towards the window so nobody could hear. 'I'm untidy. I can't have OCD.'

'Your checking, then,' he said. 'Your worrying. It's definitely got worse in the past year. I know you've been worried about whether it's too late for us to . . . but you had every right to be . . . oh God . . .'

The Eccles cake guy was oblivious to Stuart's ire, swinging the book from side to side as he chatted to his mate.

'Please talk to me,' said Jonathan, his voice now thick with tears. 'I just want to start a conversation.'

Stuart suddenly marched towards the Eccles cake guy, who still held the book. The pages were straining downwards, hanging on by a few yellowing tendons.

'I love you, Jane,' said Jonathan, weeping.

Stuart snatched the book from the guy, who stepped back in surprise, knocking into a stack of new self-help books I was supposed to have put away, which toppled, fanning in all directions.

'Woah,' said his mate. 'What the hell?'

The book destroyer furiously crammed the rest of the cake into his mouth as Stuart waved the book over his head. 'Do you know what this is?' he asked.

'A book?' replied the mate. 'Maybe you should know that if you work in a bookshop.'

'I don't work in a bookshop,' snapped Stuart. 'I own a bloody bookshop. And this is a first edition of Shelley's poetry.'

'Shelley who?' said the Eccles cake guy, spitting flakes of pastry like sawdust. 'Thought Shelley was a barmaid across the road.'

'Piss off!' shouted Stuart, hustling them towards the door. 'That's it, piss off.'

'What was that?' said Jonathan.

I suddenly realised he couldn't know I had a job. Although it wasn't in his nature, now I'd heard how deranged he was, I wouldn't put it past him to tell Martha, and maybe I'd stop receiving my three months' pay.

'Nothing,' I snapped. 'I'm in a shop.'

'Jane . . .' he whimpered. 'It literally meant nothing. It was about me. She could have been anyone. Actually, no, it was about you. It's always been about you.'

'Oh, fuck off, Jonathan,' I said, then added, 'Just send my passport, then fuck off out of my life.' Tears rolled down my cheeks: the dam had finally collapsed. 'When I say fuck off,' I continued more quietly, aware that Stuart was no longer distracted, 'I really mean fuck off. Like "I don't ever want to see you again" fuck off.'

My head swam. I kept thinking I was going to hang up, but I couldn't stop talking. Speech came out of my mouth like letters tumbling onto a Scrabble game and miraculously forming themselves into words at the last moment. He kept trying to talk.

'Because what you did—' I sobbed.

At this point, Stuart clicked his fingers and gestured for me to leave, jerking his head towards an open-mouthed woman and toddler.

I got myself outside and began blindly pacing the pavement. This was our first conversation since he'd admitted it. If you could call it a conversation. 'What you did,' I shouted, 'was fucking unbelievable! Your timing, me all over the place, and you were just thinking about someone else all the time!'

'I wasn't!' he screamed. 'I was thinking about *you*!'

'How? When? While you were fucking her, or while she was listening to your shit ideas about how Brexit could have been stopped? Did you tell her about your "human chain around Dover" idea?' I'd paced all the way to the corner shop. I turned back towards the bookshop. 'I'll never have a baby now.'

'We can . . . you can . . .' he stammered.

'What?!' I screamed. 'I'm thirty-eight – my only chance was with you, and you just thought, *Oh, it doesn't matter, it's only Jane, she won't mind—*'

'I want a baby so much,' he was sobbing. 'I want one too.'

'Well, why don't you have one with Rachel?'

'I only want one with you, Jane, please. I've not been in my right mind for months—'

'WHAT DO YOU WANT FROM ME?' I screamed. I cried thickly and clumsily into his silence, my tears running into the gaps between my phone's buttons. Mum's friend Monica sailed past on a blue bike, giving me a puzzled wave.

'Take me back,' he whispered. 'Just, Jane, forgive me.'

Chapter Nine

It hadn't been an ideal day. It was the evening of my visit to The Sphere, and I was still in my Pilates clothes, frozen in time. I had a pink notebook in my bag, and I was trying to work up the courage to ask Jonathan who Rachel Gorston-Greaves was. Maybe it would all be OK: we had friends of different genders, after all. But wouldn't I have known her if she lived in our part of London, since they'd been at The Sphere? He usually mentioned it to me if he was meeting a friend. But, no – he couldn't possibly be having an affair. He could barely remember where his keys and phone were. Yet there were times when he was worlds away from me, frenetic and edgy, and I thought, *You aren't who I first met, and* that's *who I'm thinking couldn't have done this to me.*

I'd never been in the position before of feeling anxious about something and not being able to talk it over with him. He knew before I did when I was about to worry about something. He'd catch my eye, hold my gaze and smile slowly. 'What is it?' he'd say. 'Nothing!' I'd say, and then the thought would hurtle into me, almost a physical apparition. The inevitable back-and-forth in my head always followed. *You've left the gas on and the flat is going to burn down.* We aren't there, so we'll live. *But your neigh-bours will die in the fire, and so will their cat.* Their fire alarm will go off. *What if they haven't changed the battery?* That's their lookout. *But if you hadn't left the gas on, there would be no fire.*

This could go on and on all day, running under every-thing I did, like subtitles.

'Yeah, they'll all die, even the ants,' Jonathan would say. 'Not just our flat and next door. The whole street, maybe even the whole of London.' I'd punch his arm and he'd say, 'I will try and visit you in prison, but it might be tough, be-cause I'll have met my hot new girlfriend by then, the one who runs marathons every morning.'

Sometimes I'd play out the scenario of dying after hav-ing children; telling him and them that I had an incurable illness, writing letters for them to read on their birthdays after I'd gone. He'd say, 'I will *try* and pass your letters on, but I'll probably lose them when I'm moving in with my hot new girlfriend.' And I'd giggle and pummel his ribs, and he'd pummel mine.

That night, we'd eaten dinner – well, he had – and then it just darted out when I least expected it, like a rat from a bucket. I got the pink notebook from my bag in the liv-ing room, and I found myself saying, 'You know that day I went to Dungeness with Megan?' and I knew we were in.

He didn't seem to have heard me, carried on tapping away on his laptop. We were supposed to be working on a big campaign for a washing powder company and our deadline was tomorrow. Did I really want to do this right now?

'Jon?' I said.

He stopped tapping and sighed lightly, scanning the screen to memorise the gist of his latest idea before it escaped him.

He often wouldn't speak for ages when we were working, holding his hand up to stop me from interrupting him, eyebrows knitted together, eyes darting from thing to thing in the room as the idea formulated itself. 'It shouldn't be "it's a bacon bonanza",' he'd say. And then more slowly, a smile appearing on his lips: 'It should be "a sausage in the hand is worth two in the pan!"'

'You know that day I went to Dungeness with Megan?' I repeated. 'Last Monday.' I was dismayed to find that my voice was trembling slightly.

'Huh?' he said, looking at me.

'Laura said she saw you in The Sphere with a woman last Monday,' I said, holding out the notebook, 'who left this behind.'

'Who's Laura?'

'Pilates.'

'Monday just gone? I was in meetings.'

'No, the Monday before.'

'Did she? Oh right,' he said, walking to the kitchen. I followed him, waited as he took a bottle of milk from the inside of the fridge door and drank from it in wet glugs, something I'd never seen him do in his life. He is not a nine-year-old or a bodybuilder. 'Which day?' he asked, wiping his mouth with the back of his hand.

'That Monday,' I said, 'when I was in Dungeness.'

'Um . . .' He ran his hand over his head, rubbing his hair forwards and backwards in a rough way that I used to find sexy in the early days, back when I'd have found it sexy if he'd told me that he didn't believe in bank accounts, or that he liked to eat Viennetta for breakfast. That narrow window at the start of a relationship when you can realistically ask someone to piss on you.

He denied it, of course. Then I showed him the pink notebook. After this, he tried saying they were just sitting at the same table because it was busy, but I told him how deep in conversation Laura had said they were. At this point, he started inspecting the cracks along the skirting board, but the tone of his voice had tautened.

I pursued it doggedly. I had to have details then, to twist the knife in my own stomach.

'Monday?' he said, looking up at the ceiling like it would reveal the answer. 'Could it have been Rachel from Bodyform?'

'Why are you asking me? I don't know a Rachel from Bodyform.'

'She's new. Martha wanted me to meet her.'

Of course she was new! Of course she was! The thing was, there were no Rachels in real life, apart from her, because it wasn't the mid-nineties. Rachels existed in *Friends*, and in first drafts of radio ads to sell furniture – after which they got changed to Carols – and that was it. If your partner was going to have an affair, at least let it be with a Gabriella or an Anna-Maria, going to The Ritz on a whim; a knickerless, frenetic steak before dashing up the softly carpeted stairs to a four-poster bed. Not bloody Rachel, in a Travelodge (I assumed). It was just so loaf-of-bread-from-the-shop-on-the-way-home.

Then he'd got a bit cocky, taking my silence for docile

belief. 'She's . . . yeah, actually, I'm remembering now. I didn't mention it, because it ended up being quite a long chat and she said to keep schtum, but I'm sure she wouldn't mind me telling you. She's having a bit of a hard time. She's an orphan, and she's bi, which is causing problems with her family, and she's just got loads of mental health issues.'

'How old is she?' I said.

'Huh?'

'How old is she?'

'Thirty-four.'

OK, I didn't know when her parents had died, and it was rotten luck to have lost them both at thirty-four, but when did it cease being right to call herself an orphan? I mean, the Queen didn't go around saying she was an orphan.

It took a while to wring a confession from him, but eventually he realised he had no other blind alleys to run up, and the truth came out, all sullen, staccato, sad. Rachel had recently lost her mum, and she wasn't in contact with her dad, who was believed dead. This was how they'd started chatting in the bar next to our office months earlier. They'd met when I was away at Mum's seventieth weekend, which had taken place on a bell-ringing barge holiday. I'd been so devastated about my period arriving that weekend, I'd even forgotten to say goodbye to him before I left. Rachel had been blind drunk that night he first met her, he said, and teary about her mother. The worst bit was when he admitted they'd had sex in our flat, that day Laura had seen them. 'Not in our bed, though,' he'd hastily added, both of us crying by then. 'On the washing machine.' I looked over at the washing machine then, at its innocent round door, eager to accept the washing, at its white shiny surface. Something I touched all the time.

Her version of 'bi' – I gleaned from devouring her Facebook page as Dad drove me back up to Foley later that night – involved a need to document herself snogging girls covered in glitter at Glastonbury. She didn't work for Bodyform, of course. That was a lie. She owned six houses in London and Surrey. All the way home, in the back of Dad's car (he'd insisted I go in the back so I could sleep, which I didn't, of course), my phone served up a big sloppy slice of Rachel Gorston-Greaves. The journey was about four hours, and that still wasn't enough time to view everything.

Even as I put my suitcase on my bed – I would later find that in my manic haste, I had packed two hairdryers and no socks – I was continuing to build up my fantasy of what Rachel must be like. I built her from scratch, from gold and flax and steel. It stopped me from sleeping that night, even after Mum's fruit cake and Horlicks. 'Let's do it on the tumble dryer tonight, Jonathan!' my Rachel laughed during their 10km run, before she put up a shelf, ate one edge of a doughnut before chucking the rest in the bin, then won a pub quiz without looking at her phone.

Rachel looked like someone you'd trust not to nick your phone if you needed to charge it on a train and she was sitting next to the only power point. Her dark brown hair was so straightened that it shone like a puddle. There was something dissatisfactory about her face: a Rubik's Cube one twist away from being completed. *Her eyes are too close together*, I thought at first. *That's what it is.* Then it was her chin that was too pronounced, her cheeks that were too high, her mouth that was too sour.

Contrition and regret oozed from Jonathan that evening, but part of him was protective of her. It wasn't her fault, he kept saying. It was all him. After all, she'd lost her mother only the month before they'd met, on top of all her other problems. My sugar-in-tea days paled into insignificance. Even what my head said about me having maybe burnt the house down or run someone over in the car without realising it – the thought processes simple and labyrinthine at the same time, like turning two mirrors to face each other and seeing an orange frantically reflect itself into infinity – couldn't trump Rachel for vulnerability.

Chapter Ten

'And how's your mum?' asked Doctor Lingard, washing her hands at her white sink as I took off my cardigan and put my bag on the floor, then thought better of it – germs – and hung it on the back of my chair.

'She's OK,' I said. 'Her chilblains are OK.' Mum told everyone about her chilblains.

If only I could just carry on talking about Mum's chilblains. *One's called Eric and one's called Joan, and they seem really settled.*

'She's not mentioned them for a while, I mean,' I added.

'Good stuff,' replied the doctor. She sat down in front of her computer and looked at me expectantly.

'Thanks for seeing me at such short notice,' I said. 'I'm only staying in Foley for a little while.'

'Ah, well,' she said, 'the receptionist told me you sounded a bit upset on the phone. We can always squeeze someone in.'

I smiled. The surgery had even pushed my patient application through and – because the senior partner's son, Robbie, had gone to school with me – rescinded the need for address ID, which, laughably, I didn't have for Foley, either.

'How can I help?' she asked.

I wished I'd written everything down. 'Erm, I'm having problems,' I said. 'I've had them on and off for a while, but it's worse at the moment. Since I split up with my boy-friend . . . fiancé.'

I started to cry, which incensed me. She looked so sym-pathetic, I just wanted to run out of the room there and then, to say that that small look of hers had been enough; that if I couldn't be cured by that, I was doomed.

'What kind of problems?' she asked softly. It would have been easier with someone more distant, an older male GP with fuzzy sideburns and bad breath, eager to get home to his pot roast and his family. She was only about my age. I wanted her to like me. I looked at her delicate silver feather necklace. We were currently on a par with each other, but I was about to ruin it by telling her I was mental.

I moved my attention to the window, the summer sky still blue even though mine was the last appointment of the day. My mind raced. Should I tell her about the things I sometimes *thought* I had – cancer, Ménière's disease, fibro-myalgia – or the thing I *knew* I had: the thing that made me convinced I had the other things? I took a deep breath. I'd used up enough doctors' appointments on moles and lumps over the years. I had to do this.

'Well, for a long time I've checked things are off or closed,' I said. 'Like the gas and stuff.'

She smiled sweetly and nodded. 'The gas . . . and?'

'The gas, the windows. Both doors. The front and back, I mean. The hairdryer, the straighteners, the oven. I sup-pose that's the gas, too, but – anyway, the oven and the hob is the worst.'

She started to speak, then stopped.

'That light bulbs aren't touching the lightshades, because of fire. That things in the fridge aren't touching the fridge light inside, because of fire. Flat things on one shelf, bottles on another. In the fridge, I mean. Then the TV, the DVD player, the heaters, the doors. Did I say the doors?'

'You did,' she smiled, as if I was dictating a grocery order.

'Yeah, the doors. Not the band The Doors. Although I do have to have CDs in order, too, but that one's going away now.'

'That's good,' she said. 'Why that one in particular, do you think?'

'Digitising.'

I told her that in London it was normally under control, that it was something which spliced up my day unpleasantly but wasn't that intrusive. Since I'd come back to Foley, though, I'd had bad days where I'd got into loops and had to keep going back and checking that a window was locked, again and again, say, maybe a hundred times, like I was appearing in a weird art installation and had to do it exactly the same every time. And how, if I woke up for the toilet in the night, my first thought was to check something was off or closed. And, because we were here anyway, I thought I may as well throw in how much I worried about my health, another thing that had flared up since Rachel.

'Well, that's not surprising,' she smiled. She hadn't stopped smiling, in fact. 'That's all linked. It's normally about reassurance, responsibility, control. Checking things feels like it's controlling the danger, and that includes checking symptoms online.'

'OK,' I said.

'So, currently, how many hours a day are you checking,' she asked, 'if you include the health stuff, too?'

I looked down. I felt so embarrassed, like I was having an out-of-body experience and speaking on behalf of myself. 'I guess two, three hours, if you include googling symptoms,' I said. 'Is that common? That amount, I mean. I can't stop doing it. It's like I'm in prison.'

'It wouldn't matter if it wasn't,' she replied. 'But yes, it is, to varying degrees. People are talking about mental health more and more now, and there's help. I have to ask you, do you have thoughts of taking your own life?'

'No,' I said. 'No, not at all. In fact, I enjoy life so much I want it to be perfect, but I'm always – not always, but often – worrying about something. That's the thing that stops it being perfect.'

'OK,' she said.

'There's another thing,' I started. My legs were shaking, and I focused on a tiny piece of tissue on the floor. 'I can't go into hospitals. It's bad enough coming here, to a doctor's, you know – but I can manage it, because I think of it as lots of little rooms. Like a house, where people come mostly for minor things, like maybe an ingrowing toenail.'

'Did one of those earlier,' she replied.

'Right!' I said. 'But I can't go into hospitals. It's got worse as I've got older.'

'OK,' she said. 'Is it because you haven't been in them much? Lots of people are scared of—'

'The opposite,' I said. 'Dad used to . . . sorry, do you mind me talking about Dad?'

'Not at all,' she said. 'It's confidential.'

'Dad always took us to doctors and hospitals, when we were children. He'd seen his dad die from a heart attack when he was eleven – he was the only other person there. It's not his fault. He's so . . . he loves us—'

'Of course it's not his fault,' said the doctor.

'But everything minor we had to get checked out, in case it was something serious. He trusts doctors so much, in a childlike way. Like if I'd gone in with a grazed knee and they'd said I had brain cancer, he would have made sure I was started on chemo that day. I used to look around at people with *real* injuries. We were taking up the doctors' time when they could be dying, you know?'

You know? How could she know? How could *anyone* know that our family went to A&E so frequently that we had a favourite parking space, that we knew the receptionists by name, that I knew to press D3 on the vending machine for a can of Fanta? People would ask me how my weekend had been and I'd say I'd just played in the garden, thinking of the reality: the red plastic seats and the pirate ship in the paediatric waiting room where I'd hide apple cores in the parrot's beak, which were still there the next time we visited, shrivelled up. I used to think they might grow into a tree.

Of course there was never anything seriously wrong, but that wasn't the point. The point was – Dad said – it's better to be safe than sorry.

I looked up then, expecting her to have lost interest, but she was smiling and nodding.

'When was the last time you managed to go into a hospital?' she asked.

'About three years ago, in London,' I said. 'With my

best friend, when her back went and she couldn't walk. It was A&E. I thought because we weren't going for me it might not be as bad. I ended up having a sort of panic attack in front of a vending machine. A guy was trying to buy a Twix, and I couldn't move. I was convinced my heart was beating so fast it had used up all its beats, and I was screaming, but it was as if I was screaming through a cheesecloth over my mouth or something? I don't really know what a cheesecloth is, but you know what I mean, right? I just thought, *I'm going to die here, this guy's never going to get his Twix, and my legs are never going to stop shaking, even when I'm dead.* And then Megan came out with some ibuprofen – some bloody ibuprofen – and I went to bed for three days. This is me!' I grinned, opening my hands exaggeratedly, then punching the air with my fist.

I told her how all of it was worse because of Jonathan and Rachel, but that I was never going to see him again – I'd managed a month in Foley so far. 'And I just think,' I finished, 'that it'd be good if I went back on the antidepressant I was on before.'

She checked my file on the computer. 'Right . . . so that's fluoxetine. And you haven't been on that for . . . four years.'

'I know,' I said. I'd stopped crying. *Just give me it, Lingard,* I thought. *Just give me it.* Once I had the prescription, I could run to the chemist and everything would be OK.

'You started it when you were . . . thirty-two.'

'Yeah,' I said. 'I was only on it for a few years. Until I moved in with Jonathan. I was all right before that, really. Well, I wasn't completely all right, but nobody was. It's all right to be a bit batshit in your twenties, isn't it? There was a guy at art college who used to drag a pineapple around on a lead and no one batted an eyelid.'

She smiled again. 'I want you to do cognitive behavioural therapy, too, if I put you back on this. I'd rather you tried CBT first, really.' I couldn't believe how different it was up here. In my area of London, seeing a doctor was like speed dating – you were out clutching your prescription to your chest in under three minutes with virtually no memory of having even spoken to a human being. In my old London surgery, signs on the wall for walk-in clinics read *Walking Clinics* and no one corrected them, not even with biro.

'My mum's friend's a therapist, actually,' I said. 'So you don't need to put me on the waiting list. Leave it for people who need it.'

'What's her name?'

'Monica,' I answered. I realised I didn't know her surname. 'Monica. Like Madonna.'

'OK then, I'll prescribe the fluoxetine today. Start seeing Monica at the same time. And if it doesn't work out with her, come back to me. CBT's designed to help people like you.'

I had absolutely no intention of ever seeing Monica, but I nodded.

She typed into her computer. 'As you haven't been a patient here for a very long time, I'll take a few basics today.' As she velcroed the blood pressure band around my arm, I thought, as I always tended to, that she was going to have to call for an ambulance there and then – but she tucked her hair behind her ear and said it was fine, moving on efficiently. Height and weight were easy. Then she took a small plastic pot off a shelf behind the computer. 'Would you just go and pee into that for me, Jane?' she said.

In the hot, sanitised toilet, I allowed myself a tiny smile as I aimed – and missed, for the most part – into the pot. I would just go on the tablets for a bit, to get me out of this blip. I washed the pee off my hands and put the lid on the pot, then washed them again, and then the outside of the pot, in case it had pee on it, then dried everything with a paper towel. What a hygiene-obsessed doctor I'd be, I thought, as I handed the pot back to her in her little white room and sat back down. I was just working out how often the average doctor must have to wash their hands when Doctor Lingard stopped smiling for the first time that day.

'Jane,' she said, 'you're pregnant.'

Autumn

Chapter Eleven

'And how have you been feeling, Jane?' asked Monica from her wicker chair across the room.

Not specific enough, Monica! Where's Mum when you need her? I thought I'd better try to co-operate. It was three weeks after my visit to Doctor Lingard, and I was sitting on a rocking chair in Monica's cosy rented cottage: low beams, potted plants, ornamental owls on every surface.

'Good, thanks, Monica!' I said. 'You?'

She smiled her Scrabble-teeth smile, poor thing. *Triple word score.* She put her head on one side, so I did, too. She started writing in her pad. What could she be writing? All I'd done was ask how she was.

'Do you think we should just tell Mum and Dad I'm OK,' I said. 'And we could go ice skating or something instead?'

Ice skating, with Monica? What was I saying? I gazed at my hands and tried to breathe deeply.

'Your mum and dad – why do you think they wanted you to see me?'

I thought of Dad's face when I'd told him and Mum I was going to have a baby – a momentary flash of every emotion: a children's flip-book going from happiness to disbelief to fear, then settling at cautious joy. Mum was open-mouthed, screaming, punching the air. I hadn't seen her so animated since Foley beat Bakewell at the Derbyshire Bell-ringers' Championships.

After the initial flurry of emotion, logistics were discussed, dissected, analysed and had continued to be tossed to and fro between the three of us.

I looked up from my hands.

'I suppose because I wanted to go back on antidepressants, and now I can't,' I said.

Mum and Dad had been delighted when I'd agreed to ten sessions with Monica.

'You'll be one of her first clients!' said Mum.

We'd all concurred that this was preferable to going back on antidepressants while I was pregnant. Dad's googling had confirmed his suspicions: there was the possibility of pregnancy complications with some antidepressants. He'd put his foot down then. 'Just don't do it, Jane. I know the doctor said it was your decision, but I beg you, don't take anything except for the pregnancy vitamins.'

'And you'll be a guinea pig for Monica now!' Mum had said. 'She makes mint tea, with real mint from her garden!'

Mum had told me last night that she'd thought for a long time that I'd benefit from therapy. She recalled a memory of me checking the efficacy of a fire alarm in a holiday cottage when I was eleven, my sister and cousins looking on in confusion. But I remembered it differently: Dad and I doing it together, alone. Hadn't he packed new batteries in his suitcase?

Now the option to take the pills had gone away, one

would have thought I'd be trying hard at my very first therapy session ever. After all, Monica could be the key to me being able to just live my life like a normal person. Maybe – unlikely, but maybe – she could be the one who gave me the ultimate superpower: the ability to cross the threshold of a hospital without feeling like I was about to die. But I felt ill at ease, like I'd stepped from a cei- lidh into a Quaker session, and unable to answer any of her questions. I knew my parents were going to ask for a detailed rundown when I got home. I was failing them already.

I could probably have convinced them there was no need for therapy if they hadn't been witness to all the drama with the scan.

'I'm OK,' I said to Monica. 'I really am. I've had the scan, and everything's fine.'

I'd done everything I could to avoid going to the hospi- tal for my belated twelve-week scan.

Once it had been established by Dad buying three dif- ferent brands of pregnancy test that I was in fact about fif- teen weeks pregnant, the race was on to get me into the system.

'How can you not have known?' demanded Mum.

'I don't know!' I said. 'My periods have always been all over the place, haven't they? Worse when I'm stressed.'

I'd read online that women had the right to refuse scans, but the need-to-know side of me won by a small margin. 'Just not at the hospital,' I said to Mum and Dad. 'That's all I ask.'

A midwife had reluctantly agreed to make an exception to protocol and carry out my booking appointment – the pregnancy paperwork, essentially – at the GP surgery, but I'd failed to convince her to do the same for the scan.

'Drag all the equipment here?' she'd laughed. 'If we started doing stuff like that, women would be like, "Ooh, I'm on the beach in Majorca, can you wheel it all to my deckchair and get me a lemonade while you're at it?" Anyway, we're not qualified to do it. You'll come here to the surgery for your pregnancy check-ups – us weighing you and measuring your tummy and things – but the sonographers are all at the hospital. As long as everything's OK, you'll only have to go to two scans there. It's a small department. They're lovely.' So my parents had driven me to the scan, Dad taking the morning off work.

As I'd tried to exit the car, it was like my heart was attempting to jump out of my chest. It took twenty minutes for me to make the hundred-yard journey from the car to the front of the hospital.

'I think I'm having heart palpitations,' I gasped. 'What if I'm having a heart attack?'

'Then you're in the right place!' Dad smiled.

I'd manage a few steps and then I'd see the hospital's logo on the sign outside and my legs would give way. Eventually, Mum went to reception, explained what was happening and went in to fetch a wheelchair. Dad and I sat down on the kerb. He rubbed my arm and gave cheery smiles to everyone who walked past. He recognised someone to do with work, who gave us a slightly bemused look.

'Sorry,' I said.

'What for?' he said. 'We're just having a little sit-down. I know why you're scared, Janey, but you're in the best place. They're there to make sure the baby's growing OK and nothing's wrong.' Every time he said 'the baby', it sounded like a brand-new word in his mouth.

I was positive there would be something wrong with the baby, if I ever got inside to find out. I squeezed his hand. I wondered if D3 on the vending machine still gave you a can of Fanta.

'I thought all this hospital business might have, you know, gone away,' said Mum briskly when she returned with the wheelchair. Dad studied the gravel. 'How on earth have you been surviving in London? You used to love hospitals.' She plonked me down into the wheelchair. 'There,' she said. 'We'll be in there in a minute. The little café's much better these days. We'll get you a cup of something hot, and some chocolate raisins.' She wouldn't stop talking about chocolate raisins.

Once I was in the wheelchair, the only way I could be transported was in a kneeling position, facing backwards on the seat so I couldn't see where we were going. I rocked back and forth so violently I almost propelled myself off the seat, bum first.

Mum went back in to see if they had a wheelchair with straps while Dad and I waited, in silence this time, although he rubbed my arm again. No, they didn't have one. She even asked if they'd bring the ultrasound equipment out to the car. No, they couldn't.

'You can do it, I promise,' said Dad as I paced the pavement. Mum was more blunt.

'You're a geriatric mother,' she said, 'who's about to eat a packet of chocolate raisins in celebration. Come on!'

Still I wouldn't budge.

Eventually, a square-jawed doctor materialised. He was

good-looking in a sort of lazy way, as if they'd sent the best one out to tempt me in. He spoke in a soft voice like he was hypnotising me, telling me they'd already moved appointments around to accommodate this delay, and that if I didn't go in now, even more people would be inconvenienced, their babies potentially put at risk. This worked.

Back in the wheelchair the right way round, eyes scrunched shut, I hummed at top volume the only song I could think of – 'We Wish You a Merry Christmas' – so that I couldn't hear the hospital sounds. This probably made people choke on their paninis as I was wheeled past the café into the lifts. Still, as Dad would have said, they were in the right place.

'I'm pleased everything was fine at the scan,' Monica said, 'but are *you* fine?'

I looked out of the window as she scribbled on her pad again. I should try my hardest to be honest, I knew that. I just couldn't bring myself to play into her hands.

I was surprised at how close her cottage was to The Arch – I could see the back of it clearly. The overgrown gardens with their blackberry bushes spilling over the fence, the fruits dotted in sumptuous mounds, the wooden swing seat, the stone statue of the praying woman. We didn't used to go in the gardens much, in the old days. We all had gardens at home. It was about what went on inside. It didn't look in terrible nick, considering. I could see most of the windows from here, the original velvet curtains up in lots of them. All but two of the windows were intact, which was odd, because when we'd gone there as teenagers, and even on the glimpses I'd had of it from the road since, most of them were smashed.

'Do you feel like *you're* fine?' said Monica again. 'Have you got enough support, Jane?'

'You'd be better asking if I've got too *much* support,' I smiled.

I hadn't worked out if I was even going to say anything to my parents about the baby on my short walk home from the doctor's. I was incapable of thinking anything. My legs were too busy trembling, heart too busy soaring. My laugh had echoed back at me from the surrounding hills in the pale, creamy evening. But I hadn't even taken my shoes off by the time I blurted it out, and Mum forgot to ask me to, that's how overcome she was. They enveloped me in a tight hug while the dirt from my shoes crumbled into the carpet, and I breathed in Mum's perfume and felt Dad's beard bristle the crown of my head. When was the last time this had happened? When I'd got my degree? Certainly not in recent years.

'I thought you couldn't . . .' Dad kept saying, shaking his head and laughing, then hugging me again. 'I thought you'd been . . .'

'It's what I've been telling her all these years,' said Mum, tucking my hair behind my ears and kissing me on each cheek. 'You just have to relax, and it'll happen. It only takes one time.'

'*Relax*?!!' I said.

Then, when I worked out the night it had happened, I realised I probably *had* relaxed. *One time*. The only time in recent years that I'd done it without thinking about where I was in my cycle. I'd given my brain the whole month of my birthday 'off' as a gift to myself. No peeing on the stupid sticks. No stress, and no disappointment when my period inevitably came. *One time.*

It had been at the end of my birthday night, when Jonathan had lain on the bare mattress, punctured like an unwanted football at the end of the summer. I'd come back upstairs from stuffing our red-wine-covered bedclothes in the wash and gone over to his curls, inserting my index finger through the middle of one like I always did – a game like Operation, where I tried not to touch the hair itself. I pulled him off the bed, placed a music magazine between my bum and the carpet, kissing him, momentarily lifting my hips as he removed the CD attached to the front and stowed it safely inside the bedside table. And, actually, it had been more tender than recent months, because I'd felt it as atonement. It had wiped away the mild doubt I'd experienced all day, lurking like a shadow at the corner of the lens: I was being silly to be suspicious. He'd given me a brilliant birthday. He loved me. That was, of course, before the dog shit in Sainsbury's and the Pilates teacher and the pink notebook. That was at the blissful crossroads.

'Mum and Dad are being ace,' I said.

Mum had bought some knitting patterns and wool already, and last night she'd shown me some pictures of me as a toddler, wearing a cape she'd crocheted in brown and orange. 'It's in the attic,' she said. 'I'll get it down. It's always a good idea to make things out of acrylic rather than wool. Buzz off, moths.' She giggled. She'd been like a schoolgirl ever since I'd told her.

In the cape photo, I was on the front lawn, pretending to drink tea from a china dolls' tea set she'd promised to dig out, too. Would my baby do this, just like its mum? I imagined me supporting its head as it sipped from a cup – when did you stop supporting their heads? – and kissing its eyelids. Then, quick as anything, I stopped myself. It wasn't a good idea to imagine things like this at such an early point. It could jinx things.

'I don't need much support yet anyway,' I said. 'I've been feeling a bit sick. I just put it down to stress because of Jonathan before I did the test.' I knew that Mum had filled Monica in on Jonathan. 'And I feel tired in the afternoons. But I'm only four months pregnant. And I'm not showing yet. It's still early days.'

'Are you telling yourself that a lot?' she asked. 'That it's early days?'

'Well, it is!' I said. 'My chances of miscarriage haven't gone away. I mean, it's wise to bear that in mind, I think. Right?'

'It's wise,' she replied, 'to hold both things. So, you hold the fact that it'll probably be fine, and you hold that uncertainty.' She raised both of her palms and moved them up and down like scales. 'How's all this uncertainty making you feel?'

I laughed out loud as I recalled my days since finding out I was pregnant. When I'd left the doctor's that day – even before I'd got home and told my parents – the worrying had started. I'd been eating all the wrong things, surely. I'd drunk port and copious amounts of wine on a work night out when I was a couple of weeks pregnant. I'd smoked a few cigarettes. That would be OK, wouldn't it? Didn't doctors *tell* women to smoke in the sixties? Why couldn't I be living in the blissfully ignorant sixties? On another night out, someone had had a bottle of poppers open, but it wasn't like I'd exactly leant over and inhaled. Poppers were strong, though. Even being near the bottle had given me a headache. Shit.

You can still choose to be normal, I implored myself: to tick off the months neatly in the diary, to float about and give in to cravings for – probably – chips and chalk, to glide through the rest of the pregnancy. Didn't I possess that strength, somewhere? To resist the phone and all it brought with it – the dizzying headrush of panic, periodically pierced by a short-lived sweet relief as I realised that whatever I was googling didn't apply to me? All I had to do was *nothing*. I just had to *be*. But later that night, of course, the googling had started.

On lone walks through viaducts and abandoned mills, where the graffitied angels glowed on what was left of the walls, I'd find myself abruptly halting, leaning on a fence, attempting to breathe through another panic about something I had or hadn't done to protect the baby. I would stand transfixed by the collage of cliffs and trees so treasured by me, so still they sat like a living postcard, while a tiny rivulet pulsed through my head, blotching it all. Who cared about this view that D.H. Lawrence would have killed for? Surely I'd already killed or maimed my baby by . . . by what? By just being myself.

Unless I was distracted or working at the bookshop, I was worrying and going on pregnancy forums. I went over and over the colour of the meat in a burger I'd had in The Sphere the week after my birthday. It was pink inside – it must have been. No one had burgers well done in London, and I always asked for medium-rare. But maybe they'd left it in for too long that night, overcooked it so there was no red? I got Megan to ring them, to say she'd been in before she knew she was pregnant, to ask if they typically served their burgers pink. 'He said it depended on the customer,' she said. 'But that they erred towards the rarer side. He was a bit . . . vague.' It must have been my laid-back barista with the temperamental solar plexus. My old life was now a million worlds away. 'Ask if they've got CCTV,' I said. Maybe I could get hold of the footage, decipher enough from the grainy black-and-white picture to know for sure. Megan reluctantly rang them back. No, they didn't have CCTV, and this time he hadn't been quite as friendly.

'I know Mum will have said I'm a bit of a worrier,' I explained to Monica. 'But that's not all I am.' Why did I need to justify my existence to a stranger who collected ceramic owls? 'Basically, my health's just my Achilles heel – and, believe me, if Achilles heel was a foot disease, I'd convince myself I had it.'

She laughed briefly then, flashing her teeth like some animal who has ways humans don't understand of attracting the opposite sex. Her face was so pale I wondered if she was anaemic. I felt sorry for her. I didn't need her to love me, unlike Doctor Lingard.

'Are you frightened you'd lose the good side if you worked on the shadow?' she asked.

'You can't lose the good side,' I said, 'because you can't ever lose the shadow. And vice versa.'

'*I* can't lose the good side,' she said.

'Well, exactly,' I agreed. 'No one can.' *What* is *your good side?* I thought.

'No, no,' she said. 'In session, you must use "I" when you're speaking about yourself. Not "you", as in "one".'

'Oh, OK,' I said. I wasn't going to say it all again. 'Look, the – *my* – good side and bad side: they're part of each other. It's not a question of being frightened of losing the good side – it can't be done! It's like taking the wheels off a car.'

She looked at me for a long time, so I drank some water.

'Before we finish,' Monica said, 'I'm going to ask you about Jonathan. The scan was fine, yes? Once you got in?'

I nodded, remembering the feeling of Mum's hand in mine, the cold gel on my tummy – *my tummy!* – and us seeing a shape moving on the screen.

'And how has Jonathan reacted to all of this? It's pretty big news, that he's going to be a father.'

Surely this wasn't what therapy was supposed to be. Weren't they meant to listen and nod, give you cups of tea? I deserved some sort of reward for telling her how much I'd been googling things that could go wrong – a couple of Hobnobs, at least. I hadn't been able to eat much today.

As soon as I was released from Mum and Dad's embrace on the day I found out, Mum had bolted upstairs, fetched my London phone from the material box and ceremoniously handed it to me. 'We'll leave the room, shall we?' she said. 'Unless you rang him on the way home?'

'Who?' I asked. I had no idea what they were talking about. 'Stuart?'

'God,' she said, her hand flying to her neck, which had the raspberry-coloured rash she always got when things were dramatic. 'Is *Stuart* the father?' The rash reddened. 'I mean, he's well educated, but his age, and the cardigans! Hang on, the dates don't—'

'Oh,' I said. 'No, no, it's Jonathan.'

I'd unlocked my phone and gone to Favourites. My finger had hovered over Jonathan's name. I wondered how I would say it, who he would be with, whether he'd want me back in London or whether he'd immediately drive up here. I imagined our tears, me sending him a photo of the positive pregnancy tests, how he'd scream with joy. How after the call ended he'd go into the bathroom, look at himself in the mirror and run his hands through his hair like he always did when digesting big life events.

'Actually, I'll do it upstairs,' I'd said to Mum, and she and Dad had waited for me at the bottom of the stairs, holding hands, their upturned faces full of pride.

'He was so happy,' I said to Monica, fixing her with a firm smile. 'We've both wanted this for so long, you know?'

A thick tension dropped between us like a brick. She raised her eyebrows and put her head on one side. I didn't copy her this time. 'You haven't told him yet, have you?' she said. 'Naughty, naughty.'

Naughty, naughty?

'And is this,' she continued, 'because you're not sure if you're going to keep it?'

Keep it. Like it was a car I had on loan, a forgotten sweet I'd found buried in the pocket of a coat.

There had been a brief moment, on that walk from the GP's to my parents', when I'd realised my fate wasn't completely determined – that at that point in time, my future was a blank space. I didn't have to have the baby. Maybe I could get a job at MI5, or go and open a bar in Spain.

'Jesus,' I snapped. 'Of course I'm going to keep the baby.'

The notion of doing anything other than continuing was only heady because it was implausible.

87

'Sorry to snap, Monica,' I said. 'But you don't know how long we've – I've wanted this.'

At night, I lay in bed, stroking my belly, dreaming of my baby. I just wanted it to be healthy. Once it was born, surely I could put it in a sling while I worked – I saw myself clearly, stacking books with the baby strapped to me, it dozing on the beanbag in the children's section after a feed, and us cuddling at night like two animals in their den. I saw night feeds, nappy disasters, adoring visits from friends and family. And at no point in my delicious reverie was there a whiff of Jonathan Chambers.

Chapter Twelve

Jonathan would come up behind me and smell the back of my head. Head-smelling, if it's undesired, certainly isn't ideal; but that's how it all started, and I found that I did desire it, very much.

The first time it happened was pretty soon after we first met. We'd teamed up to work on a supermarket promotion of baby food, ironically – a radio script, which the client wanted to be voiced by an actor pretending to be a baby. They'd asked for it to be like a beat poem. 'Maybe with goo-goos and ga-gas thrown in!' one of them had said in the meeting, as if they'd just discovered penicillin.

So far, Jonathan and I had spent so long taking the piss out of the brief that we'd only come up with four words, to be said in a regular rhythm: 'Goo. Goo. Ga. Goo.' A spider diagram on our pad showed various scribblings. *Organic, adventure, laughter, home, comfort, new tastes.* Crossed out were *vomit, crying, tired, hurting vagina, no sex, strained marriage.*

He'd gone to get us a couple of coffees and as he put them down – one either side of the pad in front of me – he brought his nose down onto the back of my head and breathed in deeply. Then he just sat back down and we carried on working like nothing had happened. I wasn't even sure it had.

We larked about easily, but he didn't reveal much. I pressed him in moments of softness, and found frustratingly unyielding layers. I couldn't help but ooze chatter into the gaps his silences left. With work so busy, we'd had virtually no time to talk about ourselves, but he already knew that my favourite thing on toast was boiled eggs and avocado, and that I had sixty-seven moles, and that as a schoolgirl I'd rung the Samaritans to ask whether I should do Sociology or History GCSE. It wasn't that he wasn't interested, but he didn't come forward with the equivalent. He listened carefully to everything – 'I guess the yolks have to be hard, right?' 'How did you count the moles on your back?' (exes and mirrors) – and, rather unnervingly, he sniffed out disingenuousness in me.

'That's amazing!' I'd responded earlier in the week, when I'd found him in the work kitchen swallowing two paracetamols with chunks of bread rather than a glass of water.

'Is it amazing, though?' he'd said, grinning blithely, his curls falling into line as he tipped his head to one side.

'Well, yeah,' I'd replied. 'I've never heard of anyone taking tablets like that.'

'I'm not sure it's *amaaazing*,' he'd said, mimicking my accent. 'Lots of people do it. At least five of my mates.'

I was just making conversation, you tosser, I thought, also wanting him to mimic my accent again. This was how it generally was between us back then. He'd hold out a carrot,

I'd grab it and smear it in hummus, then he'd whip it away before I had the chance to take the first bite.

The second time he smelt my hair was a few days later when we were about to go in to show our newly finished baby-food script to everyone. I'd been starting to think I'd imagined the first time, or that he hadn't meant to smell my hair. Maybe he'd been looking to see what I was writing on the pad, or perhaps he was ducking to avoid someone across the office?

This time we were standing up, waiting for our boss Martha to join us in the corridor before we went into the meeting. He came behind me and put his hand on my right shoulder, slowly moved it along to where it met my neck, and then did it.

On this occasion, there was no denying it was deliberate, and I wanted it again. I liked that he could be a bit aloof in conversation, but that he couldn't resist smelling my hair. There was something romantic about it – it wasn't me catching him looking at my body or putting an extra kiss on a text or email. In fact, he didn't put any kisses at all, to anyone. *Cheers! Jonathan* was how he signed everything off. I liked that. It was friendly, but non-intrusive. It was a circle of people chinking drinks in celebration of him.

But, of course, I liked everything about him then. Through the prism of sheer hair-smelling lust, everything suddenly sparkled. Not just him, but everything. I didn't care whether the client liked our script or not. I just wanted to work next to Jonathan and wriggle into his silences, taking the piss but not too much, constantly trying to reveal less, walking that tightrope. Seeing myself in his eyes, shunting various anecdotes to the front of the queue. A forgotten misdemeanour from my past would chime forth into my mind at the perfect moment, occasionally even coaxing out one from his. I could magnify my good bits and diminish what Monica referred to as my 'shadow', instinctively and effortlessly. Every tiny thing he *was*, I wanted to unravel and examine; match it if I could, gently mock it if I couldn't.

I wasn't to know how grating it would be in the years to come when he scrawled *Cheers! Jonathan* on the inside covers of my Christmas books and into the neat white patch in birthday cards to friends, where I'd left a little space for him to sign his name, having laboured over a personal, caring message to them. *Surely he won't do it now*, I'd think. *It wouldn't even make grammatical sense.* But there it would lie, in black and white. *Much love from Jane and Cheers! Jonathan.*

Chapter Thirteen

'Been texting you loads,' said Kelly as she clapped a wooden tray onto the café table, slopping our teas into their saucers.

'Sorry,' I said. 'I've been working.'

I looked through the café doors at a toddler feeding a goat something from a brown paper bag. I'd read that pregnant women needed to stay away from goats and sheep. I had no intention of going anywhere near them, but I had some hand sanitiser in my bag for extra reassurance.

'Remember when we used to come up here, eh!' she said. 'Bloody *heavy* petting zoo!'

I remembered nothing of the sort. At school, I had a tight group of friends like Megan: The Arch was our habitat, not the petting zoo. We all claimed we were in three bands but were normally in two, we smoked roll-ups made with liquorice Rizlas, our school trousers were baggy and frayed, and our penchant for lunching on magic mushrooms was quietly regarded by all our parents and the head, who knew each other from the bridge club, as 'a phase'. Kelly, however, hung out with the 'four-foot fringe' group: the girls who applied about half a can of hairspray every morning to make their fringes go into a rock-hard quiff like a cliff face, who misspelt all their graffiti, whose parents never came to parents' evening, and who threatened to knock you out if you so much as stepped on one of their siblings' shoelaces in the corridor.

Even so, in an attempt to numb the loneliness that had started to gather about me in the afternoons, first tentatively, as if in particles, then heavy and sodden, like fish-and-chip paper, I'd accepted Kelly's invitation to visit the park petting zoo with her two children.

Her boys were eight and ten, and they'd barely acknowledged me. The younger one, Sean, had two glossy cables of snot running from each nostril into his mouth like an eternal supply of free custard. I soon worked out ways of looking anywhere but his philtrum, but Kelly was unfazed by it. In fact, it was the least of her problems.

'Their bloody dad's gone mad again,' she said, tipping one sachet of white sugar into her tea and another straight into her mouth. 'Here! Snacks!' she shouted to the boys, who had left our booth and were running about firing water pistols at each other. 'Don't worry,' she called across to a nearby elderly couple. 'They haven't got no water in them.' She turned back to me. 'Just Irn Bru,' she winked.

Kelly chucked the empty sugar sachet from hand to hand. Her fingernails were painted the most disgusting shade of green imaginable, like she'd done it for a bet.

'Yep,' she sighed. 'Their bloody dad's gone mad again.'

She talked to me as if I knew not only everyone in Foley I'd not seen since school, but also members of her family I'd never even met. She had a repetitive sentence structure which I interpreted as the unlocking of a conversational gate I was invited to open. 'Bloody Becca's gone road rage again,' she'd said earlier as we'd wandered through the reptile section. 'Bloody Mum's got mice again.'

'You've met him, their dad,' she said, stirring her tea vigorously. 'Darren. Got chucked out the bookshop for eating a pasty.'

'Oh, him!' I said. 'It wasn't a pasty. It was an Eccles cake.'

'Bloody ooh la la,' she said. 'Wanker.'

'How's he gone mad, then?' I asked.

'Just being a wanker,' she replied, shaking her head.

Ah, I understood. I couldn't open the gate. The gate was unlocked, but I had to know the correct password to find out more. Or say nothing at all. I sipped my tea and watched with fascination as the younger one's snot dam began to disintegrate under the unrelenting stream of Irn Bru.

'Money, isn't it,' said Kelly irritably. I sighed and nodded. 'He's just bought Elliott a mobile, which I didn't want him to, but what about the stuff they actually need? School uniforms, football things. Why should I have to pester him every month, when he takes his new missus to the bloody Steps reunion twice in a row? He hates Steps. He used to say, "I want to push them *down* some steps".'

'Oh dear,' I said.

'At least they're both at school now,' she continued. 'Used to have to take Sean into work sometimes and let him play with all the post in the back. Then he got worms and you're supposed to wipe everything they've touched with a damp cloth. Worms survive on surfaces for two weeks.'

'. . . But you probably shouldn't get parcels wet,' I said,

thinking about every surface I'd touched, ever. How was the whole world not walking around with worms? I'd go and wash my hands as soon as I'd finished my tea.

She nodded, then laughed. 'I just left it in the end. Royal Mail's so shite that it usually takes longer than two weeks for stuff to get delivered.'

And much in the way that Megan had found it easier to talk to her hairdresser than her own mother about her father's death, it felt completely right to tell Kelly in that moment, with her awful green fingernails and her incorrigible children. 'I'm pregnant,' I said.

'I thought you might be,' she replied, looking down at my stomach. 'But you're on that cusp, aren't you? Didn't want to say nothing. Could be a baby, could be a Nando's.' She swilled the last of her tea. 'Well. I'll get you a chocolate bar to celebrate.'

Half an hour later, we stood gazing at Elliott, who was coming dangerously close to climbing over the fence of the pig pen. We'd finished our teas and taken our chocolate bars to enjoy the adrenaline-charged atmosphere of the petting zoo. 'Twat,' Kelly said, as he snorted in the face of an aggressive-looking pig.

'Aw,' I managed, looking at his bared teeth, trying to think of something good to say about him. 'Well, children are curious.'

'No, I mean your ex. Although he can be, too,' she said, jerking her finger towards Elliott. 'What I don't get is why men throw it all away. That's what mine did, too. It's such a cliché.' She pulled on her e-cigarette. 'OK!' she yelled as a wary teenager in uniform nervously put his hand up to stop her. 'Bloody gestapo,' she muttered, stuffing it back into her bag. 'He smack you about?'

'Oh, no,' I said, thinking of Jonathan's hands at his computer keyboard, of his long fingers with a few black hairs below each knuckle, tearing basil into a bowl.

She stared at her boys. 'Get a financial agreement set up before it's born,' she said. 'I'll help you if you want. Get down from there, Sean!'

'Well, actually,' I said, 'I haven't told him yet.'

She looked at me incredulously. 'Why not?'

I kept the tears at bay by counting the pigs. Three. Possibly one hiding in the little shed.

'I might tell him. I feel like he doesn't deserve to know.'

'And you don't deserve maintenance? What does he earn?'

'Er . . . about sixty K,' I said, looking down at her bright pink leggings, crinkled up behind her knees.

'What the fuck? You'd get more than a hundred quid a week, I reckon. You wouldn't even have to see him. Seriously.'

'I'd have to see him constantly,' I said. 'If I told him, he'd expect us to get back together like nothing had happened. He'd never leave the baby alone. Everyone's going to say I can't do it on my own, but maybe I can.'

'How will you, though?' she demanded. 'He sticks it in, then gets to swan around with this woman while you pull favours so you can work? You'll have a bloody breakdown. At least I've got regular pay. You don't even get paid at the bookshop, do you?'

'I do, actually,' I admitted. 'Don't tell anyone. I'm meant to be on gardening leave from my London job for another month.' She looked puzzled.

'How much do you get a week then?' she asked. This had never been discussed between me and Stuart. He just gave me some notes at closing time, dependent on takings, which were decreasing by the week. To tell the truth, the whole arrangement felt like a favour to Dad that would now be on the point of outstaying its welcome if it wasn't for my natural bonhomie.

'I don't know,' I answered. I would rather die than tell her my parents were basically giving me pocket money.

'You don't know? So how are you going to book your childcare hours for a job that doesn't even guarantee you money? You're truly mental, babe. Listen, my sister absolutely lost it looking after her kid when her boyfriend left, and now she's got another one with someone else. She was in the middle of the milk aisle in Morrisons in a dressing gown waving a spatula at people.' I smiled. *Bloody Becca's gone spatula rage again.* 'She nearly got the older one taken off her. You don't have to play happy families with him.'

I stopped smiling. I wouldn't need to get childcare like Kelly and her sister. Mum and Dad would keep giving me money and look after the baby for free whenever I needed them to. I couldn't say any of this, and even if I'd been able to, I wouldn't have had a chance.

Elliott had fed the pig about ten bright orange crisps, it was snorting really loudly, and the 'gestapo' was striding right towards us. We sprinted through the gate with the boys, the staff shouting that the pig would probably be sick now, that they'd have to clean it up.

'See ya soon, then,' she said as we got to where the path forked. 'You're going to ring the twat—' I started to shake my head, but she put her forehead onto mine, and her voice held a touch of cheery menace: 'You're going to ring the twat, and you're going to see how the land lies.'

Chapter Fourteen

The smell of Stuart's Pot Noodle was making me retch, but there was no escape without explanation. I didn't want him to know I was pregnant yet, so my clothes were getting baggier by the week. I wanted to keep my little secret to suck on in private; a never-ending gobstopper in my pocket. I'd told Kelly, of course, but the notion of telling people who played more of a part in my life felt very odd, like it might jinx everything. Also, I didn't want to give him a reason to sack me, although soon it would be obvious that I was avoiding lifting any boxes. He wouldn't have noticed anything at the moment anyway. He had his head constantly buried in the accounts book with his glasses resting on the end of his nose: he was concentrating.

So was I – on avoiding my phone. Kelly hadn't left me alone since last week at the petting zoo. She was texting and calling as much as Jonathan was – which was no mean feat – telling me to just make contact with him, to get the ball rolling. I'd finally acquiesced and said I'd meet her that night and call him with her there. I wasn't going to call him, though. I was going to tell her face-to-face that I couldn't do it, and then hopefully she'd leave me alone.

'Great,' she'd said earlier when we'd arranged to meet in the park bandstand, her voice rich with excitement. 'You'll feel better once you've done it. I'll get my sister to look after the kids. We can even go to The Rainbow's End after. You can have a tomato juice and I'll have the vodka.'

All everyone in the know talked about was Jonathan, not my baby. I'd admitted to my parents that I actually hadn't told him yet when Mum had started talking about calling his mum to discuss 'the logistics'.

'Just tell him,' she kept saying. 'It's what you both need. In fact, it's the *reason* he had the silly affair – the pressure of it all. Men *love* providing. It's their *raison d'être*. It'll help him as much as you.' What help did *I* need? Phone-wise, the pendulum had swung the other way: The Brick had been returned to David, and every time Jonathan tried to make contact, Mum now willed me to respond.

Then Megan would call. 'How are you feeling? When are you going to tell him?'

My sister would send texts from across the Atlantic, which contained the words 'stoked' and 'neighborhood', finishing with 'When are you going to tell him?'

Each of them revelled in the moment of the supposed unveiling, each wanted to have a hand in it. 'Best in a letter,' one would say. 'Just say it casually on the phone,' said another. 'Go and tell him in person. Try and catch him in bed with Rachel.' They all assumed it was a matter of when and how, not if and why.

The previous night, Mum had made a list of pros and cons of telling Jonathan, while I sat on the sofa eating

boiled eggs and avocado on toast. *Pros*, she'd written neat-
ly, underlining it twice. *Financial support. Love for the child.
Unfair for him not to know. Chance of getting back together.
Cons . . .* she'd wavered.

'Give it to me,' I'd said, snatching the pen, but I'd found
myself unable to think of a single word. Instead, it was a
feeling, a growing kernel, deep inside me. He thought the
score was one–nil to him – he'd done the cheating while
stupid old Jane had been in the dark – but, actually, it was
one all, and he didn't even know it. Stupid, stupid little
boy. Fuck him.

But Mum didn't let up.

'It's not right,' she said. 'He'll find out.'

'How? I won't let anyone put a picture of the baby on
Facebook.'

'He'll find out,' she said again. 'It's not right.'

'Have you just swapped them round for different em-
phasis?' I'd said, and then we giggled, but not for as long as
we usually did.

'Do you know what time they lock the park?' I asked Stuart.

A woman glanced sternly at me over the top of a copy of
To Kill a Mockingbird.

'No idea,' he said. 'Foley Joe'll know.'

Foley Joe had been in almost every day recently. 'FJ's
farting in the cookery section,' I'd say to Stuart as I passed
him in the dark theatre area, where books with their con-
tents bursting out of their skins like overcooked sausages
sat wedged horizontally, forming tiny staircases for creamy
moths to flit along.

'Stop farting in the cookery section, FJ,' Stuart would yell. 'Again.'

I liked it when Foley Joe came in because he knew a lot about books, in a way that he didn't need to show off about. In the bookshop, I showed off about anything I knew, anything at all, even directions to the museum. And I couldn't believe it if I actually knew how to spell an author's name without looking it up on the computer, or if I could genuinely recommend a book.

Today there had been an annoying never-ending trickle of what Stuart and I had come to call 'middlers'. Middlers normally didn't buy anything, but they might be a thief masquerading as a middler, so we had to be on guard. They spent ages in the shop, leaving greasy food marks on books, then trundling up to the counter and asking for 'something like – but not – Freddie Flintoff's autobiography'.

With Stuart in the kitchen, I distracted myself from thinking about my summit with Kelly that evening by placing an unopened packet of salt and vinegar crisps on the counter, then crushing and grinding the crisps within it with my elbow. I licked my finger and dipped, then dabbed the yellow shards into my mouth. And then I looked up as the door opened and there was Robbie Atkins.

I recognised Robbie immediately. His dark hair was cropped short now, and he had stubble, which was white in certain regular patches, as if a bird whose feet had been dipped in icing sugar had hopped across his jaw. But, considering it had been twenty years, he still looked a lot like the Robbie Atkins from school.

Everyone always called him by his full name – I don't know why. It had a nice cadence. *Rob bie At-kins.* He'd been in my sister's year, two years above me, and might just about know my name. At school, he was forever wearing a long leather trench coat, which he swished about as he hurried from science to maths, or concluded an argument about genetics with someone in the common room.

My main memory of him wasn't really about him. His dad was a Mason, and once a few of us had got the bus to Derby to peek through the door of a lodge meeting and spy on all the men. We were disappointed – we wanted them to be sacrificing goats, or at the very least having sex with each other, but they were just sitting around talking about people we didn't know. We went outside to smoke, and Sarah did a pee up against a really nice car, with her skirt right up over her head and her bum hovering in the air, and Robbie's dad walked out and threatened to tell all our parents. I said, 'Why? She's washing the car!' and then we scarpered back to the bus stop, where we shared a bottle of rum while Sarah moaned that the dried-on urine was stinging her inner thighs.

The next day, Robbie had come up to me in the art block and said that we shouldn't smoke, that it would kill us, then swished his leather trench coat and walked away.

The last I'd known of him, he'd been in the upper sixth about to go to Manchester to study medicine, following in his dad's footsteps, who was the senior partner at the doctors' surgery.

He recognised me at about the same time I did him, a wet index finger of salty crisp en route to my open lips.

'Robbie!' I said.

He scanned my face and smiled pleasantly, non-committal.

'I'm Jane? From school?' My name sounded stupid in my mouth, too big and too small at the same time.

'Oh, Amanda's sister?' he said.

I nodded, wiping my sludgy finger on the till drawer. 'I'm just back for a bit,' I said, wanting to get this in quickly. 'I work in London.' For God's sake, why did I care what he thought I was doing, what I had achieved? Just because he was a doctor. I plucked my T-shirt forwards from my belly. 'You living back here?'

He moved closer to the till. 'Yeah, sort of,' he said. 'I'm trying to— you know The Arch?'

I nodded. 'Of course.' *Did I know The Arch?* The Arch featured in every memory of mine from the nineties. There was a piece of me still in there.

'They want to turn it into flats,' he sighed.

'How can they?' I asked, realising I'd never given a second thought to 'they' – I was glad, for instance, that 'they' had converted a listed building opposite my London flat into a gym, swimming pool and sauna – but The Arch was hallowed ground.

'Precisely,' he said. 'I've got these leaflets – can I leave some here? I've spoken to Stuart about it before, but we got a printing press to do these so they look better. We've got a campaign to— Shit, I need to email Wendy about the banners.'

He told me the whole picture, wheeling his hands expansively. The building had been owned by the council ever since the previous owner had died in the eighties, and there were plans to convert it into expensive flats. Robbie and a few others wanted to turn it into a community centre. He'd worked all over the world in medicine, and now he wanted to do something for people who needed extra help.

He and this small group were living in The Arch, and they weren't going to move for anyone. 'We're squatting, I suppose,' he said. 'But I don't like that term. We're looking after the building. People in Foley know what the council are up to, but now it needs national media coverage.' He punched the air. 'Bigger! Better!'

I picked up one of his leaflets and skimmed it as he spoke: the building had great historical value, it was not to be sold to an outsider for financial gain, Foley was in dire need of a community centre to help vulnerable people. *Lose 'dire'*, I thought. *Negative connotations in a positive sentence.* The font didn't look right, and it was written in bullet points – all of it. Who'd designed these? I could do better in a heartbeat.

'We'll win, we'll win,' he finished, picking up an Iain Banks book and glancing at the back cover before putting it back in the wrong place. 'What can you add, Amanda's sister?' he asked, grinning. 'What can you bring to the table?'

'Erm . . .' I smiled.

He was like an express train and I was a steam engine, chuffing along. 'What do you do in London?' he asked, drumming on the counter.

'I'm a copywriter,' I replied.

'In advertising?' he said, doing a mock-alarmed face and throwing his hands up by his ears.

'No, no,' I said hastily. 'For . . . you know barbecues?'

'Who doesn't?'

What was I saying? 'I put the barbecue instructions in the right order on the manual that comes with it, make sure it all makes sense. For other things, too, like juicers and TENS machines.'

'Oh, right,' he said. He certainly couldn't take the moral high ground with that one. And really it was only a white lie: I couldn't rule out having to do that type of work in the future. 'Well, we might use you to look at how we word stuff, then.' He was leaving now. 'And tell people we're up there. Come up for a cup of tea — we've got an open-door policy. Foley Joe's there most nights.' How he regarded this as an incentive for anyone to visit was unclear. 'Oh yeah,' he added as he opened the door. 'There won't be any cars to piss on, so don't worry on that front.'

'It wasn't me!' I shouted after him as he grinned and climbed into a clapped-out van parked across the road. 'It wasn't!'

Chapter Fifteen

I'd thought being back in the bandstand would be a bit weird, but I felt at home. I hovered next to one of the white poles that held up the roof and looked at all the graffiti carved into the wooden slats. *Bazza sucks balls. Drop beats not bombs.*

Kelly emerged through the trees in heels and a strappy top, clutching a blue carrier bag from a corner shop, along with a large black bin bag. Her outfit perturbed me somewhat – it gave the evening a celebratory air. I was merely going to tell her I wasn't going to call Jonathan, then hopefully we'd head to the pub together so that I could drink three pints of tomato juice while watching her grab at local goons with her green fingernails.

She skipped up the steps. 'Maternity stuff from my sister,' she said, handing over the bin bag. 'Some of it's still got security tags on, so don't go near New Look or M&S.'

I could never tell if she was joking or not, although Mum had vouched for the fact that Becca had been seen waving the spatula in Morrisons.

Kelly produced three sherbet dips from the blue carrier bag. Her nails were a much nicer colour now – light purple, with tiny silver stars stuck on. 'Neck these in a row before you call him,' she said. 'You'll feel a bit high. It's the next best thing to all the stuff you can't have now.'

'Listen,' I said, taking a sherbet dip from her, squeezing the lolly through its paper bag. 'I can't do it, Kelly. I just can't. I hate him. I can't even read his texts. He sent me a letter with my passport, and I burnt it.' I'd had to stamp on it for ten minutes once it had turned to black ashes, in case a tiny spark set the grass on fire.

'Are you kidding me?' she said. 'You promised me you'd do it.'

'I didn't!' I replied, smiling uneasily. 'I never did! I'm only here to tell you that I can't. I need everyone to get off my back.'

'Well, I've spent twenty quid on these sherbet dips,' she said. 'They're special ones, for wusses.'

I looked at the graffiti again. 'It was a nightmare the last time I spoke to him,' I told her. 'I almost had a panic attack.'

'OK, then let me do it,' she said. 'One of us is going to do it tonight.' The sliver of menace had crept back into her voice. 'You don't even have to tell him about the baby yet, although you should,' she said. 'You've just got to be civil, pave the way. Then, when you do tell him, you won't have to go through the Child Maintenance Service to get your money. Trust me, that is a bloody nightmare. And it'll bleed through into everything, that aggro. He'll start not turning up to collect the kid on a Saturday, you'll have to cancel your trip to Ibiza with the girls.'

I looked at her.

'Sorry,' she said, putting on a 'posh' voice, 'I mean skiing with the dorks.'

'I've got enough money,' I said. 'I always will have.'

'You mean Mummy and Daddy have,' she scoffed. 'Have you ever actually done anything for yourself?' This was a gear change. She grinned sideways at me. 'How did you get up here the night you found out about him and Rachel? I'll bet Mummy told you to pack, and then Daddy came to pick you up.'

'So this is my chance!' I cried. 'Everyone always thinks I'll need help, so I take it, of course – who wouldn't? You know, *Jane wouldn't possibly know how to take care of herself*—'

'I don't think that,' she said.

'Everyone else does,' I said. 'It's only because you don't know me. I'm a bit . . . weird. Did you know I had to count all the banister things on the bandstand before I could get in?'

'So what?' she laughed. 'We're all screwed up.'

'Well, fine,' I said. 'But you've done it on your own. Why couldn't *I* manage it? I've planned it all out. I'm going to feed the baby on demand, I've read about how you can make your own purées—'

'It's not that I don't think you can do it,' she said. 'It's that you're making it hard for no reason. I'll see you when it's six months old and you've had no sleep for more than forty-five-minute chunks since it was born. You'll be begging complete strangers to take it off you so you can have a shower. You don't have to prove anything.'

'I'm not trying to prove anything!' I said. 'I *know* I can do it. My job in London, that was for myself. Hours you wouldn't believe.' So what if my friend at art college's dad knew the creative director of Brave Psyche and had got me my interview? I'd done it all once I'd got into the room. 'Jonathan took all the credit for stuff we did together. He'd just lap it up. But no one can sell something in thirty seconds like I can. No one.'

'Convince me in thirty seconds, then,' she said, 'why you shouldn't call him.'

It was precisely 7.18 p.m. when the phone connected to his and started ringing. I paced the bandstand. My skirt was too tight. Kelly kept tipping sherbet into my mouth to get my sugar levels up as it rang. I was jittery and half-dead all at the same time. *Breathe in for six, out for eight.* It was a beautiful evening, everything bathed in a heavenly golden light. I prayed he wouldn't answer. Maybe I could just pretend it had gone to answerphone, even if he did? *Hi Jonathan, sorry I missed you, don't call me back.* It was so quiet and still here in the park, though, that Kelly would be able to hear what was happening at his end through the plastic of my phone. She circled around me like a vulture, blowing smoke rings with her vape.

I wondered where he was while it rang. A restaurant with Rachel? With Rachel and our mates?

'Hi, you!' came a gasp after the sixth ring, when I was sure I'd escaped intact. I could hear the radio in the background, and little clunks, like he was moving things around. I pictured him in the kitchen.

'It's me,' I said. Kelly gave me a big thumbs-up and sat down against the bandstand, unwrapping a chocolate bar.

'Hi, hi, hi! Oh my God! Just a minute,' he said. The radio's volume faded down. I could hear someone talking in the background. A woman. It could have been the TV.

There was the sound of a door closing, then rapid footsteps.

'Busy?' I said in a voice that was not mine.

'No, no,' he said. 'Just going to my – our room.' While I listened to him pad along the hall, I did the 'wanker' sign to Kelly, who nodded.

'Who's "our", then?' I snapped. 'You and her?'

'Come on, Jane,' he sighed.

'What?'

'You were so horrible to me on our last call, screaming down the phone. It just didn't sound like my Jane. It's taken me weeks to be able to eat properly.'

'Wow,' I said.

'Are you coming back?' he asked quietly. 'Please.' He elongated the *ee* sound like a child.

I heard the sound of a door opening and an amused woman's voice saying, 'No salt, really?' She stopped talking abruptly.

'Who was that?' I said. 'Where are you?'

'I'm at home, darling,' he replied. 'Like I said. That was . . . that was a delivery.'

There was a silence as he, I assume, sank down onto our bed, where he, I assume, had been lying with Rachel before he sent her out for fish and chips and he, I assume, surprised her by only wanting vinegar but no salt – something I had also found surprising when I first discovered it.

'Don't be stupid,' he said softly when I asked him if my thesis was correct.

'Have you given her any of my clothes yet?' I asked. 'They'll be too small on the bottom, and my tops'll be too big, by the way.'

Silence.

'I haven't been sleeping,' he whispered. 'Headaches. Awful ones. I don't think you understand—'

'I'm sure Rachel'll make it all better,' I said. Kelly was standing up, coming over to me, shaking her head. 'How many blowjobs will it take?'

'It's honestly not—' he said.

'Who was that? Rachel or a delivery?'

He sighed. 'Listen . . . OK, yes, but let me—'

'Fuck you,' I said, and hung up.

Kelly sighed and gave me half her chocolate bar.

On the way to The Rainbow's End, we called in at Wetherspoon's, where I was impressed by her standard of quiz-machine knowledge about British politics.

Chapter Sixteen

My initial instinct had been to blame Jonathan entirely for cheating on me. It was black and white: we were in a monogamous relationship, and I'd never cheated on him, had I? He was searching for something that didn't exist: a partner without flaws. Or, at the very least, he was searching for the buzz you get at the start.

But sometimes, as I unpicked it all, I fantasised about the notion that I could have changed the course of things by curtailing the worst bits of myself. Not because there was something wrong with me, necessarily, but because, by making that small effort, I might have been able to stay in a relationship – a marriage – with him.

In his eyes, had I messed up in other ways, as well as pressurising him to have sex whenever the smiley face appeared, and needing him to talk me down from some panic or other on a daily basis? I wondered this slowly and often, riffling through the files of our relationship. If I'd needed him less, would he have wanted me more? These ruminations became the bass note in my day-to-day doings. Maybe if I'd been 'better', my obsession with having a baby would have just been a bit of a drag, rather than something that possessed me.

How long would their honeymoon period last before the gleam wore off? How soon before he realised Rachel wasn't even that adventurous in bed? She looked to me like the kind of woman who insisted on a pee and a wash down there within a few post-coital minutes, back at her laptop within ten. Who'd sacrifice an orgasm to order a linen sheet in an online flash sale. Clean, crisp, pragmatic, streamlined sex. Sure, she could give herself over to the moment, but precisely because she knew that when the clock struck midnight, she was going to turn a pumpkin into a studio flat in Kingston and let it out for a grand a week.

In bed at night, I would wonder if he'd introduced her to his parents yet, if they preferred her because she was more together, more like them. When I thought of his parents, I automatically smelled lamb. We'd see them a lot, for Sunday lunch at least once a month. We'd often stay over. They were the real deal, in terms of how comfortably well off they were. Not like a few would-be well-to-do Foley couples who were friends with my parents, who continually talked about lunching at 'the club', which you later discovered was a lesser-known branch of Pizza Express outside town.

At first, his mum seemed cool. My new best friend. Then I realised she was damaged – so far, so good – and dishonest – oh dear – and that she knew a lot of stuff about me from back when I thought she was my new best friend and had eagerly confided in her. Sadie had thick salt-and-pepper hair in a bob and searching brown eyes. She held onto people's hands tightly when she spoke to them and sometimes vigorously rubbed their upper arms like they must be freezing, poor things, even in summer. She put her face too close to yours. She wore long cashmere cardigans with trowels in the pockets.

I was charmed by all this to begin with. She seemed a bit dippy. She liked to reminisce about eating hash cakes in the sixties with musicians, and how she used to have her hair done next to Twiggy. She said things that sounded as if they'd been written down first, like, 'So, what's Janey made of today, then?' I used to find myself saying things like, 'Just the usual flesh and bones today, Sadie,' and sometimes something more abstract like, 'Worries and joy,' or 'Battenberg, mainly.' But nothing you said to her elicited a concrete response. Her head would bow and she'd smile sadly to herself, as if only she could see through the facade. She tended to follow it with something like, 'I'm worried about you, Janey. You look tired. A little down in the dumps.'

She was exactly the same with her sons. They'd been sent away to boarding school at seven, and my theory was that she was making up for lost time with all this arm-rubbing and not-believing-people-were-all-right-when-they-blatantly-were. Andrew, the older one, a lawyer, would shrug her off like an annoying mosquito, grinning as he did so. He'd physically squirm out of her hold and walk to the other side of the room. Jonathan, on the other hand, adored it, let her wind his curls, even placed his head in her lap.

'I hated sending you both away to school,' she said at Christmas once, as Bryan carved up the turkey. It was an unsaid rule that Bryan would silently carve the meat, even if he was in the middle of an anecdote, as if he'd lose status as the father if he relinquished this task. We'd been talking about family Christmases. 'I loved it when you came home in the hols.'

I played with my brass napkin ring, embossed with the Chambers family crest.

'Why did you do it, then?' asked Andrew, not unkindly.

Sadie said, 'It's just what was done, but it didn't make it any easier. I used to roll around the house, didn't I, Bryan? From room to room, weeping.'

Bryan didn't answer. He was struggling with an unruly wing.

I once heard Jonathan call her 'Mummy', when they were planning what veg to get for Christmas dinner before our annual shopping trip to the village. Since I'd slipped back in to check that the straighteners were off for the second time under the guise of 'getting something I'd forgotten', I shouldn't have heard it. But I did – and I couldn't forget it.

His dad was more straightforward, I suppose. A surgeon, and a good one, as I understood it. I couldn't bear to ask him about my own medical stuff, apart from a mole on my back once, which was on a 'watch and wait' with my GP. It felt odd to lift up my vest and show it to him in one of their spare bedrooms upstairs. I could hear his breath whistling in his nose.

'Two colours, like he said,' he'd mumbled, running his finger over it. 'No need for anything drastic.'

Later that night in bed, Jonathan had held me and stroked my forehead with his thumbs as I'd gone through all the various outcomes again. Two colours on a mole could be nothing, could be something. Had it got bigger?

I didn't know. It was on my back. Jonathan tried his usual 'You'll be dead within a month' business, but it didn't work that time. I felt I couldn't go on living unless I knew one hundred per cent definitely that I wasn't going to die, the irony of which was not lost on me.

'There's no way the GP would have said "watch and wait" if he thought it was urgent,' was the best he could offer.

My ear started to itch and I became momentarily concerned, realised the worst it could be was eczema, then came back to the mole. Although . . . 'Is ear cancer a thing?' I asked.

'Haven't *heard* of it,' he replied. 'Geddit?' I let him kiss me on the nose and mouth. 'Do you want to go for therapy, by the way?' he said. 'I don't mind paying.' This was the first time he'd suggested therapy.

I was defensive, of course, thinking he meant he didn't want to hear about my various potential illnesses anymore. He didn't, of course – who could blame him? – but would never say this. We got back to being silly.

'I won't come to your funeral!' he shouted, tickling me. 'Fuck that! Funerals are boring. You don't want Leonard Cohen played, do you? You want "Ghostbusters", right? Oh, "The Birdie Song"? Cool, cool. I'll tell the vicar.'

I started to kiss his neck and stroke his belly where the hair got darker. He opened his eyes suddenly.

'Or Mum? Hey, why don't you talk to Mum? You can do it while you're here, and she's so wise.'

It wasn't at all hard to set up. After dinner the next time we visited, she took me by the hand to the sofa next to their fireplace as Bryan, Andrew and my beloved went up the road for a drink. I dearly wanted to put on my wellies, too, crunch my way along the lane to the warm pub with them; breathlessly peeling off hats and scarves, sipping half a mild and playing pinball. But it wasn't to be. I was going to be cured by Sadie.

'Darling,' she said, stroking my arm. 'We all know you're a bit of a worrier, but Jonathan says it can get quite debilitating. So, what's Jane made of tonight? Right at this very moment?'

God, the odd *what's Jane made of* question again. I knew I had a choice – either be honest or answer in the same strange mode as I normally did. She was to be my mother-in-law, and sometimes when you're honest, it gives the other person room to be. So, I was.

I told her I never felt truly free of my worries – that each one seemed as real as grass or pencils or coconuts until I received ample reassurance for it to move aside and be replaced with a new worry. Sometimes I had a heady, wonderful patch where I felt normal, but you could be sure a seed had been planted somewhere. There might be something on the radio about how dropping things can be the first sign of motor neurone disease, I might overhear someone say that her colleague had been diagnosed with something called New Daily Headache, where you get a headache every day, which sounds bad enough, but in actual fact it was a brain tumour! Then there were the worries about having left the straighteners or the gas on, or the door unlocked.

I said how work helped because it absorbed me so completely, and how Jonathan helped because he took the piss. This worrying was just a part of me. Was it even a part of me? Should I regard it as something from outside? Maybe that would help?

She held my hand throughout and didn't break eye contact once. When I'd finished, I looked at the fire poker. I was going to know her my whole life. I was going to marry her son.

'Well done for admitting all that,' she said. 'I think you're absolutely brilliant. I do hope you feel better, darling.'

She got up to load the dishwasher, and I thought, *Well, that was short and sweet, but I do feel a little better.* No one had ever done this, said 'I hope you feel better', not even the Samaritans when I'd rung them that time about my GCSEs. They were only there to listen, which was annoying, because I could really have done with someone telling me that History was a sturdier subject.

Later, when we were all going to bed, I crept downstairs to check that the back door was locked when I overheard Sadie saying to Bryan in the kitchen, 'The thing is, this constant fretting is all very well with Janey now, but what kind of mother will she be?'

I had the mole removed privately in the end. Out of sight, out of mind. The next time we went over, Sadie asked with a sympathetic look about 'that pesky mole'. 'Oh, it's all fine now,' I said, grinning at her. 'Everything's fine.'

Despite my various worries, I loved Bryan talking about his operations, which he did with aplomb at every opportunity. Maybe I felt more armed with information as a result, and also, he just told us about the funny ones with the good outcomes. You only had to ask what sort of week he'd had to start him off. 'Do you really want to know?' he'd say, with a glint in his eye, and I'd beam and nod yes, while Jonathan

shrugged and Sadie tutted into her lamb, her mouth twisted upwards into a half-smile. Unlike his colleagues, who
favoured classical music, Bryan liked to listen to the ship-
ping forecast in the operating theatre. A friend who worked
at the BBC had made him a CD which he played on repeat. He didn't laud his expertise over anyone; it was almost like a slight burden he viewed from the outside as his
lot in life.

He'd told us once, early on in my and Jonathan's relationship, as Sadie served up home-made stargazy pie, that
the perfect circle of pilchard heads reminded him of a patient's circle of warts he'd removed at the start of his career. Sadie had shown utterly no reaction, just sliced into
the pie. Jonathan had squeezed my leg under the table and
we'd given each other an 'eeek' look, and I couldn't wait to
be alone with him to laugh about it.

Was that what he and Rachel were doing right now?
Had she made it to the stargazy pie stage of their relationship? I hadn't even heard of stargazy pie before that day.
It's a fairy-tale pie, golden brown with a lid, containing
potatoes, eggs and pilchards. The fishes' bottom halves are
submerged and their heads protrude through the pastry
as they gaze blissfully at the stars. Like they don't know
they're dead.

Chapter Seventeen

'It's a good view from here,' I said, breaking the silence.

What? Was I fifty? I was sitting in Monica's rocking chair, looking across the valley, a patchwork of yellow and olive green. Although it was my fifth weekly session, I still felt that all her responses were too studied to be genuine, and I remained on the defensive, counting down the weeks until I didn't have to come here anymore. We'd spent the half-hour since my arrival at her cottage discussing 'nurturing my relationship' with Mum, who had, to put it lightly, not accepted that I wasn't planning to tell Jonathan about the baby. *Nurture. Ugh.*

'There are so many buildings in Foley, but also so much space,' I continued. I started to rock in the rocking chair, then immediately stopped, as it felt a bit casual and – oddly – made me feel too powerful within the dynamic, like I thought everyone in the town should flock to hear my views on views. 'I like how the light hits the back of The Arch.'

'What's The Arch? My gate?'

Not your gate, I thought. *You're not from round here. You don't know anything.* Then I felt bad, because she was a long way from home, and probably lonely, and I hoped Mum and Dad were paying her for these sessions. I expected they probably were. I didn't want to know.

'It's that abandoned building over the fence,' I said. 'It was originally a hotel, The Archibald, but we called it The Arch. Because of its name. And because . . . it's got an arch above its front door.' This suddenly seemed ridiculous. Didn't every front door have some form of 'arch'? 'We used to go in there a lot – an awful lot – when we were teenagers.'

'What for?'

'For . . . what teenagers do. Hang out, smoke, drink snake-bite.'

'Tell me about that.'

'You mix cider and lager together. Some people are pretty meticulous about it being fifty-fifty, but—'

'Tell me about that period of your life.'

At least she wasn't asking how I felt about the fact that I used to drink snakebite. I told her about how going to The Arch was just something we started doing, like breathing.

And I was back in room six, sitting cross-legged in the corner in a long purple tie-dye dress, Ed Millet using the dip the dress made in my lap to assemble a joint before sparking it up, inhaling, then beckoning me towards him with a flick of the finger like Patrick Swayze does to Jennifer Grey in *Dirty Dancing*. He held my face to his, our lips together, breathing grey smoke into my mouth.

Then in room one, which had tartan eiderdowns, where Ruth Swinburne told us her stepdad came into her room at night and that when she'd confided in her mum, her mum had said nothing and cooked him a Sunday roast with six potatoes on his plate.

One Saturday afternoon, Ed's older brother had dropped a daddy-long-legs into a jam jar and then lit a candle, slowly dripping the wax into the jar. We'd all watched in horror as it frantically flew up the sides of the glass. It was still trying to escape when the last of its legs became entombed in cherry-red wax.

It's possible someone's older sibling had taken us there first – I couldn't remember. As a teenager, it had been like a treasure trove, albeit a treasure trove where you were more likely to find a used syringe than a diamond necklace. There was unfinished business in that building, like someone had stopped typing halfway through a sentence. The walls were packed with secrets. Maybe shit secrets, like the fact that someone who used to stay there had liked cheese and pickle sandwiches, but secrets nonetheless. And then the biggest secret. What had happened in room three.

'It was good,' I said. 'It was . . . I was content.' In photos from those days, I wasn't always smiling, but I looked *present*. I hadn't had to check the gas was off before I'd set off to get wasted at The Arch. I'd just gone. On the walk there, I hadn't had to click my teeth together every time I passed a blue car. I'd just walked.

'How did you used to feel, being in The Arch?'

Hadn't I just told her? I was content. She was going to ask me how I felt about every single topic that came up, wearing me down until . . . what? What did she and Mum want from me? Although Monica had promised everything would remain confidential, I was sure they were colluding.

And I couldn't be sure that Mum hadn't told Monica about room three, even though my parents and I had barely said a word about it since the night it had happened.

'By the way,' I said, 'where's this all getting us? Do you know what I mean? What do you expect the outcome to be?'

'Oh no,' she replied, 'I don't have any expectations. I'm just here for you to talk to. If I can help you and your mum see eye to eye, that's a bonus, but it's all got to come from you.'

'Why?' I said. 'It should come from her, too, shouldn't it?'

'I feel like you're getting annoyed, maybe even angry,' she smiled. 'Tell me more about that.'

'You're nice,' I said. 'I get that I'm not the easiest – but . . . I'm really going to be all right. I mean, I *am* all right. Mum and I will be fine. You don't know her.'

'Oh, I do,' she said.

'You don't,' I laughed. 'You think you do, because of church, but you don't really. I've always been a perfect project, much more so than my sister. So she digs into me and scoops out the soft stuff, then plays about with it and puts it back in. And sometimes that suits me a lot, and sometimes it doesn't, and it doesn't at the moment – that's obvious – but the point is, she always has to have *something* to squirrel away at.'

'And this is what she's squirrelling away at, yes? Your reluctance to tell Jonathan?'

'This is utterly perfect for her! The lists of pros and cons, the drama of it, the analysing of the relationship. It's the gift that keeps on giving. Some of the things she tells me to do, I do. Like, she made me tell Stuart last week, in case I get ill at work or something.'

Stuart had patted me on the arm, saying, 'Right you are, duck, right you are.'

'But there are things I won't do, and she can't accept that because I normally just do it all. They want me to marry Jonathan as well as tell him. They're always saying, "At the very least, he must know."'

'Couldn't this be the girl who cried wolf? This time, it's a valid argument from her? He needs time to get used to the idea before the baby comes? I'm merely playing devil's advocate.'

'She does really believe I should tell him, yeah. She always has to have an opinion, but don't think she doesn't love it, too. Mum and I will be fine, though. As long as we don't talk about Jonathan. And I'm not definitely not going to tell him. I just haven't *yet*.'

Unexpected, and certainly unwanted, tears started to flow down my cheeks but didn't affect my voice, like silent backing vocalists.

'This is really good, Jane,' said Monica. 'I feel like we've made a breakthrough this session.'

'How is it good?' I laughed. 'Because I'm crying? Look at my hands.' I held out both hands, palms down. The end of each finger was crimson from being bitten and chewed, like I'd been dipping the tips in a vat of strawberry juice. 'OK, if you want to do something for me, stop this.'

She smiled. 'I wish I could work magic. I know you're in pain, believe me. How's your anxiety, would you say? When you visited the doctor to get antidepressants, you felt it was worse at that time because of Jonathan cheating.'

'I don't know,' I said.

I spent about an hour a day on pregnancy forums, in conversation with women in Louisiana who'd had five miscarriages and were praying their baby made it to term, with women in Germany whose husbands were jealous of the baby before it had even been born. For once, I felt like I wasn't the odd one out for worrying about everything.

'You know you can talk to the doctor again about antidepressants, don't you? Even if you're pregnant. People think all therapists are against medication, but—'

'I'm not taking them,' I snapped. 'I've talked to Dad about it.'

'OK,' she said. 'Well, if all else fails, this is what I always say to myself, Jane: this too will pass.'

'I think it's "shall pass",' I said.

'Ah, it is indeed,' smiled Monica. 'I've just put my own spin on it.'

She said it felt right to stop there until next week's session, but there were still ten minutes until Dad was coming to pick me up – we were going to the Waitrose in Buxton! – so she asked me to come into the garden with her to collect some herbs. I reluctantly acquiesced. And there, beyond Monica's brown fence, was the back of The Arch. The house with no key, the party with no curfew. Ivy snaked up the outsides of the walls, which were cracked and discoloured where they had once been candy pink. It still looked pretty dilapidated.

Monica bent over at the waist to pick some mint, yanking it out at the root, which I thought probably wasn't right.

'Has he tried to call you much recently?' she said casually. Great. This was supposed to be 'downtime'.

'Yes,' I replied. 'Of course. He calls every day. Maybe you shouldn't be pulling that out at the root.'

'Ah! But I am,' she said, continuing to yank whole plants from the earth and place them into her wicker basket.

Her back to me, I studied The Arch again. I saw movement in an upstairs window, which I reckoned was room ten, and my eyes settled on it. Robbie, in a white T-shirt. He was gesticulating to the room, absorbed; perhaps giving a speech to people I couldn't see, who were sitting below the level of the windowsill, on the floor.

'It's interesting,' Monica began, kneeling back, her hands on the small of her back, 'how mint grows.'

My eyes stayed on Robbie.

'Elephant mint can grow to one metre high,' she went on. 'The mint was the clincher for me renting this cottage.'

Christ, I thought. *Imagine living a life where mint is the clincher.* Maybe this was what counsellors should really do. Have such lame lives that it made their patients feel better about their own. Robbie was laughing, pointing at something I couldn't see within the room.

'Do you want to help me?' asked Monica. 'It's very therapeutic. We can make some tea with it, if you like.'

'You're all right,' I said, shaking my head.

She bent over the soil, raking into it with both hands, and I glanced back to the window. Robbie had turned away from the room and was looking directly at me. He mimed 'I see you' by pointing at me and 'peeling' his eyes with his fingers. I smiled, then so did he, a warmth spreading across him. I pointed at Monica, her bum turned towards me, and did a thumbs-down. He laughed. Then he folded his arms, like he was waiting for me to mime something else. I couldn't think of anything. If only the church charades lot were here. I could have done every *Beverly Hills Cop* in quick succession. So I folded my arms, too. He beckoned to me, a big swoop of his arm. *Come here.* I shook my head, and mimed walking around with a shopping trolley taking things off shelves. He looked puzzled, then after a few moments he smiled, stepped backwards and was swallowed up by the room.

Afterwards, when I tried to think back to the interaction between us, I found I could only recall it in pictures, like a crime.

Chapter Eighteen

Stuart and I sat at the cash desk, watching the rain fall in torrents against the window. 'Lesser spotted teenager,' he muttered as a lanky boy hurried into the bookshop, his wet hair glued to his forehead in blond locks the width of fish fingers. 'Be wanting *Fifty Shades of Grey* for his girlfriend and turning fifty shades of crimson as he asks for it.'

I'd started to make up categories of customer pretty soon after starting in the bookshop, to Stuart's delight. 'Dead-eyed parent,' I'd say, just out of earshot of the poor mum in the children's section, a whining five-year-old tugging on her arm. *It must be so tedious to be a parent*, I'd think, disconnecting myself from my own body, even once I knew what was growing inside it. To me, babies and children were separate entities.

Our only other customer was an elderly lady – 'walnut in wisteria' – who'd been looking at the pictures in the same origami book for twenty minutes, nodding to herself as if recognising a bunch of old friends. All day, nobody had come in with the intention of buying anything – we were just a glorified bus shelter from the rain. We were truly into autumn now. It had only been a week earlier that I'd

spied Robbie from Monica's garden, but the whole landscape seemed to have become grey overnight. I'd skipped
today's therapy session, said I couldn't manage it. Nobody
dares to challenge a pregnant woman who says she can't
manage something, I'd found. What Monica didn't know,
along with my parents, was that I wasn't going to another
session with her, ever. I always felt worse when I came out,
I wasn't sure how much I trusted her and anyway, the contact from Jonathan was gradually tailing off as he got the
message. It had now been three months since I'd left London, so the idea of him finally backing off couldn't come
soon enough.

Fancy coming to the cinema tonight? texted Kelly. *Can't
manage it*, I sent back. The truth was, I couldn't afford it.
Now my gardening leave pay had stopped, money from the
bookshop was proving tight to get by on – even though I
wasn't paying rent, didn't own a car and had most of my
meals cooked for me. I also had Dad putting a bit of money
into my account every month, of course, but this quickly
disappeared on online maternity clothes, my phone bill,
food and drink at The Rainbow's End after work, and the
odd day or night out with Kelly.

'Chuffing hell, it's the ladies in Lycra,' said Stuart, as the
group of cyclists who rode through Foley every Thursday
afternoon sped past. 'I don't know how they do it in this
weather. Right, another hot chocolate, Jane? It's so bloody
quiet, we'll have to let you go at this rate.'

I looked up for the twinkle in Stuart's eye, and there
it was. Not quite as twinkly as I'd have liked, but it was
there. I opened Sharon Osbourne's autobiography and he
mounted the stairs towards the kitchen, but he was near

enough for me to hear him say, 'Doctor Stubble' as the door dinged. I stuffed my book back under the counter as Robbie approached.

'All right, Amanda's sister?' he said. 'I need your eyes. Don't worry. I'll give them back afterwards.'

At the biggest table in The Rainbow's End an hour later, Robbie unrolled the developer's floor plans and mock-ups for The Arch, which he'd somehow acquired, explaining that the enemy's aims were to modernise the building to an unrecognisable extent. The main hall would be gone, chopped into quarters and made into living rooms and kitchens and bedrooms for the various flats that would lie side by side.

'But this could be literally any building,' I said. 'Why does he have to use The Arch?'

'Exactly,' he said. 'This guy owns loads of property all over the country. He couldn't care less about the original features or the history of the place. He'll talk in the brochure about the majesty of the building, blah blah blah, course he will, but really, it's just something else in his portfolio.'

I thought of Rachel's properties on her website: expensive scatter cushions on cheap sofas, all the walls an inoffensive dove grey, white fruit bowls containing only green apples.

Robbie showed me hand-drawn plans for what his group would do. They'd hardly change anything at all structurally, just knock a wall through to make the kitchen bigger. The cavernous main hall, where everybody ate and socialised around a mammoth wooden table, would stay as it was.

The bedrooms would serve different functions: computer lessons, exercise classes, a recording studio, a needle exchange.

He looked at me during long sentences, to check I was listening. We hadn't had much of a chance to look at each other yet. I'd been busy tidying away and cashing up the little we'd made, while he'd waited patiently for me to finish, sipping tea from his battered flask on the beanbag and replying to all his emails about the development, in between eagerly telling anyone who came into the shop about the protest march this coming Saturday.

I watched him as he fished out papers and messily spread them onto the table, wishing that I, too, could have such passion for something that held absolutely no benefits for me. He had a habit of rubbing his hands together like a child when he got excited. Every time he did so, the scrolls of thick paper would spring together again, so I took to holding them down for him. He leapt from one diagram to another, pointing with wide, weather-worn fingers so different from Jonathan's, constantly more excited by the next element of the plan. I fought the urge to ask him about what I hoped was just round ligament pain in my tummy rather than anything serious. In order to do that, I'd have to tell him I was pregnant, which I was sure was now reasonably obvious, but if I wore baggy T-shirts it still wasn't entirely clear. The idea of telling him – even how and when to mention it, not just the very fact of it – felt like breaking a brittle spell.

It was as I was looking through the wording on the flyer that I noticed I had eighteen missed calls from Jonathan, but no answerphone messages. Well, I wasn't going to ring him back. This must be a new tactic, trying to make me think there was some kind of emergency so that I'd contact him. I put my phone firmly in my bag and zipped it closed. Everything I needed was in Foley.

'I'd change the "Foley is in dire need of a community centre" bit,' I said to Robbie, crossing it through with a pencil and starting to write. 'That sentence has always bugged me. Can you get changes made in time for the protest?' He nodded. 'OK . . . how about: "A new community centre would benefit everyone in Foley, providing services the council has backtracked on, time and time again"?' I thought for a moment, sucking the end of the pencil. '"The Arch Centre would make sure that Foley supports the members of its community no matter what their story, rather than merely directing tourists straight to the museum gift shop and rejoicing as they buy yet another pencil sharpener."'

I looked up. His eyes were glittering. Green, with darker flecks towards the pupils. 'You're wasted on barbecue instructions, Jane,' he grinned. 'We'll make good use of you yet, love.' His smile was like the fairy lights on a Christmas tree – it made the rest of his face make sense.

Of course I'd be there on Saturday, I said, as he packed his things away. I'd agreed to keep score for the bell-ringers' charades final at the church that morning, but I'd go straight to the bandstand to meet them all afterwards. We'd march through Foley, handing out flyers, and wind up at The Arch – if I could find it in me to step over the threshold, of course – for tea and cake.

As we walked out, I told him my friend from London was in her second trimester of pregnancy and was concerned about recent pains in her abdomen. 'She's a bit of a worrier,' I said, rolling my eyes.

'Is there any blood?' he asked.

I shook my head.

'And the anomaly scan was OK?'

I'd been for it a few weeks ago with Kelly, factoring in extra time for me to get myself into the actual building. Her complete indifference to my freaking out and the fact that she had had to leave promptly for the school pick-up meant that it had gone much more to plan than the first one, although at one point I'd thought I was going to throw up onto the pavement with fear. 'Best get you some water when we get in there,' was all she'd said, distractedly patting my back as she searched for a 'packed lunch' emoji to text to her school WhatsApp group. Dad had been sad that I didn't take him and Mum. I couldn't explain that it was simpler with Kelly. Part of the reason it was easier to go in than the first time was because I knew I'd never have to go in again. I'd been promised a home birth.

I nodded. 'No problems at the scan.'

'Then she's fine,' he said.

We didn't hug. I turned and started walking away, then heard him call my name in a soft voice. When I turned, he mimed 'I see you', like he had when I was in Monica's garden last week. I mimed back 'I see you, too'. Then he beckoned me back towards him and, without a word, placed both his hands on my stomach as gently as you would on a newborn lamb.

Chapter Nineteen

The bell-ringers stood huddled together in a scrum, David's brow glistening with sweat, a frown of concentration on his face. *Book*, he mimed. *Three words. First word: 'the'. Second word: rhymes-with sign.*

I sat in the front pew with my stopwatch and my clipboard, which Mum had prepared by marking out a convoluted grid of score boxes, and watched as David stiffened his right arm and swung it backwards and forwards. Foley had done well to get to the final, but I didn't share the enthusiasm of the meagre crowd behind me, who bubbled with anticipation and had started to whisper excitedly. 'Rhymes with cricket bat!' I heard. 'Rhymes with arthritis!'

The vicar turned and shushed them for the fourth time. This was on my list of jobs, but I didn't have the nerve.

'Door!' shouted Mum.

David shook his head, but Mum was like a woman possessed.

'The Door . . . The Door Opens!'

'It's rhymes with!' hissed Dad.

Someone in the rival team from Tibshelf guffawed.

It was chilly outside, but I was wrapped up in a cosy

scarf, and I had a brick of green floral foam next to me that I couldn't refrain from repeatedly sticking my finger into. Instead of my usual *Did I turn the hairdryer off?* and *Was my egg properly cooked this morning?* Robbie's face kept popping into my head unbidden, the sensation of his fingers softly resting on my rounding belly two nights earlier.

'Door . . . rhymes with . . . boar!' shrieked Mum. '. . . Floor!'

'Whore!' screamed Lynette.

The vicar looked up sharply from his sudoku, then straight back down, like a weary dog who hears its name being called by a new owner and decides to ignore it. I knew I should probably dock Lynette a point, but my right index finger was encased in a cocoon of wet foam. I decided this foam couldn't be harmful for the baby: it couldn't seep through my pores. It melted away like watermelon as I swirled my finger round and round. This afternoon I'd be on the march, and then, if all went to plan, back in The Arch. I'd let Robbie show me round, tell me more about the project. I'd get him to smile again. Maybe I'd sit next to him when we were having tea and cake. I texted Megan. *Not ever telling Jonathan*, I said. *Just decided. Then no blurred lines.*

Mum glanced over at me for a bit too long, like she was trying to work something out, then looked away. This had happened a lot recently. Dad seemed even more distracted than usual. I'd vaguely wondered if the two of them were having marital problems, since they never appeared to spend much time together. Perhaps that had always been the case since Amanda and I had left home, though.

I'd never returned for more than a few nights at a time, until now.

I was getting more used to sitting down. Stuart didn't let me do any lifting now he knew. I mainly spent my time sitting at the front desk drinking hot chocolate, eating chocolate biscuits and trying to resist going on pregnancy forums. If Stuart wasn't around, various men from The Rainbow's End would silently materialise in the doorway as the delivery van drove away. They looked genuinely cross if I tried to help them, so after the first few times, I didn't. They'd often put the books in the wrong places, so I'd do many trips to and fro after they'd left, clasping six or so books to my chest and weaving through the shelves I'd come to know so well. I'd sidestep past tiny pieces of paper pinned to every surface – newspaper clippings, literary trivia, little competitions, Stuart's version of lonely hearts comprising a passport photo of a customer with their favourite book and contact details underneath.

David had once again taken up his mime of moving his arm about, only with more gusto. *Move on, mate*, I thought. *It's not working*. They only had forty-five seconds left on the stopwatch. One of the Tibshelf team unwrapped some malt loaf and sucked at it, grinning.

Still moving his arm, David began tipping his head from side to side with a faraway look in his eyes. Somehow this did the trick.

'Gate!' shouted Dad.

David did a thumbs-up and finally put the sweeping arm down. The onlookers applauded.

'Gate . . . rhymes with Kate! Late! Great!'

David did a thumbs-up for 'great'.

'So it's a book,' said Monica. 'The Great something. Third word . . . two syllables . . . first syllable rhymes with . . .'

David got down on all fours and pretended to lap from a bowl, then rubbed his bum on the font as if it was itchy. We all laughed and I glanced at the vicar, but he was completely focused on his sudoku.

'Rhymes with cat!' There was a shriek of joy from Mum's team.

I rotated my finger lazily inside its lush green snuggery, thinking back to the baby moving on the scans, how it was kicking and dancing inside me right now.

David hooked his little fingers into each other.

'Plural!' said Lynette.

'Cats? Is it cats?'

'It's gats. *The Great Gatsby*,' said a voice from far behind me, a voice so familiar it seemed to echo inside of me, a voice which sounded so incongruous in this church that it took me a split second to absorb.

The bell-ringers stopped, frozen. Dad looked down, Mum squared her shoulders and I turned to see – flanked by his mother, his father and his brother, practically skipping down the aisle towards me – Jonathan.

Chapter Twenty

Everything went into slow motion. I remember turning away from Jonathan and his family to face the bell-ringers, who were livid.

'We were about to win there!' David shouted towards the back of the church. 'It'll be disqualified now!'

'You wouldn't have won anyway,' piped up someone from the Tibshelf team. 'You didn't even get *Frozen* earlier! That was someone standing there, literally shivering!'

I didn't dare turn to see how close they were. To see if they were really there. Perhaps it had been some awful apparition. Then Mum, as if snapping out of a trance, sprang towards them and ushered them backwards, speaking in hushed tones about charades protocol. The vicar joined them, and as a scrum they moved to the back of the church.

I looked at Dad, still in the cluster of bell-ringers, which was now beginning to disperse in defeat. He looked as shocked as I was. Why were they here? The whole family? When I'd first arrived in Foley, I'd feared that Jonathan might make the trip up to try and win me back, but the chances of this happening had appeared to diminish as the weeks had gone on.

I wished Dad and I could just run, run, run through the side door and keep running. But then Mum was at my side, her drama-rash crawling up her neck like poison ivy. Everybody started to shuffle out of the pews, aware there was something afoot.

'Tea,' she said to me, taking my hand and poking her face down towards me. She was breathing so shallowly I thought she might faint.

'Mum?' I managed to gasp. 'Why are they here?'

She looked towards them, then back to me. 'We'll all have tea, darling,' she said. 'Back at the house.'

Twenty minutes later, my cup and saucer lay untouched in my lap as everyone fluttered about my parents' living room.

I hadn't actually looked at Jonathan yet, which had been hard. The end of the charades was a bit of blur. I remembered the vicar presenting a trophy to Tibshelf with a quick mumbled speech, Jonathan and the rest of the Chambers family still at the back of the church with Mum, and David leaning on the lectern, glowering at everyone.

Then we were all somehow standing outside in the churchyard, me flanked by Mum and Dad like we were about to play one, two, three, jump, the Chambers clan in a clump behind us, a few bell-ringers orbiting, talking animatedly. Once we set off for home, Jonathan materialised beside me and whispered, 'Have you been OK?' but I pushed him away, almost knocking him off-balance, and he scuttled back to his family.

Mum flitted from person to person, leaving Dad and me in silence as we all trudged down the cobbled lane that led the short distance to my parents' house. Dad was biting the skin around his nails, something I hadn't seen him do for years. He kept trying to talk to Mum, but she was too busy flitting, and then she raced ahead to the house. I could feel everyone's eyes burning holes in the back of my neck. Dad, in a forced, jovial tone, started to point out things from my childhood to me that I already knew. 'That's where you cut your hand open when Mum made you carry an umbrella and you fell over.' 'There's the manhole cover you and Amanda thought Mr Draisey lived under.'

Then here we were, in the living room: me, Jonathan, Mum and Dad; his parents and Andrew; and, for some inexplicable reason, Monica, who I hadn't even noticed had left the church. She sat smiling into the middle distance, stroking a crescent-shaped pendant around her neck. I'd been wedged next to Jonathan, who tried and failed to take my hand with his own shaking one. I clamped my hands together between my knees and fixed my gaze on a gaudy sand ornament I'd made on the Isle of Wight as a child.

Everyone kept sneaking sideways glances at my belly, so I placed an embroidered cushion over it. Dad and I caught each other's eyes in disbelief, then he began gnawing at his fingers again.

God, they didn't do things by halves, did they, this family? Just one of them – even Andrew – would have been too much to handle. Silently, I made to get up and leave. The protest march had only just started, and I knew their intended route. This plan was scuppered by Mum getting up and making her way to the mantelpiece.

'Well, I think I'll begin, if nobody minds,' she said.

Begin what?

'Oh, would anyone like any more scones first?'

Some people murmured no thank you, others remained silent.

'Andrew, you're gluten-free, aren't you?' she said, her hand clapped to her mouth in shame. 'Oh God. You must be starving.'

'Oh, it's OK, Nora,' he replied. 'I've got some gluten-free oatcakes.' He tapped a shiny burgundy briefcase and I thought, *How much of a lawyer do you have to be to use a briefcase as your everyday bag, on a Saturday?*

'I don't know what you're starting,' I suddenly felt able to say, 'but I'm going.'

'I'll come with you,' Jonathan said, getting up.

'The fuck you will,' I snapped. I still wouldn't look at him, which felt good.

'Jane, Jane,' he said, moving his head to try and come into my field of vision. 'We're all here now. Please, we just want to start a conversation.'

'Oh my God!' I said. 'Who's told you to keep saying that – Derren Brown?' I could see the dark outline of his hair from the corner of my eye. 'This feels too much like an intervention.'

Sadie and Bryan had only been to Foley once before, for my thirty-fifth birthday; Andrew, never. I started to feel a bit 'pulled under' – a new pregnancy thing, where my mind would get vague and I'd just need to sit, like a magnet was pulling me down.

'Come on, Jane,' came Sadie's saccharine voice from the pouf. *So, what's Janey made of today, then?* A scone on a willow plate sat untouched on her lap. 'Sit down. Don't get worked up. It's not just yourself you've got to think about now.'

And from the way she said it – with no surprise in her voice – I realised they'd already known about the baby before coming up, and that this, rather than a general mission to try and persuade me to forgive Jonathan, was the reason for their arrival. Sadie was looking at me, smiling, her eyes glistening. Bryan had his mouth in a grim line and kept looking to Dad as if for some fellow fatherly solidarity, which he was denied. Andrew was riffling through his plastic tub of oatcakes for an unbroken one, and Monica looked like she was breathing it all in, enjoying it, almost.

I glanced over Jonathan to Mum, who was now clinging onto the mantelpiece for dear life. I turned and ran upstairs to my room. I kicked the door shut and flopped onto my bed, on my side to prevent stillbirth.

Immediately, Mum and Sadie burst in, like we were all girls in a nightclub toilet cubicle, there to discuss Jonathan's unsatisfactory shoes or overzealous dance moves. They sat on the end of my bed and Mum started to rub my foot. I knew she was slyly trying to reach an acupressure point for calm.

'Get off my foot!' I shouted, pulling myself up into the duvet. 'I need to talk to Mum,' I said to Sadie, who was gathering her cashmere cardigan around her and burrowing her neat bottom into the space where my feet had been.

'OK,' she said, holding up her hands. 'I'll be downstairs when you're ready. Lovely wallpaper in here, Nora,' she whispered to Mum as she left. 'Laura Ashley?'

Mum couldn't help but briefly smile in gratitude, but as the door softly closed, her face became solemn.

'They knew already, didn't they?' I said. I couldn't

believe it hadn't dawned on me when I'd first clapped eyes on them.

'What?' said Mum. 'Absolutely not. They just came up here to – I'm sure – to see if you'd get back together with him.' She started to trace the pattern on my duvet with her little finger. 'You're just showing a bit now, so there's no denying it. No way did they know already.' Her shoulders squared a little. 'No way.'

There was a knock on my bedroom door. 'Sorry, Nora, sorry, Jane,' came Sadie's voice. 'We were just wondering if there might be any lunch. It's just Andrew's blood sugar – he likes to know in advance, you see. We'll have to pop out and grab something if there's nothing but scones.'

'I'm not sure,' Mum answered, her voice wet with imminent tears and, perhaps, a sprig of indignation. 'Don't know about that.'

There was a pause from the other side of the door. *Ha!* I thought. *Should have brought a picnic with you, shouldn't you?*

'We'll just see, then,' said Sadie, not satisfied. 'We'll probably pop down the road shortly, I think, after we've spoken to Janey.'

Mum turned back to me on the bed, her eyes now wet. 'See, darling? They're going in a minute. Will you come down and talk to them?' Her voice trembled. 'That's all you'll have to do. Then they'll go to get lunch.' She winked at me. 'I'll even take the scones away, so they'll have to.'

I buried my face in my pillow and screamed.

She tugged the pillow away. 'They won't leave Foley until we all sit down,' she said, stroking my hair. 'Come on, darling. Ten minutes, max.'

Chapter Twenty-One

I made my way back into the living room, where everyone sat in exactly the same positions, like waxworks, silent.
When I came in, they all smiled at me as if I were some
sort of fragile goddess. Mum took up her place at the mantelpiece again. I stood in the little archway between the
dining room and the living room.

'Let's start again,' Mum said. 'Monica, do you know
everyone now? Monica's here – impromptu – as a friend of
mine, and as Jane's therapist.'

'I've only seen her a handful of times,' I told everyone.
'And the last one involved her pulling up mint by the roots
for half the session.'

'By the roots?' said Sadie to Monica. 'You'll damage
the—'

'She still knows Jane's feelings on things,' Mum inter-
rupted. 'So I think we're all glad she's here.'

Monica sat with her elbow on her knee, staring at Jonathan and me in turn.

Mum cleared her throat. 'Um . . .'

'Come on, Nora,' prompted Sadie, 'Andrew's drooping
somewhat.'

'Well,' said Mum, starting to cry, 'this is all unexpected, but it's become clear, and there's no denying it . . . Jane's going to have a baby in the new year! It's amazing news.'

'Actually,' I said, 'I'm not pregnant. I've got a massive tumour in my stomach, the size of a watermelon, and my dying wish is to never see any of you again.' I looked at their faces, all shocked apart from Jonathan, who was grinning. 'Except Mum and Dad,' I added. 'No offence, Monica.'

'You don't change,' said Jonathan. 'I do love you.'

'How do you know it's not true?' I asked.

'Well, because,' Andrew piped up from the sofa, 'I'm holding a letter I've just found from the hospital, about your recent anomaly scan.' I'd never regarded Andrew as a potential traitor. I'd always pretended to be interested in his cricket trivia, his endless anecdotes about how many hot dogs were eaten at Fulham football matches by people I'd never meet. Last Christmas, I'd given him a linen scarf, and he'd given me a Network Railcard. I'd *still* smiled as I opened it. And this was how he repaid me.

'Well then,' said Mum. 'I mean, I think we all thought . . . I think that's . . . that's . . .' She started to flutter her hands about. Mum was good in a crisis, but – crucially – only those of her own making. She loved to create, analyse and then solve a crisis all on her own – not to get the glory so much as the satisfaction of having solved it. She was, to put it simply, incapable of throwing together a shepherd's pie when someone had a breakdown. I'd never seen her this frenetic. Someone needed to take over. Not Dad, who looked on the verge of tears himself. 'It's, it's—' she stuttered.

'It's, it's what?' said Sadie. 'Look, the bottom line is, Jane's going to stop being silly, and – look, we've all done things we shouldn't. Jonathan's paid the price. Honestly, Jane, you should have seen him since you left. Believe me, he's paid for it. Who here's got a truly clear copybook? Well, we'll go first. Bryan, remember the nurse from King's? The one with awful hair and fat fingers you took to our place in Suffolk when you were on that training weekend? It was just a silly little thing, wasn't it?' Bryan looked distinctly uncomfortable. 'Janey, you should have seen her fingers. Like sausages. She could barely even draw blood samples from patients!' She tossed some grey fluff she'd found in her pocket from hand to hand, laughing to herself. Dad had gone pale, as he always did when blood was mentioned.

'I mean, are you expecting to stay, Sadie?' The words cascaded from Mum like light, untethered beads. 'It's just, ever since you asked about lunch I've been worrying – we weren't expecting you all, and we're using the bedrooms for other things now. I could put a Zedbed up, but I can't move the printer. Jonathan'll go in with Jane – we all hope, don't we? – but can the rest of you perhaps all sleep in the same bed?'

Why would they be staying in Foley at all? Everyone kept saying to me I had to talk to them for ten minutes and that was it.

'No, no,' said Bryan. 'Not sure it's a good idea for everyone to be under the same roof. We've booked The Folly.'

So they wouldn't be going back today. Of course they wouldn't. Probably not tomorrow either. And of course they'd booked The Folly, a self-contained Victorian lodge

in the grounds of The Fox At Foley, the only remotely posh hotel for miles around. Only people from out of
town booked The Folly, thinking it would give them priv-
acy to be across the gardens from the main hotel, un-
aware of its intermittent hot water and invincible army of
spiders.

Monica stood, placing her empty teacup on her chair.
'You have a break, Nora,' she said to Mum, who slumped
down like all the air had gone out of her. 'Let's change
things up a bit here. How does everyone feel about doing
some role play?'

'Sounds good,' said Sadie. 'We should be able to manage it, having just come from a charades competition!' She
stood up eagerly.

Monica clapped her hands together like a teacher and
Sadie sat back down. 'No explaining,' she said. 'The only
rule is, you have to act truthfully. I'll be Jane – and who
wants to be Jonathan?'

'How about Jonathan?' said Bryan, shrugging.

'That's not the point of role play,' replied Monica. 'How
does Andrew feel about being Jonathan?'

Andrew finished his mouthful of oatcake and stood
up slowly. He walked to what had somehow become the
'stage', in front of the mantelpiece.

I only need to get through this utter bullshit, I thought, *then
they're going to go.*

Monica instructed Andrew to sit on a chair and to tell
her his thoughts as if she were me. He kept glancing at
Jonathan, who looked away the whole time like he was
about to burst out laughing, or, perhaps, crying. I looked
at Jonathan then. He seemed a bit thinner, otherwise the

same. He was wearing his favourite grey sweatshirt that had to be washed at zero degrees.

'Don't look at Jonathan, little tinker,' Monica laughed, slapping Andrew lightly on the back of the head. He looked completely affronted, and I wondered if this kind of thing happened to him in chambers. I'd never seen Monica like this. But then I'd never seen her interact with a younger man, and I realised with a horrified fascination – she wasn't to know he was gay – that this was an attempt at flirtation. 'Eyes on me,' she said to Andrew. 'You're in Hollywood. Shine!'

'I'm doing this for you, bro,' Andrew told Jonathan, who nodded in gratitude. Andrew cleared his throat and stared at Monica. 'I'm Jonathan Chambers,' he mumbled, in a quiet voice. 'I'm thirty-nine. I'm sad.'

'Don't worry about changing your voice,' said Monica. 'I just meant get into the meat of it.'

'Let's look forward, Jane,' he said to Monica, continuing in the voice. 'Just let me see the baby, or at least have access. Maybe we could make a Parenting Plan with a mediator, for example. I know what I did was wrong, but I'm not seeing her anymore.'

I looked at Jonathan, who was staring at the carpet. 'Bollocks,' I said.

'Oh, Jane,' tutted Monica. 'Try not to swear, and if you want to interrupt the role play, tap one of us on the shoulder and take our place.'

'I just know that to be wrong,' I said. 'I rang him the other day and I could hear her in the background.'

'No, you couldn't,' said Jonathan. 'You thought you could—'

'Well, who else were you telling not to put salt on your chips? The Dalai Lama?'

Now Andrew looked at Jonathan, and Sadie followed suit. Bryan kept examining his hands as if realising for the first time that he had hands.

'No, no, no,' Jonathan cried, looking livid with us all.

'Let's pause the role play, everyone,' instructed Monica. 'You must be honest now, Jonathan. That's what we're asking from everyone today. Was she there or not?'

Jonathan ran his hand back and forth over his hair.

'She stayed for one night. One night. Seriously. I didn't even tell you guys, it was that irrelevant. *Nothing* is happening. She's sofa-surfing. Hasn't got anywhere to live.'

'Oh yeah?' I said. 'Apart from her ten thousand properties?'

'Actually, she wouldn't be allowed to live in them,' said Andrew, rather gently, in his normal voice. 'She'd have got buy-to-let mortgages.'

Bryan stood up and tapped Monica on the shoulder. 'I'll be Jane,' he told her. He was breathing shallowly, through his nose, like a bull. Monica moved back towards the mantelpiece as Bryan towered over Andrew. 'You promised your parents you'd never see Rachel again, didn't you, *Jonathan?*' he thundered. 'You told your parents that was *it*.'

Andrew looked from Bryan to Jonathan. 'Er . . . erm . . .' he spluttered.

'It *is* bloody over!' shouted Jonathan. '*It is!*'

I had never seen him properly shout in my life, I realised, and I'd also never witnessed either of us swear in front of our parents until today.

He stood up and strode swiftly out of the room, then

out of the back door. He tried to slam it behind him, but it bounced back off the door frame with a weak 'ooeee' sound.

I then saw, with a hot flush of delight, his faithful burgundy trainers lined up next to all the other shoes in the kitchen. Jonathan Chambers was going to walk around Foley in just his socks. He'd be best friends with Foley Joe by the end of the day.

'It was a good time to take a break,' said Monica. 'We can try again tomorrow.'

I looked at her, this woman I barely knew, standing up in our living room, telling two families what to do about a baby she had no relation to. She loved the drama of it all, the power.

'And it could have gone worse,' said Mum. 'That's what we all need to remember.'

Sadie gave an ironic laugh. 'How?' she muttered to herself.

Bryan was still towering over a shell-shocked Andrew, who was staring at the place on the sofa where Jonathan had been sitting. Dad, who hadn't spoken a word for ages, looked pressed into himself, like those photographs of rabbits at cosmetic testing centres.

'How the hell could it have gone worse?' said Sadie, getting up and putting on her jacket.

'Well, there are eight scones left,' replied Mum. 'And we're all still alive.'

'Actually,' I said, then I walked forward and tapped Bryan on the shoulder. He stepped backwards onto Jonathan's scone, which had been left on the floor, then stumbled back into an armchair. The heel of his sock was covered in jam. I took Bryan's place opposite Andrew.

'OK . . .' said Monica. She glanced to Mum, satisfied. 'Let this run, Nora. What would you like to say to Jonathan, Jane?'

I stared at Andrew. 'Who told your family about the baby?' I asked.

I'd been endlessly running through the possibilities in my head ever since I'd realised they knew. My parents, Stuart, the bell-ringers: no way. That left Megan, my sister Amanda, Monica and Kelly. Megan was sending me weekly packages from London, containing messages on tiny squares of pastel card about how I'd get through it all. It wouldn't make sense for her to have done it. Amanda and Leo were too self-absorbed and stressed with their own lives. Monica? There were codes of conduct therapists had to stick to, and even she wasn't arrogant enough to risk getting struck off.

There was only Kelly left. Out of anyone, Kelly was the one who challenged me most about not telling Jonathan. Her every other sentence to me was about how hard it was going to be without his support. I didn't think she'd do it to me, but how could I be sure? Until recently, she was just someone from school who'd coloured their leg in blue. What did we really have in common? Just loneliness.

I repeated my question. 'Who told your family about the baby?'

Andrew looked from Monica to his parents, then at Mum and Dad. 'Are you asking me, or Jonathan?' he said to me. 'Am I still Jonathan?'

'Who told you, *Andrew*?' I demanded. 'And who told you two?' I turned to Sadie and Bryan, who were both looking down.

'Look,' said Mum, 'no one told anyone. We've established this.'

'What do you mean, we've established this?' I said. '*You* established this. I've played the game, haven't I? I've watched this – this second game of charades today, all quiet like a good girl. So, I've got a right to know. I *know* they knew. Who fucking told them?' Mum physically blanched at the word 'fucking'. I experienced a great wave of something swirling inside me, and it was not unpleasurable. 'Who?'

Mum started crying again. Dad got up, mumbling something about needing the toilet. Andrew looked at his shoes. I was already planning how I was going to march to Kelly's and confront her. Everyone thought of me as soft and weak, weighted and tethered by my various wobbles – well, I'd bloody well tackle her about it. She couldn't hit a pregnant woman. Could she?

Andrew looked up at me. 'I think you do have a right to know, actually, if we're going to proceed with any mutual respect. Our families are glued together forever.'

Mum stalked out into the garden with her slippers on. I watched her pick up a rake and start bashing it into the side of the shed.

'I'll give you a clue,' he said. 'They've just left the room.'

Chapter Twenty-Two

'Fuuuuuuuck,' breathed Kelly, vape smoke curling lusciously out of her mouth.

'Yeah,' I said. 'Yeah.'

'I bet they didn't expect you to just go,' she said. 'I bet they expected you to drop into their laps.'

'Definitely,' I said, thinking of the shock and sadness on Dad's face as he'd returned from the toilet only to watch me run from the room like Jonathan had minutes earlier. I leant forwards and let my forehead fall into my hands, closing my eyelids and kneading them with my palms until I saw interlinked spirals in the blackness, wagon-wheeling into infinity, teenage LSD's farewell kiss.

'We need to work out your options,' Kelly said. 'Tonight. They'll be planning their move as a unit, so we need to get there first. It's a pity it's come to this. If you'd told him back when we were in the bandstand, we wouldn't be dealing with all of them.'

I brought my head up slowly and she shoved a chocolate toffee bar into my mouth. I bit into it, meaning to tear a bit off ferociously like a lion would, but the consistency made this impossible, and stalactites of brown toffee concertinaed between my mouth and my hand like limp puppet strings. 'Can't you get some, you know, *people*, to go round there and threaten them?' I asked.

She laughed. 'Who? My mum? My nan? Yvonne from the Post Office?'

'Surely you know people,' I said. 'Don't you? Someone who'd just – not *do* anything, but make them leave town?'

She laughed again. 'We're not in a western, babe. This is Foley. And his brother's a lawyer. That's why I've been on at you to sort this. The longer it goes on, the harder it gets.'

'All right, Kelly,' I sighed. 'I know.'

She got up and went to the kitchen and I remained cross-legged on the floor, her boys on the two-seater sofa behind me, deep in the throes of a cartoon about fighting robots.

I looked at them, their complete absorption in the TV show, somehow in *themselves*. They took their trays of cheese on toast from Kelly wordlessly and settled back on the sofa. It looked like a good life. Warring robots, food, bed.

'It's me and you, babe,' Kelly said to me. 'We need to make a plan.'

'Burn down the Folly?' I said.

Elliott, the older one, flashed a quick look at me as if to say: *I'm in.*

'Too obvious,' said Kelly.

'Oh, I was joking,' I said hurriedly. Who knew who these kids would tell at school? And what if The Folly happened to burn down that evening, by coincidence? It was old and would probably burn down easily. Even if they couldn't prove I'd done it based on statements from the kids – which I wouldn't have! – it would be like I'd willed it somehow. Was there some way I could protect The Folly from burning down? I could go and keep watch over it all night, but I'd probably fall asleep. Call the fire brigade anonymously, just in case?

'I don't want Jonathan to come to any harm,' I announced loudly, so the boys would note it, too. I sighed. 'I really don't. I just want him to go home. All of them. You don't know how determined they are.'

'You know what we need to do, don't you?' Kelly said, breathing out a cloud of blackcurrant vape smoke. 'Get him on his own.'

'Did you know Robbie Atkins is trying to turn The Arch into some community centre?' said Kelly as we drove past it, starting our climb towards the moors.

I peered at it in the darkness. There were numerous banners on the front of it outlining the campaign: ways to help, to donate, to give time. The curtains were drawn for the evening. They'd all be eating cake by now in the main hall, dissecting the day's events.

'Yeah,' I said. I hadn't even texted him to say I wasn't able to go on the march. 'I just can't believe Mum did it,' I breathed, gazing at The Arch in the rear-view mirror until it disappeared from view.

'Here we go again,' said Kelly, grinning. Then she said more softly, 'I know, babe, I know.'

She and I had spent all afternoon going over the hows and whys. I must have said 'I just can't believe Mum did it' upwards of fifty times. Kelly maintained that I ought to hear Mum's reasons, but I was too angry to even answer her phone calls.

There was a bit of Mum that had fallen in love with Jonathan back when I had. It was a barbed, sharp, deep affection, like she fantasised about being thirty years younger, and she and him having the sort of relationship where she pelted him with saucepans for buying her the wrong type of necklace, or some similar bullshit that only happens in films. Even when he'd mucked things up in the past – when he'd mistakenly called me his ex's name once, or that year he'd forgotten my birthday – there had always been an *Oh, Jonathan, what have you done now?* bobbing below the surface. With Rachel, though, it had been different. I'd felt for the first time that Mum hated him, that she was completely on my side. Which made her betrayal in telling him so hard to understand.

Dad had never been sure about him. He'd never stated this, but the fact of it was just known and absorbed, like these tiny familial dissatisfactions are: one drop of vanilla essence in an enormous cake. Jonathan's presence filled the room even more when Dad was there – and Dad would sometimes be silent for hours, listening to Jonathan's stories about mishaps at work with a slightly suspicious detachment.

'I don't think it's about sides,' said Kelly. 'She's still on your side if she wants him to know. In fact, she's done you a favour.'

'You're only saying that because you think she's in the right,' I said.

'At least my mum's never been there for me,' she smiled. 'I can't feel let down by her if I've never been let up by her.'

I nodded.

'Bloody gone mad *again*, my mum,' she continued.

'Kicked my sister and her kids out again, and there's only cat food and dolly mixtures in the cupboards.'

'Can we have some dolly mixtures, Mum?' asked Sean as Kelly backed the car into a mini car park across the gardens from The Folly.

'Afterwards you can,' she said. 'If you do what you're told. Right, here we are then. The Folly at The Fox At Foley. Bloody stupid name.'

I wasn't quite sure how our plan was going to work, but Kelly assured me it would as she adjusted the boys' masks. Halloween was only a few weeks away after all, she said, and Batman and Robin were pretty typical trick-or-treat costumes.

I'd never actually been into The Folly, only seen it from the outside. As a teenager, I'd helped at various functions in the main hotel. I'd carried trays of canapés like Bambi might, skittering into tables, trying to make myself invisible. The Folly was slightly downhill from the imposing main building, across a vast ornamental garden.

Kelly and I hid behind a hedge that bordered the car park as the boys crept towards The Folly, all the lights of which were on, which boded well. The four of us had been monitoring the building for a good ten minutes, and had managed to establish whose bedroom was whose, that Sadie liked to examine her neck from lots of different angles, and that Andrew watched a lot of rolling news, in a dressing gown much fluffier than you'd expect for a lawyer. Finally, we saw Jonathan moving about in the kitchen, getting his squash. He always took a pint of orange squash to drink while he read in bed, then complained that he had to get up to pee in the night.

We lost sight of the kids as they pelted round to the side door.

'Don't worry,' Kelly said, bringing out her mobile. 'Elliott's downloaded a baby monitor app thing so we can hear what they're saying.'

I heard some knocking, then the sound of a door opening, Jonathan's voice saying 'Yes? Can I help you?' and Elliott and Sean shouting, 'Trick or treat?'

This wasn't part of the plan – they were just supposed to hand over the note I'd written, unless someone other than Jonathan answered, in which case trick or treat was a back-up, a way of playing for time, during which, hopefully, Jonathan would come to the door to see what was going on.

'Er, you're a bit early for Halloween,' we heard Jonathan say. Then, 'Does the hotel know you're here?'

Kelly and I smirked at each other. I could imagine him with his pint of orange squash in his hand, wanting to close the door. Perhaps a little scared. We listened intently to her phone, our heads cocked together in the moonlight. Then it was happening before we could stop it.

'Come and meet Jane in the car park,' Elliott hissed. 'Or we'll burn down the house like she said, you sad motherfucker.'

Chapter Twenty-Three

Jonathan was still out of breath five minutes in, his cheeks bright red against a pale, frightened face. We stood together on the lawn beside a defunct stone fountain with cherubs carved into its base, which we were taking it in turns to kick. He was in the same type of dressing gown as Andrew, and I realised they must have been provided by The Folly. I could see Kelly and the boys eating sweets in the car, avidly watching us. I had her phone in my pocket so they could listen on the app.

The two of us stood with our arms dangling limply by our sides like empty sausage casings. Finally, the silence was broken.

'I had a dream about you last night,' he said.

The first text I ever sent him wasn't related to a client or a deadline, it was: 'I had a dream about you last night.'

This was after all the hair-smelling business. I'd had a dream that we were in a nightclub in front of all our clients, and we were holding each other and whispering together. Nothing else. When I'd woken up, I couldn't remember what we'd been whispering. It was about the proximity, and the fact that no one could say we were doing anything wrong, but we knew we wanted to be alone together. It was the promise it held.

As I'd prepared to go into work – showered, eaten breakfast, checked my straighteners were off – I was buzzing off the feeling of being in his arms, even though it hadn't happened. I was nervous about seeing him. And then the dream started to fade – the memory I was carefully turning over and over like a tiny jewel became fuzzy around the edges. Soon I could only remember the actions, rather than the feelings, and then just that our clients had been watching us hug, and then barely even that. Just a ghost of a memory of a feeling. Desperate to breathe life into it, I texted him on the way to the Tube.

I didn't put a kiss. Or a full stop. I mean, I didn't have many eggs in my basket as it was. It had to look casual. As I rode up the escalator at Oxford Circus Station, I was almost trembling with anticipation, at the same time chastising myself for sending it on the way to work. I was going to see him in fifteen minutes! What was I going to do if he hadn't replied? Megan would be the one who'd pick up the pieces over lunch in Soho. I almost felt sorry for her in advance.

When my phone lit up as I ran up the steps towards daylight, I could feel my heart thumping in my ears like a caged bird. *Text Message Received.* It would only be Mum, saying that black pudding was in fact a superfood, or Martha telling me about a changed deadline. I unlocked my phone. *Jonathan C Mob.* If only I could remain on this delicious precipice forever, never opening the text, but knowing I could.

I opened the text. *Did you now?* it said. No kiss.

My fingers flurried over the letters as I typed. *Yeah,* I put. *We were hugging in a nightclub and whispering to each other in front of people, but they couldn't hear.*

I'd turned the corner onto Great Marlborough Street. I was going to see him in five minutes. We'd have to talk about the difficult beer company who wanted one of their own staff to write the scripts. His reply came back quickly. *What were we whispering, Jane?*

I thought about all the things I could put, but decided to stick to the truth. *I don't know,* I wrote. *I want to know so fucking badly.* It came then, like a sudden burst of bright light. A crystal-clear sensation of his lips brushing my earlobe in the dream, almost feeling his tongue on my skin as his mouth formed those elusive words.

The first time we'd slept together, a few weeks later, I wanted it to be as erotic as the dream. But, of course, it was vastly different. We'd stayed late in the office and had ended up going to the pub, drinking pints and sharing crisps, and our hands had snaked towards each other until it was inevitable that we'd kiss. Later, I felt relief as I realised the sex had been better than fine: we hadn't upset each other, we'd both enjoyed it, there were no awkward moments, and we appeared to understand each other's bodies to a basic extent. It wasn't adventurous in any sense, but then no one wants to say, 'Hey, let's pretend I'm a bored housewife and you're a sexy plumber,' to their work colleague the first time.

As I lay there afterwards, repeatedly flicking the neatly knotted condom into his side – which he didn't seem to mind – I ached for the feeling the dream had given me. I vowed next time to ask him to hold me for ages, and to whisper in my ear slowly and gently, before we did anything at all. But the next time we did it we were at the yearly advertising awards, in a toilet cubicle. I'd just stopped a completely wasted Martha from drawing out 500 pounds from the cashpoint so she could 'make it rain' at our table when we inevitably won our categories. Shortly afterwards, I was straddling a sweaty Jonathan, whose curls brushed my chin as he took my top down with one hand and my tampon out with the other.

Now, five years on, it was his turn to use the 'I had a dream about you last night' line. He stood before me with his chin tilted upwards, hands plunged deep into his dressing-gown pockets.

'Did you now?' I said flatly, sliding down against the cold stone of the fountain to sit on the edge. He looked marginally less miserable, and I realised this was the first time I'd shown a shred of interest in anything he had to say since I'd left London.

'We had a baby boy, in the dream,' he said, smiling for a moment. 'I was constantly . . . I was trying not to make you two leave me. I was worried he was too small to go on the slide.'

It struck me he could be making this up.

'I think it's a girl,' I said. 'Apparently you want carbs and meat if it's a boy. I only want to eat loads of cake and strawberries.'

'We've always eaten loads of cake and strawberries,' he said.

'Shut up,' I snapped. 'And a newborn wouldn't go on a slide, you bloody idiot.'

'Can I feel it?' he asked, gingerly sitting down next to me.

I didn't say anything, and he put his hand on my stomach but kept it still, didn't stroke it.

'I'm your dad,' he said softly to my black coat. 'Hello, I'm your dad.'

I stared straight ahead.

'*Frère Jacques, Frère Jacques, dormez-vous . . .*' he sang in a faltering voice. He trailed off and pulled his hand away. 'Shouldn't it be kicking?' he said, his voice uneven.

'It does kick,' I answered. 'Just not on demand. Don't make me worry any more than I am.'

'OK. Sorry. I . . . I . . .' he stuttered, making a swirly pattern in the gravel with his heel. He was barefoot, I realised, and this fact was somehow like some final clue slotting into place. 'Can you remember how much we both wanted a baby? I just want to know that you remember that, before you decide what to do.'

I didn't say anything. Of course I remembered. *We'll get there together. We will, we will, we will.*

'I think we got a little bit . . . separate about it,' he said. 'But please, just remember that.' His head drooped down and his ridiculously fluffy shoulders hunched forward. 'Can I touch it again?' he asked, looking at me sideways from under his hair.

I nodded and he put his hand on my tummy again. Both of us were crying.

'I've got you something,' he said. 'Back in the . . . the place. A hypnobirthing CD. And some folic acid.'

'I've got loads,' I replied. 'I take a pregnancy multi-vitamin thing.'

'Course,' he said.

'You didn't expect me to just take folic acid, did you?' I said. 'When there's a multimillion-pound pregnancy in-dustry a mere tap away?'

We smiled and stared in silence across the gardens, at cars arriving and tipsy couples outside the hotel's main en-trance, a man giving a woman his jacket and lighting his cigarette from the end of hers.

Jonathan rubbed his hand to and fro over his head, then turned and told me in a low voice that he felt the affair had been some form of breakdown. The whole thing was a blur. All he'd wanted since I'd left was to talk to me in person, alone. He, too, was bewildered about the role-play thing earlier that day. What was Monica think-ing, and who was she anyway? he said. He couldn't stop them from all coming up. He wanted to give me a thou-sand pounds tonight, and then more when I needed it. But only on the condition that he could see the baby once it was born.

I glanced to Kelly's car. The three of them were nod-ding vigorously and doing the signal for 'higher' with their hands.

'OK, so in the evenings, you and Rachel – what? Eat together?' I asked. 'Decide who loads the dishwasher?'

'No, no,' he said. 'We don't eat together—'

'So she *is* still living there!' I snapped, getting up. 'All that bullshit you said earlier about her staying for one night!'

He reddened. 'OK, listen,' he began, 'I said that before

because Dad would have killed me. She's been staying to help me. I can't be alone since you've gone, Jane. I can't sleep. I've been feeling dizzy—'

'Dizzy?!' I said. 'Boo-fucking-hoo!'

'She's not like us, Jane. She seems so strait-laced, but . . . she's kind of unpredictable. She's already seeing someone else – an artist from Hackney, a woman. Capricorn. She stays, too. They look after me. They'll go whenever you want. You'd really like Capricorn. She's got an exhibition where she's emptied gravel all over Tory— it doesn't matter . . .'

I started walking towards the car. Elliott was totally gripped, a pink dolly mixture frozen halfway to his mouth.

'Just go back to London, all of you!' I shouted back to him. 'You're incapable of living without women telling you what to do! It doesn't even matter who!'

'That's not true!' he yelled.

Our voices had carried across the pond. The couple smoking at the hotel doorway turned to look at us, visibly interested in the spectacle unfolding. Ah, in for a penny, in for a pound.

'You know what?' I turned around fully to tell Jonathan, to tell Kelly and the boys, to tell all the guests in the vicinity. 'I hope it *is* a girl, then it won't be anything like you.'

Chapter Twenty-Four

'Nah, it was when he started crying the first time,' said Sean, rocking with laughter in the back of the car as we drove towards town. 'It was so lame.'

'No,' said Elliott. 'It was when he was like, "Now, can I offer you a grand to see this bluddy babby when it cometh out?"'

'I bet his mum still wipes his bum!' sniggered Sean, spitting sweets all over the back of my seat in his mirth.

'Looks like we're going to have to do plan B,' said Kelly. 'Burn down The Folly. Why didn't you just take the money, babe?'

I looked out of the window across the moors. Kelly wasn't using her full beams at all, which was making me nervous. There were very few other cars on the road, it being so late at night.

'Want me to operate the headlights?' I asked. 'It's another thing to think about, isn't it? I wish there could be some sort of sensor—'

'Broken,' she replied. 'It's OK. I know these roads like the back of my twat. And' – she smirked across, whispering

– 'these roads know the back of my twat like the backs of their hands.'

I remembered coming up here with Waggy when I was about seventeen. What had been his real name? Something Wagstaffe. Phil? James? He'd had a van, as his family had run a building business. I used to find it so uncomfortable trying to do stuff in a car, gearsticks jamming into flanks and windscreen wipers being set off by elbows. He was always talking about how he was going to 'get out' of the family business and become a rich gangster in Manchester, have a suit specially made for him.

'What's Waggy doing now?' I said to Kelly.

'Working at the quarry,' she replied. 'Nights. Wears tracky bottoms halfway down his arse. On New Year's Eve, we stuck a daffodil from the middle of the round-about down his bum slit and he didn't notice all night till someone said it needed watering.' She cackled and banged the steering wheel with her fist, her other hand lying limp-ly in her lap like a fan of playing cards. I swore never to get into a car with her again.

'Who?' said Sean from the back. 'Who watered it?'

As we approached the crest of the hill, there was a parked car at the roadside with a dim light on inside. 'Oh, that's Lyndsey's car,' she said, slamming on the brakes and wind-ing her window down. 'Oi-oi, Lynds!' The other window inched down slowly, then back up again. 'Naughty little piglet!' Kelly shouted, driving off with a roar of laughter.

We passed the convent, The Arch and Monica's cottage, then the bookshop, then the end of the alley that led to my parents' house, dappled with pale pink flowers, like stars; then along the river, towards our old high school and, ultimately, Kelly's, where the invitation was open for me to stay. She had a small spare room, but her sister, Becca, was staying in there tonight with her two children, so I'd be on the sofa. Apart from how uncomfortable the sofa would be to sleep on, I'd seen what Sean and Elliott put down the backs of the cushions. Food, bogeys and worse, probably. They were constantly putting their dirty shoes all over it. I'd be breathing that in. The baby would be breathing that in.

I looked to my left up the hill and waited for the roof of The Arch to materialise. Making itself the full stop in the sentence, the cuckoo in the nest.

We pulled up outside Kelly's. 'Hey, listen, I'm going to go and try and talk to Mum after all,' I said. 'I'll walk home.'

'Good move,' she said.

Half an hour later, I was stationed in the bus shelter opposite The Arch, clutching my overnight bag and shivering a little. The building was still very much alive with people. Lights on all levels blinked on and off like doors on an advent calendar opening and closing. I watched from the darkness as Foley Joe stumbled out of the front door, shouting his goodbyes. The noise carried crisply across the still night air. 'It were a good day,' he said over his shoulder. 'It's all in the hands o' the spirits now.'

Robbie came out onto the pavement and clasped him in a bear hug. 'It's in the hands of the council, mate,' he said. 'And the developer. We'll get there. I can feel it. You made a difference today, Joe.' He released his grip and waved him off before closing the door. Foley Joe tottered down the hill, periodically stopping to wave at the moon.

My phone bleeped: Kelly. *Home yet babe? x.*

Yep, I typed. *Thanks for today x.*

There were thirty-three missed calls from my parents' landline, and even more from Jonathan.

I carried my bag up to the door, which was the same old scarlet colour but now plastered with information about the campaign, and stood beneath the grey arch. I was so tired I was stumbling over my own feet. I was starving. Robbie had said The Arch was 'open door', but the door certainly wasn't open. I tried pushing it. It didn't budge. I'd never had to knock before. I clasped my hand around the rusty knocker and held it tight.

The curtains to the main hall were drawn, but I could see a blurred view through the stained-glass porthole cut into the door. I could just make out the staircase, where Megan and I had sat cross-legged and pricked each other's fingers with a pin, clasping them together to become blood sisters. The green sofa was still there, the battered leather one I'd always curl up in after rows with Mum and Dad. Then they'd come in and haul me out, kicking and screaming, sometimes take me to hospital for a check-over, in case I'd 'inadvertently inhaled marijuana'.

My memories of the building fell into two boxes: the bit of The Arch that wasn't room three, and room three. At the thought of the latter, my heart started beating sickeningly fast, and I put my forehead on the cold stone until I felt able to stand unaided.

My parents were ringing me again. I let it go to answerphone again. I breathed in for six, out for eight, and I raised the knocker.

Chapter Twenty-Five

'Round and round the garden . . .' crooned Foley Joe from above my head as I rubbed my eyes, easing myself up onto my elbows in the dry bath, where I lay fully clothed, covered in blankets. Where was I? Blinking, I took in the familiar tiles of the bookshop bathroom.

He was holding a long wooden scrubbing brush above my head. 'Hair's looking a tad greasy,' he said.

'Piss off, FJ,' I mumbled, clambering out of the bath and pushing him from the room. I looked in the mirror: he was right. I'd do it myself in the sink later.

My entrance back into The Arch after my twenty years of absence had failed catastrophically. Instead of letting go of the knocker so that it actually made a noise, I'd placed it softly back down and skulked along the road to the bookshop, using my key to let myself in. The bath, filled with towels and blankets I'd found in the cupboard, had been the only suitable place I could think of to sleep; I certainly wasn't going to knock at Stuart's cottage. In fact, it would be better if he didn't find out I'd slept here at all.

'What time is it?' I shouted through the door to Foley

Joe, splashing cold water on my face. I needed to charge my phone. My ribs ached.

'Well, the shop's open,' he said. 'Stewpot's got a red face and his glasses are on the wrong end of his nose. And he says you've got to get up now. All the cardboard stuff's come.'

Oh God, it was Sunday. The biggest book event of our whole year. Philip Pickering was due to come tonight to discuss his latest book, *Re: Relationships*, a collection of essays on love.

I scrabbled in my washbag for my toothbrush and pregnancy tablet, and emerged a few minutes later. Foley Joe was waiting outside the door, holding the scrubbing brush aloft. 'I could just do your back if you like?' he said, waving it as I hurried past.

Downstairs, Stuart was assembling flat-packed display stands, vigorously thumbing open cardboard slits and slotting them together. I was confused to see Monica there, too, piling up copies of *Re: Relationships* on the counter. Had she just come in for a book and taken pity on him? I cleared my throat as I descended the last step.

'Oh, good. Two cups of tea, please, Jane,' said Monica. 'You shouldn't be doing any of this work.'

I looked at Stuart, grunting with exertion. 'You'd better not sleep in the bath again,' he said. 'I could get done for that.'

I nodded. I'd have to start getting up at six, getting dressed and out of the bath long before Stuart trudged down from the cottage to open up.

'I prayed for you this morning, Jane,' said Monica

quietly, holding her hands out towards me. 'Oat milk, if you've got it.'

'One for me, too,' piped up Foley Joe from the beanbag. He knelt on the floor, unzipped the beanbag and reached inside, stirring the tiny polystyrene balls round and round. 'Put either salt or sugar in. Don't tell me which.'

As I filled the grimy kettle and allowed myself a brief smile at the impossibility of Stuart buying oat milk, I worried what my function would be here, now that the bump was getting bigger and I couldn't do as much physically. Had Monica been coming here on my days off, while I was taking walks along the cliffs, hand to my bump, imagining my baby's face? How could I justify secretly sleeping in the bath if I wasn't even working here?

I had to make myself indispensable. Perhaps by upping my knowledge of literature so I could sell a book better than Monica could. But I still hadn't finished Sharon Osbourne's autobiography, let alone read any of the latest releases. Apart from this evening's book, which was lucky, because I'd be asking all the questions again. I could barely contemplate anything other than the present moment, though, with everything that had gone on yesterday. When I opened the fridge, I was surprised to find a carton of oat milk tucked into the door.

The afternoon was taken up with preparations. I was put on sedentary duty at the counter, while Stuart and Monica jolted about the place, moving chairs and shelves. I swotted up on Philip's book, then got my phone out and google-imaged Robbie Atkins – there were articles about him online due to his considerable humanitarian work – while ignoring the repeated interruptions from my parents and Jonathan, who were about neck and neck in terms of how much they were calling. Jonathan would be in the back of his parents' car on the way home to London by now, strapped in next to Andrew like a child.

'What's Monica doing here, by the way?' I asked Stuart in the kitchen when I got a chance.

'She's offered to help out a bit, voluntarily,' he replied.

'She offered voluntarily, or she's helping voluntarily?'

'Both. She's not got enough to do. Good at seeing stuff from a new angle, she said.'

'Yeah,' I laughed, nudging him. 'Big-ass boaster.' That's what we called anyone who came in assuming they knew more about books than us. Although they usually knew more than I did, but that didn't fit our narrative.

'Mmm,' he said, forking a sardine onto a piece of burnt toast. 'Have you read the book this time? We can't muck this one up. We've only managed to get him because he wants to visit his sister in Hebden Bridge.'

'I have actually, Stuart, yeah,' I said. 'It was a bit abstract for me.' I stared after him as he left, then ate the rest of the sardines from the tin, including the bones.

The first thing we learnt about Philip was that he was not a 'Phil'. 'Cup of tea, Phil?' Foley Joe chirped from the bean-bag as the author walked through the door – greying hair, thin smile – and greeted Stuart. Yes, he would like a cup of tea, he wanted to know how many people we were expecting - and it was Philip, not Phil. 'Philip, I feel the same when people call me Mon,' Monica said, as we all took him upstairs and directed him to sit on the toilet – seat down, draped with one of the blankets I'd slept in, my overnight bag stashed in a cupboard. I vowed to call her Mon every opportunity I could.

'Philip, before I go down to seat everyone, I have to say I loved your essays,' gushed Monica. 'They reminded me of Saul Bellow.'

'Never heard of her,' said Philip drily. 'So you'll be asking the questions tonight, will you?'

'Oh, I'm afraid not,' replied Monica, leaving the bathroom. 'Jane will be.'

Philip gave me a brief, unsmiling nod.

I just have to get through this evening, I thought, *wait for Stuart to lock up, and then go back to sleep in the bath you're gazing scornfully at.*

'This green room is . . . rather quirky,' Philip said to Stuart, dubiously accepting a mug of grey tea from Foley Joe.

'There's nowhere to sit in the kitchen,' said Stuart. 'And at least you're in the right place if you get nervous! Right, people'll be starting to—'

'Oh Stuart, I've been doing this too long to get nervous,' replied Philip dismissively, picking up the bar of Imperial Leather and dropping it with a splat.

The bathroom door began to creak open from the outside, and Stuart got up, saying that whoever it was would have to go somewhere else, but it was too late – it opened fully. Jonathan stood before us.

'Hi, darling!' he said to me, as if this were our house and we were the only two here. White-hot adrenaline coursed through my veins. 'Is this the customer loo?'

'You'll have to go to the pub across the road, lad, I'm afraid,' said Stuart.

'Pub it is,' said Jonathan, skipping back down the stairs. 'See you afterwards, Janey! Break a leg!'

I bundled Stuart into the corridor, my pulse hammering in my throat. 'Get him to leave,' I said. 'Get him to leave! He's my ex.'

'People are downstairs now,' said Stuart. 'Let him watch, then he can go. I don't want a scene. We need to seat them all, we need to give out the wine. We'll put him at the back. You can stay up here until just before it starts.'

'Please, Stu,' I begged, gripping both his arms. 'Please.'

Foley Joe popped his head out from the bathroom. 'Phil says he wants to start in a minute,' he said to Stuart. 'He needs to get to Hebden Bridge before the chippy shuts for the night.'

Fifteen minutes later, Philip and I sat on our stools, the applause finally dying away, our shiny black microphones resting in their angled stands in front of our mouths.

Philip, not Phil. Forget about Jonathan. Philip, not Phil. Philip's been a prick so far, but he'll be all right on stage. It turned out fine with Fenella, plus you've read the book this time. Forget about Jonathan. He'll be going home tomorrow. Just don't look at the audience. Philip, not Phil. Philip, not Phil.

As I fixed my gaze on the back wall and opened my mouth to start, the door jangled and I saw Mum and Dad creep in and squeeze in at the end of a row – next to Robbie. Bloody hell. These three, on top of Jonathan already being here? I felt faint. Could I pretend to be suddenly ill? I was pregnant, after all. Then I imagined the look of glee on Monica's face as she saved the day by stepping in, followed by me inevitably losing my job.

My heart was pounding. I breathed in for six, closed my eyes for a moment, then said into the mic, 'Hi Jane, I'm Philip.'

There was an awkward chuckle from people, which died away quickly.

'Well, let's start that again,' I stammered. 'I'm certainly not Philip – you are – and you've written yet another . . . another great book. Moving, and at times funny.'

'*At times* funny!' he replied. 'How kind! I've had . . . hmm, let's see . . . "Brutally fragile ruminations on what makes us human" – *The Spectator*; "So moving I felt like I was on a high-speed car chase" – *The Times*; "Not as good as *His Dark Materials*" – my nephew.'

A warm bed of laughter came from the crowd. Good, he'd do all the work for me. Then it would end, and I'd never have to see Jonathan again.

'Let's have a reading to start us off,' I said. This had worked with Fenella – in fact, the whole thing had been dominated by her readings.

'Oh, I don't do readings at events like this,' he replied, smiling. 'I'm only here as a favour to Stuart. He should have told you that, Philip.'

I thought he was joking, but he just stared back at me to silence from the audience.

'My name isn't Philip,' I said.

'Oh, sorry,' he said. 'It's just you said your name was Philip at the start.'

'It's Jane,' I said, my cheeks reddening. The indignity of the situation would be so much easier to bear if my parents, Jonathan and Robbie weren't among the people watching it unfold. 'OK, well, why don't we talk about what inspires you?'

'God, anything but that question,' he sighed. 'I'm just a man. I'm not a bloody genius, Philip.'

Silence. My mind was blank. Stuart was doing manic arm gestures from the back of the room. Everything was an exact repeat of what had happened with Fenella. But this time I'd read the book, so it wasn't anything to do with me. Were all writers just absolute morons? Would this end in the same kind of ritual humiliation, Philip bellowing words at me to whoops and cheers from everybody?

'Well,' I said, 'we're all here because you've got an impressive body of work—'

'So's she,' said Philip, gesturing towards a pretty woman in her twenties on the front row, who laughed reflexively. 'Oops, naughty Philip! Stop it!' He slapped his hand theatrically.

'. . . Novels, plays,' I continued, in slight disbelief. 'And now this new book on love, which is really varied. I've read all the essays in your book—'

'You've read *nearly* all the essays in my book,' he corrected. 'There's a new one going into the paperback, about a stolen night in Berlin. Or a *stollen* night in Berlin, if you like bread as much as I do, sweetheart,' he chuckled to the same woman.

I shot a glance to Robbie, who did the 'wanker' sign while pretending to scratch his face.

'Have you ever tried stollen?' Philip asked the woman.

She shook her head, not smiling anymore.

'Get your passport, we're going to Berlin tonight!' he said. He laughed to himself. 'I've *got* to stop doing this!'

My palms were slippery with sweat. He wouldn't even look at me. I tried again. 'I was struck by the story,' I said, 'about the man and woman leaving secret notes for each other under the leg of the wobbly restaurant table.'

'You've obviously not read the book properly,' he said. 'In my essay, the notes are left inside the menu.'

As he spoke, he was staring at the woman again, his eyes roaming over her breasts under her grey vest top, her legs, her hair. She'd started to look self-conscious and crossed her arms over her chest.

My hands began to tremble. I swallowed hard. Stuart was doing swooping arm gestures again. I neither knew nor cared what they meant. Monica was grinning her rictus grin and physically straining towards the stage. Jonathan looked full of despair, Robbie looked angry. Mum and Dad were gazing down, embarrassed. I saw it all. And I thought of the shitty forty-eight hours I'd had: the intervention; the fact that Mum had betrayed me; that Rachel was still living with Jonathan, who wouldn't just go home; that I couldn't even pluck up the courage to knock at The Arch so had slept in a fucking bath.

Everyone thought I would return to my parents' within a few days. Kelly hadn't even queried it last night when I'd said that was what I was doing. And they all thought I'd cave in and marry Jonathan, because I was too weak to stick up for myself, to go it alone, to brave a storm so that I could see what was on the other side. Stuart hadn't been bothered about me sleeping in the bath because he didn't think I'd do it for long. He'd only asked me to do the interview tonight so that I could be a punching bag yet again. Good old Jane, she can take it – she'll bounce back, she's damaged enough as it is – what difference does it make if she's humiliated by a misogynist writer in a tiny bookshop in Foley?

'It's funny, Phil,' I said, my voice clear for the first time that evening. 'From the moment you got here, you saw me as insignificant – probably because I'm pregnant, and obviously older than your usual type – and from the moment you saw this woman, she was just a plaything. It's made me realise the reason I couldn't relate to your book. The men are the complicated ones and the women only serve one function – beautiful, haggard, jealous – and when any of them seem to have changed, they haven't. It's just someone else has told them what to do, pointed out where they're going wrong. Well, that's not a story to me. And my name's not Philip, as you know. It's Jane.' I threw his book into his lap. 'My name is *Jane*.'

Chapter Twenty-Six

I only went to The Rainbow's End afterwards because Robbie made me. He told me I'd done a really good thing as he clasped my shoulders upstairs in the history section, where I'd been hiding since Philip had curtly wrapped things up, signed far fewer books than we'd predicted, then promptly got into his Audi. Robbie said that Philip had obviously never been challenged on his behaviour, and that this was the sort of thing that needed to happen. I should hold my head high. If he were my parents, he'd be proud. Now, what did I want to drink?

It felt like a good time to officially 'tell' him. There, in the quiet, just the two of us between the dusty shelves.

'I don't normally drink tomato juice,' I said. 'I'd be on the pints with you. I'm with child. As you just heard.'

'I've suspected for a little while,' he replied. 'Congratulations.'

'I don't know why I said "with child",' I smiled. 'It wasn't the Immaculate Conception. But I'm not with the dad.'

I didn't mention that 'the dad' was downstairs, that I could hear him holding court with the story about how he'd once stood next to Melvyn Bragg at a urinal at the Hay Festival.

'No questions from me!' Robbie said, holding his hands up and grinning.

'OK,' I said. 'No answers, then!'

We snuck out the back way and looped through Stuart's garden, past the bits he called 'squares of interest', where he'd plant seeds when he was too drunk to remember which types, and what grew would be a complete surprise.

In the pub, I got a few claps on the back from audience members as I walked in. I managed to get Stuart on his own straight away, as Monica went off to get their drinks. There was no sign of my parents or Jonathan yet, but then everyone was still dribbling over from the bookshop. Why should I leave, though? This was my pub.

'Pint of mild, was it, Stu?' Monica shouted back to him from the bar, knowing full well she could ask any regular or the landlady herself.

'Nothing for me, thanks, Mon!' I shouted. She frowned and turned to order. 'The baby did a big kick during the Q&A,' I said to Stuart.

'Did it?' He looked around the room, took a deep breath in. 'No bloody wonder.'

'Sorry if you think I shouldn't have said anything!' I said. 'But—'

'Look, I know he's not perfect, character-wise, but if something sells, it sells,' he said. 'We needed it to sell. We needed him to come back again with his next book, tell his mates we're a good place to do an event. It's all very well to have people like Fenella come, but that doesn't really put money in the till, does it?'

'So what are you saying?' I asked. 'That money should always come before principles?'

He sighed. 'When it's the difference between putting food on the table or not, then, yes, I think so.'

There didn't seem to be anything more to say, so I walked over to Robbie and his group as Monica returned. She looked at me with pity as I passed her, like I was an insect fallen on its back.

'Think Stuart's on Philip's side,' I said to them all.

'He'll get over it,' said Robbie, handing me a tomato juice with exactly the right amount of Worcestershire sauce in it.

I hadn't been introduced to any of them yet. There was an older woman with long, wild hair who smiled as if she'd seen it all before – Wendy, I would learn; a vaguely familiar guy in his forties with a gold earring who nodded a lot, Bramwell; and a young woman, Nell, with long, languorous limbs, like a resting puppet's, and the self-assured air of the kind of person you find out on their deathbed is fluent in Norwegian, but 'it never came up'.

'I've always had good dealings with Stuart,' added Robbie.

'But it's about what people do when it comes to the crunch, isn't it?' said Nell. She had a southern accent. 'Like, yesterday, loads of people we didn't expect turned up to the march, and loads who said they *would* come actually didn't.' This felt like it was directed at me, even though she couldn't possibly have known I was supposed to be coming – unless Robbie had mentioned me to them all?

'*I* was supposed to come, actually,' I said. 'But my family basically went crazy and tried to stage an intervention because I didn't want my ex to know I was pregnant. And then I had to sleep in a bath!'

They all nodded like I'd just told them I liked ham and crisp sandwiches. 'It's OK, Jane,' said Robbie, briefly touching my arm, his eyes crinkling at the sides in concern. 'You're one of the good guys.'

I thought, *You think I am, but would you say that if you knew how I'd worked on campaigns for massive tax-dodging corporations?*

'Anyway,' continued Nell, 'there'll be more protests. Shitloads more, if yesterday's anything to go on.' Nell and Robbie started talking animatedly to each other about the campaign.

'Incoming woman and man,' said Bramwell, and I turned to see that Mum and Dad were behind me, with Jonathan standing at the now-busy bar.

'Jane, Dad's getting you five different drinks,' Mum hissed as Dad peeled off towards the bar. 'We didn't know what you wanted. And I can now see you've already got one, but you'll need another one, and I know you'll say you don't want to talk to me, but if you don't, I think Dad's going to have a panic attack. He didn't sleep at all last night.'

I looked over at Dad, who was peering behind the bar at the range of soft drinks. Jonathan, hunched next to him, moved his head up eagerly when he saw me looking over and banged it on a tankard hanging from one of the beams.

Mum and I sat side by side on the drystone wall outside the pub, a tray on the ground holding my six drinks. I let her put her cardigan round my shoulders. My condition for talking to her was that an indignant Monica didn't accompany us for 'family mediation'.

'What a night!' she said. 'What a character Philip was!'

I kicked the wall with my heels.

'We nearly called the police last night,' she said quietly. 'When you didn't come home. Dad went round to Kelly's, and she said you were at our house! It was like you were fifteen again. Didn't you see any of our calls? Then we rang Stuart and woke him up and he found you in the bath. We all thought it would be better if you slept.'

I didn't say anything. I was thirty-eight.

'Gosh, I had no idea the church charades was going to end so dramatically yesterday!' she giggled. 'I don't think the bell-ringers will ever forgive Jonathan for shouting the answer!'

'Why would they ever see him again?' I said. 'She's actually living with him, you know. It wasn't just one night.'

'I don't want to get into an argument,' she replied carefully. 'All we want is for you to come home and be safe. You don't have to decide anything else for now. Just see it from our point of view. You're pregnant, you're not coping well – surely you agree – and now you've left home. It's all his family wants, too. Just let us look after you! I'd love it if you still married him. It's so different now there's a baby involved. Look, it's up to you, though. Small steps. At the very least, come back. You haven't been managing for a while, Jane. And look how hard you found it tonight with Philip.'

'Mum!' I said. 'I had hardly any sleep, in a bath, then I had to interview a sexist pig! I actually thought I did very well! And I've got nowhere to live—'

'Yes, you have!' she said.

'No, I haven't!'

'Where are you going to sleep tonight, then, if you won't come home?' she asked. 'It's already after nine o'clock. Not the bath again, please. Kelly's sister's always at her house, she said. You're not going to The Arch, are you?' She was starting to work herself up. I'd been wondering when it would happen. 'Please don't tell me you've been back in there, darling. I know they're all in the pub. I remember Robbie from school, he was really going places. Did you know one of them was caught stealing Sellotape from the library the other day? I mean, what do they want Sellotape for?'

I swirled my tomato juice. 'To make signs,' I replied. I looked through the window to see Stuart with two chips tucked under his upper lip like vampires' fangs, waving his arms like claws to make Monica laugh. He must be tipsy already.

'It won't work, all that protesting,' Mum said, smiling. 'We know the developer. His son's the organist at Winster. He's a lovely man. Look, we've all got to make money. It'll provide good homes for so many people. And it's best that place is gone, in its current state. I can't walk past it without thinking about—'

'Leave it, Mum,' I said.

There was a pause, and she squeezed my shoulder. I could smell her perfume.

'Come on, silly billy,' she said. 'I've put your favourite duvet cover on your bed, the one I hate, the rough one with the sequins. And Dad's so sorry. He's furious they all came up like that. He didn't tell them we were at church. They must have guessed.'

'What do you mean?' I said.

'He only told Jonathan. We forgot what a' – she whispered emphatically – '*mummy's boy* he is.'

My mouth went dry. '*Dad?*' I said. 'Dad told him?'

'You may as well know who it was. We're all going to be honest from now on. It wasn't just for the sake of the baby; it was for your sake, too. Jonathan understands your funny ways better than us – this business of not having the baby in the hospital. It was done from love. Please, darling, *please.*'

I couldn't breathe. Mum doing it was abhorrent enough, but *Dad?* 'No!' I said. 'You're lying. It was you. Andrew said so yesterday.'

'I don't know why he would have done, but if he did, it wasn't true,' said Mum.

She's just left the room. That was what Andrew had said, wasn't it? I thought back to the moment carefully, to me standing in the middle of the living room, post role play, Andrew packing away his oatcakes into his briefcase. *They've just left the room. That* was what he'd said. And Mum and Dad had both left the room. Mum to go to the garden, and Dad to lock himself in the toilet, because he'd had enough. Now I knew why.

Mum was crying, trying to get me to sit back on the wall. 'Look at it this way. He knew you'd hate him for it, and he still did it. That's how much he loves you.'

In the coming weeks, I would be haunted by Dad's pinched face watching Mum and me through the pub window that night, like a child helpless in his parents' divorce. I would picture it as I was stirring my tea in the bookshop kitchen listening to Stuart reading poetry to Monica downstairs, as I sat with Robbie and the others in The Rainbow's End, as I laughed at Jonathan's text messages saying he was back in London but would get a helicopter up to Foley if I needed him to, and as I laid my head down at Kelly's every night, in whichever bed I was offered, and where I could have seven or so hours of breathing without thinking.

Chapter Twenty-Seven

'It's definitely not bone cancer, babe,' said Kelly as I pressed the skin under my right kneecap and let it spring back. 'It's more likely to be a witch's curse than bone cancer.'

'How can you be so sure, though?' I asked. 'It definitely looks a bit swollen, doesn't it?'

'But anything can be cancer,' she said. 'It's always at the bottom of any list. Headaches, back ache, foot ache, trouble sleeping. Look, you're pregnant. Your knee hurts. The end.'

'Yep,' piped up Kelly's sister from the sofa, where she lay in a black velour tracksuit feeding her baby a bottle. 'It was your headaches yesterday. All roads lead to cancer. Why leave the house? Just scan your body for any aches and pains, then get googling.'

Kelly's sister, Becca – *bloody Becca's gone road rage again* – was Kelly squared, if such a being could exist. She could materialise at any time of the day or night with her two children, fourteen-year-old Taylor and baby Stella, and I would immediately be moved from the spare room into Kelly's room, to share with her. These nights of sharing with Kelly I adored, despite Stella waking frequently down the hall. Just me and Kelly in her double bed, logging in to her Facebook account to gawp at people from school and Rachel's stupid outfits. She'd vape out of the window while I let the icy wind whip across my face with the smugness of someone whose body is cocooned in a thick duvet. It was like *Grease*, if you didn't count her snoring and me checking the window was locked sixteen times. Sometimes, in her sleep, she'd place her hand on my shoulder like a little paw.

The only downside was that I had to see Becca. I wasn't sure how long she expected me to be staying. I don't think anyone else was sure, either. It had already been three weeks.

Becca and her children were officially living with Kelly and Becca's mother, but recently Becca's arguments with her had got worse. I'd assumed that this would make us kindred spirits, but she obviously didn't think my predicament was as serious as hers.

'God, I'm not looking forward to this bit!' I giggled as she pinned a screaming Stella down with her knee in order to change her nappy. Becca rarely washed her hands after nappy changes, which meant I couldn't let her cook for me. Not that she ever offered.

'Yeah, but I'm not being funny, though, yeah,' Becca said. 'When you decide to forgive your dad and all that, you get to move back into a nice big house and they'll look after the kid. I mean, you're still taking money off him, right?'

I looked down.

'So this is all play-acting. I'm sharing a room with both kids wherever I am, and Mum keeps putting all our dirty washing into our beds when we're not there. And when we are there. Did you hear that, Kel? Mum's seriously losing it.'

'Can't their dads help more?' I asked.

'Do you think all dads offer to give you thousands of pounds to let them see their kid?' she laughed, knotting the nappy bag. 'Some would give you that to never meet them.'

'Darren had had a few and he set Sean down on a work-top when he was six months old,' Kelly said. 'He fell off and broke his arm. I've never trusted him since. It's like having a bloody third kid.'

Becca didn't understand. She didn't stop to think, ever. Everyone was wrong and she was right. When I'd first arrived here, the night of the Philip Pickering event, she couldn't fathom that Jonathan was only down the road, at The Folly, and that I was refusing to see him. She had har-assed me so much about it that I was doubly relieved when the Chambers family had finally gone back to London a few days later.

'Come on, what else are you worried about?' said Becca.

I ran through the Filofax in my mind. Bone cancer; skin cancer; gestational diabetes; pre-eclampsia; stillbirth; that I would somehow kill everyone in Kelly's house by inad-vertently starting a fire or leaving the door unlocked for a madman to break in. The list was endless. 'The birth, I guess,' I settled for. 'I don't care about it hurting, I just want the baby to be OK.'

'Hear that? She doesn't care about it hurting,' Becca said softly to the baby, who was trying to pull down the zip on her hoodie. 'What you doing? What you doing?' she whispered. 'You're getting twat-all milk out of them.'

I'd been trying not to think about the birth. If it had to come out, it had to come out, didn't it? They knew I couldn't do a hospital birth – it was in my notes.

'Don't know what all the fuss is about with births,' said Becca. 'Just get all the pain relief you can.' She put Stella's dummy in and stroked her nose. 'Next thing to worry about,' she sang to the baby. 'Next thing!'

'Births are on another level,' said Kelly. 'You don't know what's going to happen next. Anyone who says it's the best day of their life is nuts.'

'Well, that's nice for her to hear, isn't it?' said Becca. 'Look at her. She's a bloody mess as it is.'

'There's stuff no one tells you,' replied Kelly. 'And she should know it beforehand.' She counted on her fingers. 'One, you'll feel like you're being punched in the stomach with a concrete fist with spikes on.'

'Great,' I said.

She continued, putting her hand up to silence me. 'Which rotates slowly once it's punched you, from the inside and the outside at the same time. Two, imagine your body's a tube of toothpaste being squeezed, but instead of toothpaste inside, it's shit and blood.'

'And the baby,' added Becca.

'Oh yeah,' said Kelly. 'And the baby. But you won't even be thinking about the baby then, you'll be thinking let-me-die-let-me-die-let-me-die.'

'Cool,' I said. 'Cheers.'

'Stella was so big she just didn't want to budge,' said Becca. 'Five days of labour after a failed induction, and then an emergency caesarean.'

'You didn't exactly *labour* for five days, Becca,' Kelly said. 'It was just five days from start to finish.'

'Yes, I did!' snapped Becca. Stella began to whimper. 'You weren't there.' She put Stella's bottle back in her mouth. 'I did,' she muttered to herself. Then, '*She* kept pooing after Sean,' she continued, pointing at Kelly.

'So what?' replied Kelly. 'It's not my fault. I had a third-degree tear, which means the fanny and the bum muscles, but not up to the hilt, if you get what I mean.'

I didn't in the slightest. What was the 'hilt'?

'Why didn't you just have a caesarean then, to avoid it?' I asked. They both laughed and ignored the question.

Kelly said, 'After Sean was born, they sewed me up, and I was so high from only breathing gas and air for half an hour – no real air – it was like in that film *Inner Space*, like I was inside my own body and could see all my organs and stuff.'

'Bollocks,' sniffed Becca.

'You always say that!' said Kelly. 'It's true. Anyway,' she paused and widened her eyes, 'when I got home, I couldn't stop pooing. I don't mean on the loo, I mean lying in bed, feeding the baby – I just couldn't stop. I had to go back to hospital and let this really fit doctor stick his finger up my bum to see if it was a *missed fourth-degree tear*, and I was like, he was so fit – if this was any other circumstance – I was still with Darren then—'

'Dependable Darren,' Becca muttered to Stella.

'Then,' Kelly continued, 'Mum was like, "Well, it might never stop happening, and you'll have to have a colostomy bag. But don't worry, because Darren can't leave you now you've had two kids with him." And then it stopped after a few weeks, but Darren went anyway!'

'Maybe he *wanted* you to have a colostomy bag,' Becca cackled. 'Oh darling, can I change your bag for you before I go to the pub and look at all the lovely ladies? You'd better not come, darling, cos of your *bag*.'

They both roared with laughter and I smiled, gazing at Stella. I never saw mums I knew in London behave like this. Their husbands were always lingering there, bearded, nervy, offering earnest advice to everyone. Becca picked up Stella with one hand to wind her and drank from her cup of tea with the other. The mums I knew worried about their babies all the time because they had the means to. When Kelly and Becca got a chance to be alone, the last thing they were going to do was wonder if their child was hitting all their milestones. They were going to drink Baileys and play Candy Crush. They definitely laughed more than the mums in London. They were *living*.

Becca was right. If I really was going to do this alone, I needed to put my money where my mouth was – or, rather, back into Dad's bank account.

Chapter Twenty-Eight

'Yet another delivery for you,' said Monica from where she was stacking books as I walked in. 'I've put it in the bath with everything else.'

'Cheers, Mon,' I replied. I would never tire of the frown this nickname elicited.

I walked into the bookshop bathroom to find a four-foot bright-blue teddy bear with a bow around its neck and a T-shirt saying *Hugs for Free*. I didn't even bother to read the message. The bath was now crammed full of gifts from Jonathan, and I'd already given away so much over the weeks, to Stuart, Monica, Robbie, Kelly, and even a few customers. Hampers full of chutneys and crackers and cocoa, gigantic cuddly toys, balloons and boxes of choco-lates, a basket of cupcakes from yesterday. They came at least twice a week. I didn't know what to do with any of it. All the messages were along the same lines, as if nothing was wrong in the slightest: *Love you so much. Can't wait to meet the baby. Jonathan and co. xxx* The fact that there was no *Cheers! Jonathan* made me think they were actually coming from Sadie, but I wasn't about to try and find out.

I never knew what to expect when I got into work these

days, aside from an unwanted gift. Businesswise, Stuart appeared to have moved on from The Philip Incident, as Monica referred to it, but he hadn't asked me to host any events since. We'd had two writers in conversation with each other, and last week Monica had led a discussion with local artists and writers about the best books to buy for Christmas presents. This hadn't led to as many sales as Stuart was hoping for. I felt privately that this was because Monica had started virtually everything she said with, 'For *me* . . .' but I couldn't tell him that. Stuart and I were like strangers, and I was almost relieved when Monica came into the kitchen to break up the tension. I thought back to the days when we'd laughed until we'd cried at the man who insisted *The Magus* was pronounced '*the ma-goose*', and when we'd take it in turns to make each other lunch with whatever was at the back of the kitchen cupboard. Now, the two of them worked deftly at the front of the shop, while I hovered, moving the odd book back to its rightful place, not allowed to lift anything now I had a big bump. 'Put your feet up, Jane,' Monica would say to me, handing me Sharon Osbourne's autobiography from where I kept it behind the counter. 'Read Sharon's book.' I was helping Robbie with the wording of the campaign, so I always had things to do on my phone, but I didn't want Stuart to think I was skiving.

Stuart was sidestepping around me even more than usual today, which I presumed was because he was distracted by the fact that it was Monica's birthday. I'd seen him in the kitchen wrapping books whose titles corresponded to each letter of her name. There were two hidden helium balloons bobbing in the cupboard under the sink, not the droopy ones we used for book events.

On the shop floor, Monica tore open large boxes and gleefully assembled a pyramid of books with the titles *God? No Way!!* and *God? Yes Way!!! The Sequel to God? No Way!!* right next to the door, which was probably in breach of health and safety. Doctor Lingard sent a dozen or so of them tumbling as she walked in.

'It's all right!' said Monica, although no apology had been uttered.

'Hello, Jane!' said Doctor Lingard, beaming. 'I've just popped in for a present for my niece.' I hid my bitten fingers in my pockets as I joined her in the children's section. 'How are things?' she asked quietly, picking up a storybook. 'Not long to go now, have you?'

'Good,' I said, smiling. 'Good, good.' *Good, as long as I have my phone with me at all times to check every single possible pregnancy condition and as long as I check Kelly's door's locked, that the gas is off and that all the windows are closed, which involves me sneaking into the boys' bedroom every night, where I've never even opened a window, and risking waking them up.* 'I'm checking things a bit less these days,' I said, after making sure Monica was out of earshot. 'I know you're not supposed to talk about this stuff outside the surgery, but... there's a tiny bit of progress. And it's in my maternity notes that I need a home birth, so I'm not worried about the hospital thing anymore.'

My evenings were spent lying on the sofa with Kelly and Becca, whom I'd grown quite fond of now I'd got used to her. 'Her bark's the same as her bite,' Kelly liked to say of Becca. 'What you see is what you get.'

Doctor Lingard chose a book and took it to the counter to pay.

'She's refusing to come to therapy anymore, if you're wondering,' said Monica as she scanned the barcode. 'I know you're from the practice. I'm Monica, by the way, her *ex*-therapist.'

Doctor Lingard got out her credit card.

'And what kind of therapist are you, Monica?'

'Oh, a talking one,' replied Monica. 'I trained under Peter Radford in Newton Abbot, who devised his own method of—'

'Well,' said Doctor Lingard, 'I should imagine Peter Radford told you to adhere to the confidentiality clause, didn't he?'

'But this is for Jane's own good, and you're a fellow professional,' said Monica, leaning towards her. 'She turns all the plugs off in the kitchen every night here. I have to turn them on when I come in. It's very sad to see. She never completed her course with me, you see. And she's moved out of her parents' now. She hasn't really spoken to them since, and she won't take money from them. She won't enter a hospital. We're all worried.'

'I'm sure Jane'll ask for help if she needs it, Monica,' said Doctor Lingard, taking the book in its brown paper bag. 'From anyone she feels can help her.' She accidentally-on-purpose knocked into some more of the God books on her way out.

'It's all right!' laughed Monica after her, and I excused myself to go to the kitchen and do some deep breathing.

I leant over the sink. *In for six, out for eight.* Whenever I stepped out of Kelly's, there was nowhere I could go where I wasn't being suffocated with seemingly good intentions.

The gifts from Jonathan, the missed calls from Mum and Dad, concerned messages from Megan and my sister, the way the Arch lot wouldn't let me buy my own drinks when we met in the pub to discuss the campaign. Even Monica, in her stupid way.

While the initial rage towards my parents had now faded, I just couldn't bring myself to make much contact with them. If I were to give them anything substantial, Dad would be picking me up within the hour, my bag packed from Kelly's, just like the night I found out about Jonathan and Rachel; Mum cooking shepherd's pie to be on the table the minute I stepped through the door. I knew I could do this: it was much harder without Dad's money, but now Becca couldn't say I was sponging off my parents. Nobody could.

The first time I'd returned Dad's weekly allowance to his account, he'd immediately put it back into mine, like it must have been a mistake. So I'd returned it again. Then he'd knocked on Kelly's door. Since no one ever called for me there, I'd answered. He looked surprised, as if he expected me to refuse to see him. 'Hi, love,' he said, looking at my feet. 'Did you mean to return that money?'

'Yeah,' I said, 'I don't need it anymore, Dad. I'm not spending much money.' He looked doubtful. 'Kelly doesn't charge me rent. I get all my clothes from her sister. I just do babysitting in return.' The boys paid literally no attention to anything except the TV and iPad, so it was a pretty cushy deal.

'What about when the baby's been born?' he mumbled.

'Just trust me,' I said. 'I'm OK. I'll think of something.' He looked like he might crumple in half at the waist, so

I held open my arms. For some reason, even though he was the one who'd betrayed me, it was easier to forgive him. The idea of Mum shovelling healthy pregnancy soups down my throat made me want to scream. Each one of her texts contained a minimum of six questions.

'I'm sorry, love,' he said. 'I was just so worried about you coping with him not knowing.'

'I'm all right, though, Dad, aren't I?' I said, grinning.

'When are you coming home then, love?' he asked.

'Dad,' I replied, 'I'm not coming home.'

I could do it. As long as I didn't think about tomorrow, or the next day, or a year's time, which I did, every hour of every day, which made me dizzy with worry and fear, but these were familiar bedfellows to me, and I could operate pretty well with a kaleidoscope of chaos swirling constantly just under the surface. I always had done.

'Jane! Just the woman,' said Stuart, walking into the kitchen carrying an obviously home-made cake. All morning I'd watched him struggling with plates of clingfilmed food, carrying them from his cottage through the shop to The Rainbow's End, so that Monica could inspect each one of them on the way. I wouldn't have been surprised if she'd sanctioned her presents herself. He stood on the stool to reach into one of the top cupboards, pulling out a dusty plastic cylinder containing birthday candles. 'Listen, duck,' he said, clambering down. 'There's no easy way to say this.'

Chapter Twenty-Nine

'I don't get it,' said Robbie from across the table. The Rainbow's End was empty apart from one local, and the blue teddy bear, which I'd brought with me. Stuart had said it had fallen out of the bath earlier and scared some kids. The bar staff were bustling about, setting out the food for Monica's party. Robbie's computer sat open on the table, where he'd been working before I trudged in. 'Christmas is next month!'

'He said that was the problem,' I explained. 'He's not expecting to make enough. And Monica'll work there for free, plus she's blatantly his girlfriend now, so how can I ever compete with that?'

'You'll be OK,' Robbie replied. 'You grab life. You *grab* it.' Was he talking about me, or people in general?

'What am I going to do?' I said. 'Sell the stuff from the hampers? How? Who wants to buy a teddy bear the size of a ten-year-old?' I couldn't bear to ask Dad to restart the standing order.

'Let's look at it clearly,' said Robbie. He closed his computer, which meant I'd really got his attention. This was what I'd wanted in all our meetings, for him to notice *me*.

'You've got two weeks' notice. You're talented. Look at what you've done for the campaign. You can do so much more than barbecue instructions. You're going to be OK. You're Jane bloody Wildgoose.'

Then I cried, and he moved his chair round to beside mine and held me. My face was squashed into his shoulder, and his fleece smelt of fires. His stubble felt like sandpaper on my head.

'People'll start arriving for Monica's party soon, probably including your mum and dad,' he said into my hair. 'Do you want to stay for it?' I shook my head, staying where I was. 'Nor me,' he said. 'Shall we get out of here?'

We pulled up in his van on the moors road between The Arch and The Folly, the place where you went to do things with blokes when you had no access to a functioning bedroom. I felt a bit calmer now. I licked my fingers and wiped the smudged mascara from under my eyes. I sat next to Robbie, the blue teddy bear squashed in on my left, its seat belt on. We looked out across the hills, at the lights glimmering in the distant towns. It was almost December and the air was completely still. I'd been back in Foley since July, living at Kelly's for a month and a half, due to have a baby in February. The London me wouldn't recognise me.

'I missed these hills so much when I was away from Foley,' Robbie said. 'Each one's a slightly different green.'

I nodded. 'Me too.'

'Then I realised that the only reason most people yearn for the landscape they grew up in is because they connect it with the people they miss,' he said. 'This view isn't particularly special, it's just symbolic to us, because we're from here.'

'Bullshit,' I said. 'Foley *is* special. Do you reckon you get people lying on a beach in the Bahamas, thinking if only I could have a view of that concrete slab from my childhood because it reminds me of my nan?' He grinned. 'Did you used to come up here, to, you know?' I said to him.

He laughed. 'I was too busy with schoolwork. Did you?'

'Yeah, of course I fucking did.' I smiled. *'And* I still got straight As.'

I don't know who kissed who, but it was a long, slow kiss, which involved me swivelling around to a kneeling position on the seat because of the bump, without breaking contact. He held my face in his hands.

'You're a sexy, wonderful, intelligent, kind girl, Jane,' he said to me. 'I had to kiss you. Sorry. You're powerful, you've got another life in you. You can do anything.'

'Why are you saying sorry?' I smiled. 'It was lovely.' I kissed him again.

'I've been thinking,' he said, his palms still on my cheeks. 'Why don't you move into The Arch? You're helping us loads anyway, and you wouldn't have to pay for anything because we grow or forage it all. You could have room three – it's one of the biggest—'

I shook my head. 'I can't.'

'Why not?' he asked.

'I've just . . .' I paused. 'It probably seems weird I haven't been in there yet, but I can be very funny about everything being clean, and—'

'It's clean, honestly. It's cleaner than my parents' place,' he said. 'Bramwell goes on these ten-hour cleaning sprees.'

Tears started to flow down my cheeks.

'Did something happen in the building?' he asked. 'I've been thinking that maybe it could have. You completely change at the prospect of coming in. Honestly, you can tell me if it did. It *is* a weird place. I know stuff went on there when we were kids. But we've made it so nice inside.'

'No,' I said. 'No, nothing happened.' I sat back in my seat. 'Can you take me back to Kelly's?'

I couldn't think of a single thing to say on the drive into town, even though we normally never stopped talking, our sentences tumbling over each other. The silence descended steadily like a blind.

Then, after about two minutes, we saw a car broken down with its hazards on. A figure was bent over the engine, which was obscured by the open bonnet. Robbie wordlessly pulled in and got out to help, and I slowly opened the door and climbed down, hoping a blast of cold night air might reset everything.

I heard his voice before I saw him. 'Thanks so much for stopping, mate! It's a mate's car. I thought it might be a flat tyre, but now I think – I don't know. It just lost power. Can't get any reception.'

My stomach lurched as I rounded the car. There he was, in his best flannel shirt he wore for pitching sessions, and new jeans, his ever-faithful burgundy trainers on his feet. He'd lost weight.

'Jane!' he cried.

'Robbie,' I said, 'this is Jonathan.' I had a fleeting vision of Robbie punching him, or vice versa, but instead they shook hands. Jonathan immediately eyed the van, The

Arch's campaign logo painted on its side. 'What are you doing here?' I asked.

'Oh,' he grinned, 'I was invited to Monica's party. Are you not going? I'm only here to see you, really, of course. Left you alone for long enough. I'm staying at The Folly again, if you want to pop in.' He spoke as if he'd only popped over from Chesterfield, not made the three-hour journey up from London.

'Heard a lot about you, mate,' said Robbie. That wasn't actually true. All he knew was that Jonathan had cheated, how and when, that he tended to take all the credit on work assignments, and that I was never going to speak to him again. Apparently.

'All bad, I hope, mate!' replied Jonathan, bouncing his head from side to side and doing an 'eeeek' face.

'Actually, weren't you at the Philip Pickering thing?' said Robbie. 'I think we sat near each other.'

'Yeah!' said Jonathan. 'Didn't she do well? What a prick he was.'

'He was a prime arsehole,' agreed Robbie. 'I was very proud of her.'

A look crossed Jonathan's face. 'Yeah, me too, mate,' he said. 'Me too.'

They bent over the bonnet, and Robbie tinkered around, while Jonathan stood back, trying to catch my eye. I turned to look at the hills again.

'I think it's your tracking, mate,' said Robbie. How many times could they call each other mate? A peal of hysterical laughter almost escaped my lips. 'Garage in town'll do it. It'll be closed now, but I know Fred. He only lives above it. He'll come up and tow it. You won't get phone reception till the convent anyway, so I may as well drive you there. I can take you on to the party after if you want, mate.'

I sat squashed in the middle of the two of them as Robbie drove towards the town centre. The blue bear was now banished to the back of the van, and I hated that Jonathan had seen me with it. He wanted to know lots about Robbie – whether we'd been at school together, stuff about his work abroad as a doctor, what The Arch campaign was about. 'Bump's getting big now, Janey!' he said as we rounded down towards town.

'Yes,' I replied. *Do you want to know what I was doing just before we found you?* I wanted to say. *Kissing this beautiful man, who could have changed your tyre in thirty seconds if you'd needed him to, while you worried about getting oil in your hair.*

'Did you get all my hampers and stuff?' he asked. 'Obviously you like the bear, but it's just I haven't heard from you.'

'Yeah,' I said. I started to feel hot and dizzy. I just wanted to get away from him. This wasn't right. It wasn't in the plan.

'We've had some of the chutneys up at The Arch, actually, mate,' said Robbie. 'Went down an absolute treat.'

'Right, so . . .' Jonathan looked confused. 'You're *living* there, are you? In this Arch place?'

'No!' I said. 'I'm not.' He couldn't know I was living at Kelly's. 'I'll jump out here,' I said as we pulled into the garage. I raced off down the alleyway towards Kelly's as fast as I could, bump allowing, the wind whipping my hair into my face.

'Jane!' they both shouted in unison as I ran. 'Jane!'

Winter

Chapter Thirty

'Look after yourself,' Stuart said as I handed him the bookshop keys. The idea that I'd ever slept in the bath here seemed ridiculous now I had Kelly's. 'Once business picks up, we'll have you back in no time.' Monica hovered behind him, but that didn't stop me from hugging him.

'I hope things pick up, Stu,' I said. 'I've loved it. You've really helped me. Thank you.'

'You'll be all right, Jane,' he said.

'You can keep any new hampers,' I said, although we both knew that no more would arrive. 'I'll come and collect my post when I can.'

The upside of my and Robbie's roadside encounter with Jonathan a fortnight ago was that no more gifts had come since. The downside was that, instead, the letters had started. They arrived at the bookshop almost daily. Some of them talked about the past in awful sentimental sentences. *Remember in Alicante when we drank rosé and ate paella at the same table at the same restaurant every night and I promised you the world? Well, maybe we both fucked up, right?* Others were more passive-aggressive. *I know something's going on with Robbie. When he said he was 'proud of you' taking on Philip Pickering. You're pregnant. It's a bit weird, isn't it? Just tell me. Rachel and Capricorn have moved out, by the way. Thought you might like to know.*

I'd showed a few choice ones to Robbie, but he didn't ever find them funny like Kelly and I did. Since he'd met Jonathan, I sensed he was a little perplexed as to why I didn't want him involved in the baby's life. 'Why did you run off like that?' he'd said afterwards. 'We were both so worried.'

I decided from then on to keep him and Jonathan totally separate. It was all right for Kelly and me to piss ourselves laughing at Jonathan's letters, but it wasn't exactly a bad thing if Robbie didn't see that side of me. Anyway, all he talked about was The Arch these days. In the past few weeks, a potential benefactor had made contact, saying they were interested in donating a large sum of money to the campaign. They wanted a say in what the community centre would be used for, so we were now spending lots of time detailing the plans from Robbie's and the group's point of view, wording them in the right way. It seemed like I could have imagined the moment we kissed, he was so engrossed in things. Luckily I was instrumental to it all now, and had started to really enjoy being in charge of the writing side of everything. It wasn't the same as when it was just me and him, though. Something monumental would have to happen to me to tear him away from it, or I would have to make myself bigger and better and more appealing.

Dad had been to see me a few more times at Kelly's, and he'd even come in and had a cup of tea with us all on the condition that no one spoke about Jonathan. Kelly and Becca had made a fuss of him, giving him three custard creams – which Mum would never have bought – on the only unchipped plate. 'Your mum would love to see you,' he said. 'It's breaking her heart that you're going to have a child out of wedlock, but she'll not make you do anything. That's how much she loves you.'

'Hey!' Kelly said. 'If you say something like that again I'm taking away a custard cream.'

'Oh, sorry, girls,' he said. 'But I didn't mention his name, did I?' I think he enjoyed coming in.

'Tell Mum . . .' I said as he left. 'Tell her I do love her.' Why couldn't I let Mum back in? I realised it was because Dad was such a worrier he'd had no choice but to tell Jonathan, whereas she knew exactly how to pull all my strings. And Dad's.

When I'd got back from seeing him off on his most recent visit, there was a yellow Post-it note stuck under the leg of Kelly's kitchen table. *Your idea was much better than Philip's*, it said in biro. He'd remembered Philip saying about the notes in his book being in the menu, not under the table leg. *Anytime you want some money, you call me. Day or night. Dad x.*

As well as the slight anticlimax of my last ever bookshop shift, the strange fruits of which I carried in the form of two bags full of clanking jars of chutney refused by Stuart, I had two matters jostling for attention in my head. I didn't think the baby had kicked enough that day, which was something I thought fairly frequently, but Kelly had a way of making me breathe deeply before feeding me something sweet and getting me to lie on my side until it did. The other thing was that I was convinced I had a lump in my breast, and I wanted Kelly to look at it before Becca inevitably got to her house that night. It was at the bottom of my right breast, and completely rigid. I'd even thought of texting Jonathan, that's how in need of reassurance I was. I'd been on cancer anxiety forums all day. The only thing that made me feel mildly better was the number of ailments other people on forums tended to have.

I turned my key in Kelly's door and smelt the familiar smell of fish fingers and waffles, but it was Becca shovelling them onto plates and handing them to the children, all clustered around the little table in the kitchen. It was Becca slapping their hands away as they picked up fistfuls of spaghetti hoops and threw them at each other.

'Kelly's at Waggy's,' she said, before I'd even asked. 'Fish-finger sandwich?'

Of course she was. She always was, these days. Kelly had started 'properly seeing' Waggy, who no longer had a daffodil lodged in the back of his trousers; instead Kelly's thumbs, hooked under the waistband. In fact, he'd left the daffodils far behind him, and was now in junior management at the quarry. He wore dotted burgundy ties and carried football cards in his pockets for Elliott and Sean, which they took silently before retreating. We'd all be standing around chatting about something serious, and then the memory of his tongue in my ear like a hot, lazy slug twenty-odd years earlier would pierce my attention, and I'd have to repress the urge to burst out laughing like a teenager.

Later, while the boys watched a film and Stella played in her cot, Becca and I sat in silence on the bed in the spare room. 'Bloody hell,' she muttered as she ran her finger along my skin in the manner of a plumber diagnosing a leak. 'It's a new worry every day with you. No wonder he bloody cheated on you.'

She winked, as this was close to the mark even for her, and I held my top up and tried to still my heart as she examined the lump from all angles.

She stopped dead and looked at me with wide eyes, her face close to mine. 'I reckon you might have a few years left in you yet,' she said.

'A few years?' I gasped. 'How do you know?'

'Because . . .' she said, shaking her head, 'that lump . . . is your fucking top rib.'

I almost cried with relief.

'Do you think so?' I asked.

'Yeah, I think so,' she replied, looking away. 'I know so. Listen—'

I felt the lump, running my finger back and forth along it. Of *course* it was my rib. It was just my rib, doing its job of holding my ribcage together, with all my juicy organs inside! But should one rib stick out more than the others? What could that mean?

'Should it stick out like that?' I asked.

'It doesn't,' she said. 'You've just been feeling it all day, haven't you, so it seems like it does. Doesn't your mind ever sit still?'

'That's all I want it to do,' I said. I was praying for the baby to kick now, then surely my list of worries for the day would be done.

'You know you can't control the baby's life by trying to keep Jonathan away from it, don't you?' she said. 'People always do stuff you don't want them to do. Just saying.'

She took a sip of tea from her mug on the bedside table. She kept her hand on my ribcage as she spoke, which was very weird now that she'd done her job, but you could never tell Becca what to do. She pressed it absent-mindedly, touching the underside of my slackening maternity bra.

'Listen,' she said again, 'I'm going to be staying here properly for a bit with the kids. Move all our stuff in. Mum's lost it again.'

'Well, you're here more or less all the time anyway,' I said. 'But welcome! I like being in Kelly's bed.'

She looked at me strangely. 'Well, thing is, Waggy's moving in for a bit, too – problems at his place – so, y'know, you can't go in Kelly's bed no more. She says you snore anyway, but that doesn't matter now. She didn't want me to tell you about that.'

I snored? '*She* snores,' I said. 'Hang on, where will I go?'

'I'm thinking ahead really. You're going to have the baby soon, so we need to get this sorted now.'

'So where can I sleep then?' I asked. Even if I cleaned it thoroughly, the sofa in the living room would be too narrow for me and the bump now. 'I don't think I can manage the boys' room.' How could that possibly work? There was already a mattress on the floor for Taylor, and no room for another, even if I could stomach the smells that emanated from there in the mornings.

She was silent.

'Where am I going to go?' I said quietly, trying not to cry. 'It's nearly Christmas.'

I couldn't go to Mum and Dad's, the tree decorated with Auntie Polly's knitted figurines, Mum planning a celebratory meal with Jonathan and his family for my return. I couldn't go to Stuart's freezing cottage, with Monica watching my every move like a scrawny hawk. I couldn't go anywhere Jonathan might materialise, including Megan's.

'I don't know where you'll go, Jane,' Becca replied, finally removing her hand from my trusty, stupid old rib, which I felt was somehow complicit in all of this.

I pulled my top down over my bump.

'There's a women's shelter in Derby,' she said. 'My mate stayed there once or twice. It's not too bad. You'll get some sleep. There's showers. Tea. Maybe some food.'

'It's OK,' I said. As I took a deep breath in, the baby kicked. Hard. 'I know where I'll go.'

Chapter Thirty-One

Stepping over the threshold wasn't how I'd imagined. For a start, Becca had come with me, leaving Taylor in charge of things at Kelly's. I'd forgotten she'd been in the same school year as Robbie. He'd greeted both of us with a bear hug and hustled us in. Before I knew it, I was in the main hall, full of paraphernalia for the upcoming protest that Nell, Wendy and Bramwell were busy working on. Some of the furniture remained, like my favourite green leather sofa, but on the whole, things looked very different. This was good.

I was given a choice of room three or room eight, and of course I picked room eight, even though it was smaller and colder. Room eight was where Megan and I had once done a Ouija board and asked to speak to John Lennon, then told him to tell Bob Marley he was a 'legend'. He'd refused.

'Probably pissed off you didn't ask him about the Beatles,' said Robbie when I told him. 'Everyone only wants to talk about themselves, really, don't they? Even spirits.'

'Tell me about yourself, then,' I said, sitting on the bed next to him. So far, I'd found that as long as I was near

Robbie, I could disassociate myself from what had happened here the night of my eighteenth. Robbie hadn't been part of my life back then. And now, he was. He fizzed with energy.

'I'm the most annoying kind of arsehole there is, Jane,' he said, stroking my cheek. 'I'm devoted to helping the many, not the few. And I include myself in the few.'

I looked around my new room. Bare floorboards with a rug, one of Wendy's abstract paintings, a sink with one working tap and another to which Bramwell had fastened an empty toothpaste tube to stop it from dripping. I looked up at the chandelier, wispy cobwebs running down from canopy to candelabra, its own set of mini suspension bridges. There was the odd unpainted patch on the walls, and cracks in the corners, but, apart from the cobwebs, it was clean. Despite the repairs and painting they'd done, it was still The Arch. Being back in here after twenty years made me feel almost nauseous with the weight of it. Surely the Germans had a word for this: *naustalgia?*

I walked over to the window and looked out at the gardens, alive in the moonlight. When I used to come here, they were overgrown, full of planks of wood, shattered glass and old wiring. Now, the wooden swing seat looked in much better condition, and the statue of the praying woman was free of moss. Pastel-coloured fairy lights looped over trees and posts, creating glowing constellations.

The others were dotted around outside on a break. Wendy and Nell were on the swing seat, laughing in unison at something or other. Bramwell was smoking a joint on the veranda – everyone had received strict instructions not to smoke in the house any more now that I'd arrived.

Foley Joe stood beside him doing what looked like tai chi moves.

Robbie joined me at the window and we stood together, watching them all. He clearly wanted to be near me. I could smell the fire on his fleece. I felt serene. Almost like this might be our house, our mansion, and we were looking out over the place where our child would play and grow. I breathed deeply, drinking it in. Then I remembered room three, and a sharp panic pierced my gut. I could just close my eyes whenever I walked past the door. But how would I carry the baby past it with my eyes closed? Surely I could do it. Blind people had babies, didn't they? I could learn the route. I still had two months before the baby would be born.

'It really looks like this money's going to come in,' Robbie said. 'From the donor. Come January, the council won't know what's hit it. We'll get them the week they're back at work. We had hundreds at the last protest. Maybe we'll get thousands this time. If we get enough of it prepped now, we can take Christmas off. I don't think I've ever been so excited.'

'I love Christmas, too,' I said.

He laughed. 'Oh, Jane,' he said. 'Now listen, you're not to worry about anything, OK? You've not got long to go now. We're all here for you. I mean, no heavy lifting, but I can carry on working you like a donkey on the paperwork, yeah?'

Becca's parting words to Robbie had been about how I was 'a bit of a worrier'. She'd stayed for at least an hour, nosing about, admiring their Christmas tree and record player, asking him non-stop questions.

How did they get electricity? There was a nail to bypass the meter lying across the wiring. Couldn't they just get chucked out at any time? No, because it was a commercial property. What if the owner came? He could be arrested if he used force or violence. I smiled and nodded solemnly at all his answers, sometimes – as if *I* had a clue – laughing a half-laugh from the back of my throat, like in the theatre when an audience member wishes to demonstrate to everyone that they understand an obscure reference in a play.

She introduced herself to everyone in the hall, admiring their signs, and immediately rolled up her sleeves to help Nell make the papier-mâché effigy of the developer, which was to go in a wheelbarrow at the protest. I sat in the rocking chair next to the Christmas tree, surveying the room, hunting for things that might endanger the baby once it was born. It was going to be hard to find a stairgate wide enough for the staircase, which was so much grander than I remembered.

Leaving Becca to aggressively slap strips of paper and glue onto the developer's nose – a man she had never met – Nell took my hand and pulled me over to another part of the table, where there lay a messy pile of cardboard, pens, tape and paper. 'Help with the wording on these template placards, will you?'

I sank down wearily into a chair and picked up a pen.

'All these weeks you've been working with us now,' she said, 'and I don't know exactly what your job used to be in London?'

I looked around for Robbie, who was laughing heartily at something Bramwell was saying, his eyes wide and incredulous. I racked my brains to remember what I'd told him about my job in London. Something about the wording for barbecues and TENS machines?

'I worked with words,' I said solemnly. 'In an office.' This seemed to suffice, for the moment.

People not profits, the first card read. It was a bit hack. *Fuck off shit head don't do this*, said one with CND signs drawn around the edges. I started laughing.

'That's Foley Joe's,' Nell explained, holding her hands up. 'I know it's . . . but everyone's got to feel they're being heard. That's really important. How many protests have you done?'

None, I thought, *unless you count moaning with the rest of our old street about how the school opposite was being expanded, curtailing our view of the London Eye.* 'Oh, lots,' I said. 'Probably not as many as you, but – y'know, Don't Attack Iraq, animal testing, too many to remember.'

She nodded.

'Extinction Rebellion, of course,' I added. Thank the sweet Lord for Extinction Rebellion. 'How about you?' I asked.

'An average of one a month since I was thirteen,' she said, gazing at the Christmas tree. 'Do these placards, then you can probably reword the statement we're reading out to Gareth, the council guy, at the protest. Get the points across quickly. We're going to try and get him on lunch. He goes to Boots every day at the same time and gets a prawn mayo sandwich meal deal – we've got intel. The *Foley Herald* should be there when we get him. Maybe you know someone who works for them? We also need to draft another email to Simon, the developer, but we can do that tomorrow.'

I scanned the statement. Why did everything always carry a price? I wanted to settle into my room. I was so tired.

Robbie wove his way over, high-fiving people on the way, rubbing his hands together in glee. 'Yes, yes, yes!' he said, punching the air, his eyes glittering. He reached us and grabbed Nell by the shoulders, rotating her from side to side and walking her towards the effigy and Becca, who was still making the nose. 'Hello, mister developer!' he said to it. 'Haven't these girls done a good job on your lying, stinking face, Simon Sinclair?'

We laughed, and I waited patiently for him to take his hands off Nell's shoulders.

After Becca and I had been shown a line of showers – 'It's a tad Russian roulette' – Becca announced she should be on her way. The three of us paused at the top of the staircase to the bustling hall. I took in the dilapidated grand piano they'd somehow managed to get through the door, the huge, messy table, the cornicing thick with extra layers of plaster, like Christmas-cake icing.

'Look after this one, eh,' Becca said to Robbie. 'She's a bit of a worrier.'

'Aren't we all?' he replied, walking us down the stairs either side of him.

'I don't think you understand,' she said. 'She thought her rib was a—'

'Thanks so much for everything, Becca,' I said hastily. 'To Kelly, too.'

I itched for her to leave and felt embarrassed, like she was a parent dropping me off at university for the first time.

She'd pulled him aside then, and there was nothing I

could do to get Robbie away from her. I'd fiddled with the baubles of the Christmas tree and unsuccessfully tried to eavesdrop while they spoke quietly.

'Becca's a bit scary, isn't she?' I said to him as we gazed out of the window of my new bedroom. Foley Joe was still doing his tai chi moves, and Bramwell had joined in. 'You ought to get her to do your PR.'

'Good idea,' he said. 'Yes, Jane!'

'What did she say to you, as she was going?'

'She asked me what was going on between us,' he said. 'Between *moi et vous*.'

'And what did you say?' I asked, turning to face him. 'And I'm *tu*, not *vous*.'

'I said that you're someone who's going through a lot,' he replied. 'That you're a little bit stubborn and very, very brilliant, and I reckon if you feel loved and appreciated here, with the gang, you'll have a much easier labour.'

I turned back to look at the gardens. Robbie was standing just behind me, our bodies very close but not touching. I wanted desperately for him to put his arms round my neck from behind, for me to lean back into his chest and reach up with my arms, still not looking at him; for him to move his hands slowly down to my breasts, to stroke them gently through my top, then to scoop his hands down inside my bra more roughly as I turned to place my mouth on his. My nipple in his mouth, him biting tentatively, then harder, and harder, until it obliterated everything in my head, just for a brief moment. Until it obliterated the fact that I felt sure I was going to die of cancer before the baby was one, that I had probably damaged its brain because I'd eaten that rare burger back at The Sphere, that I knew I would somehow kill it through negligence – by letting something fall into the cot, or during the birth, somehow, by refusing or accepting something medical that I shouldn't. That I couldn't open my eyes as I walked past room three, all because of something that had happened two decades ago, that I leapt from secret crisis to secret crisis like they were stepping stones, each a new shape and texture, each telling me 'those ones were all practice – I'm the *real* danger'.

I wanted infinitely more of him. I wanted him to see me as a precious jewel only he had true access to, to notice me over and above everyone else, to see me as more than 'very, very brilliant', but unless I could come up with as much money as this donor, how could I make that happen?

'What about my bum?' I said, looking over my shoulder. 'Did you mention to Becca that I've got the best bum in Foley? Even in maternity leggings?'

He laughed and headed for the door. 'There's no doubt about it, Janey,' he said. 'Now. How good are you at making wool hair on effigies?'

Chapter Thirty-Two

Robbie was right: I had a family now. I had my place at the table, and my plate and my cup. I learnt the unspoken rules within the building. How to tell when Wendy was meditating. That it was better not to try to interject when Nell was talking about the campaign. The way Bramwell went to forage in the woods early every morning and wanted to base every meal around what he found, but that the others liked to use up whatever was in the kitchen; there were a lot of hotchpotch dishes every day.

There were spoken rules, too: rotas on the walls, detailed ones. I made sure I did bits and bobs, but not too much. Robbie and nimble Nell went to the skips outside Morrisons every night or so, jumping over the wall behind the bus station and gathering a wide array of binned food, almost always intact within its packaging. Occasionally they drove the van to the Waitrose in Buxton to do the same, and that was very exciting: Welsh cakes, extra-creamy butter, Derbyshire oatcakes. 'We're not taking anything that's not being chucked anyway,' Nell said. 'Even if we *were* stealing, it's all they deserve, these big supermarkets.' We all nodded our agreement and I put firmly to the back of my mind the myriad supermarket campaigns I'd worked on. I started to relax in the building. I did some painting with Wendy and began to take joy in the unpredictability of cooking with a lucky dip of ingredients.

Letters arrived from Jonathan, who must have learnt from my parents where I was living – I'd seen Monica over the fence in her garden and given her a reluctant wave – and I threw them into the fire without reading them. Christmas cards dribbled in – some forwarded on – from Stuart, the Chamberses, Megan, a few London mates, my sister Amanda, saying that she and Leo couldn't wait to meet the baby, and lastly, my parents. *We'll always love you,* it said in Mum's neat writing. Dad had written a P.S. *Important. Keep well. Seek medical advice even if you think it's something small. If they try to fob you off but your instinct says it's serious, ask to see someone else.*

'Bit full on,' said Nell, reading over my shoulder.

'Yeah . . .' I said with a flash of irritation. 'It's just my dad. We all have to humour him.' My dad, with his head always slightly bowed, eyes darting, in the room but not in the room. My dad, hugging me, teasing me, telling me about an accounting client who handed over his receipts in a clean sock. My dad, talking like he was in the present but living in the past, where symptoms may have been missed, and a price paid.

When I grew tired, Wendy and Bramwell would massage a foot each, Wendy's touch light and deft, and Bramwell's more intense, his large thumbs digging deep into my skin. On our breaks from the campaign work, Robbie talked to me about how amazing babies were, how they knew how to breastfeed without being taught, how he knew I would be such a creative and instinctive mother. I managed to draw down Nell's defences, and soon had her waxing lyrical about bivouacking and wild swimming, two things I would never do if my life depended on it. After dinner, Bramwell would sit at the big dining table, building spliffs and whittling tiny wooden figurines and making cheerful affirmative noises every minute or so, like a children's toy that makes a generic bleep when you haven't played with it for a while. I got good at closing my eyes when I walked past room three. I learnt the irregularities on the wall, which meant I could move along it using touch as a guide, knowing that when I hit the third creaky floorboard it was safe to open them again. If anyone saw me doing this – which I'm sure they did – they said nothing to me about it.

On Christmas Eve, Robbie was playing the piano and Nell was teaching us – rather too strictly, I thought – a dance she'd learnt in Brazil, when there was a loud knock at the door. I prayed to God it wasn't Mum or Jonathan. When we opened it, there was nothing there except the biggest turkey I'd ever seen resting on the doorstep in a tin-foil tray, studded with cloves of garlic and sprigs of rosemary. Who'd left it? Who cared? Bramwell was so stoned he couldn't be sure he hadn't put it there himself. We whooped and cheered and danced around the hall, Robbie spinning each of us in turn. Even Nell beamed from ear to ear.

Christmas Day passed slowly and quickly at the same time. I found myself wondering what it would have been like to work in the bookshop over Christmas and hoping it had been busy and not too stressful for Stuart. I could imagine Monica foisting *A Christmas Carol* upon people, jumping in before they'd even started browsing. Mum and Dad had left some presents on the doorstep for me: clothes for the baby, books, slippers. I felt very uncomfortable opening them, but Wendy made me, telling me there was a difference between closing a door on a situation and locking it. Bramwell gave us whittled versions of ourselves, Wendy gloves she'd crocheted, Nell home-made lanterns and I a silly poem for each of them. Robbie didn't get any of us anything. None of us expected him to. He lived and breathed the campaign, working on the online fundraising deep into the evenings.

After eating, we played Pin the Horrible Tie on the Property Developer with the now-finished effigy, and a game I think Bramwell had made up, where you rolled hazelnuts into empty toilet rolls. I even had an inch or two of red wine, at Robbie's behest.

'Enjoy yourself,' he kept saying. 'This is the calm before the storm.' I didn't know if he was talking about the protest or the baby.

If I was feeling wobbly, he'd climb into bed beside me and hold me until I went to sleep, tracing circles on my back with his fingertips, spelling out words I tried to decipher but never could. I always hoped he'd be there next to me in the morning, but he never was.

Jonathan and I had always joked that he'd proposed on Christmas Eve because me saying no risked ruining future Christmases forever. The ring had appeared on the Christmas tree, hanging on the ear of a decorative reindeer he'd diligently painted at a ceramic café alongside scores of het-up children and parents trying to get gifts done before Christmas.

When I'd first set eyes on the ring – a simple diamond on a gold band – I'd felt like an elderly relative was telling me everything would be all right. No fireworks, no alarm bells. Just that contented feeling like when you sit in an armchair at someone else's house, and you realise it's one of those with a lever which tips the chair back into a reclining position.

We went for a late Chinese meal – we were among the only customers there – and held hands under the table the whole time, which is quite easy to do when you're using chopsticks. Tinkly Christmas music played, and there were red paper chains pinned up. When we told the owner, who knew us as regulars, he brought us fortune cookies and beers.

'You're making me look bad for not hiding the ring in a fortune cookie!' Jonathan had said, and we'd all laughed. I said I'd keep the little slip of paper from the cookie forever. But it was in our flat, in a plastic bag along with the ring, next to the hordes of ovulation sticks and pregnancy tests at the back of the airing cupboard.

Whenever anyone cried – Bramwell cried very easily, with joy, mostly – Robbie acted as though nothing was different, like the person had just sneezed or yawned. Crying was merely another bodily function – the system ridding itself of the emotion so it could get on with living.

Tonight, he held me and carried on tracing the mysterious words onto my back. 'It wasn't meant to be like this,' I sobbed. 'Just, sometimes, it's like I'm still in shock. If he hadn't cheated, I'd probably be living in a four-bedroom house in Putney by now, the nursery all done up in yellow, stupid boring neighbours dropping off baby stuff and banana cake.'

'No one knows what anything's meant to be, Jane,' he said. 'You still might have that life. In fact, I think it's likely. But you don't know. That's the joy of it all.'

'Is it?' I asked.

'Would you really want to control,' he whispered into my hair, 'everything about your future? Know exactly what your baby's going to be like, what it'll end up doing as a job, what you were going to die of, and when?'

'That sounds fucking great,' I said, squirming into him.

'Tell me what happened to you here, Jane, in room three,' he said. 'You're safe. Tell me.'

I closed my eyes and pretended to be asleep until he stopped asking, and I listened as he got up, left the room and softly shut the door.

Chapter Thirty-Three

On Boxing Day evening, as I sat in the rocking chair wearing one of Wendy's gigantic crocheted cardigans, she knelt down next to me and volunteered to be my doula for the birth.

'What exactly *is* a doula?' I asked. 'Like a mortgage broker?'

'A guide, I suppose,' she said. 'I'd be your eyes and ears throughout labour, talk to the midwives on your behalf, offer calmness and snacks, that sort of thing.'

'I can't pay you,' I said.

She hugged me. 'Don't be silly. I've done it for both my daughters. It'd be my gift to you, Jane.'

Her long hair brushed my shoulder as I clasped her hands. 'I've got to have a birthing pool, Wendy,' I said. 'It's my only stipulation, apart from not going into hospital.' I spoke quietly, so the others wouldn't hear as they bustled about us with mismatched crockery and silverware. 'I've got a problem with hospitals. It's to do with my dad.'

'Home births are much better,' she agreed. 'And I was going to suggest a pool. My friend in Nottingham's got one. I'll collect it nearer the time.'

I told her a home birth had been agreed at my antenatal appointments at the GP surgery, and that they knew about my fear of hospitals, but that they still thought I was living at my parents'.

'All your scans and appointments have been fine?' she asked.

I told her yes. 'They had to take my blood pressure twice last time, but it was OK the second time. I get a bit nervous, you see.'

'They can't make you go in, no matter where you are when you go into labour,' she explained. 'It's your right not to.'

We immediately began to plan where the birthing pool would go.

'It's got to be a big room,' she said. 'They're quite big, those pools, you know. Your room's way too small. What about room three?'

I went cold, then hot. 'No,' I said. 'Can't it go in Robbie's room?'

'That's not big enough either,' she said.

'OK,' I said, panicking now. 'This hall, then?'

She looked incredulous. 'You mean . . . I don't think you'll want everyone to see you, will you? This is a communal area. It can go on for hours.'

'We don't mind seeing,' Bramwell called through from the kitchen, peeling carrots. 'I could paint it, if you like, duck.'

I would rather everyone saw me giving birth than set foot in room three, I realised. I was so weak, so pathetic. I started to feel dizzy and even hotter.

'You can go in my room, I guess,' Nell said. 'I reckon it's big enough.' I barely registered her words.

'Just going to the loo,' I said, tearing off Wendy's cardigan and running upstairs.

In my room, the door shut behind me, I phoned him without thinking about it. My body knew what my mind needed. I waited for it to connect, my heart pounding in my chest, facing the window where the swing seat swung wildly in the wind, where the stars hung like glittering fish caught in a net. I saw none of it.

'Come on, come on,' I hissed into the silence. I listened as it went straight to answerphone without ringing. Of course – it was Boxing Day. He would be with his family, probably at their holiday cottage in Suffolk. The mobile reception there changed with the weather. I couldn't ring the landline, risk speaking to Sadie or Bryan or Andrew. I'd have to leave a message, hope he'd go up to the attic room at some point this evening, where you could normally get two bars of reception if you waved your phone next to a picture of an elephant. 'Jonathan,' I said. 'It's me. The baby's OK. Listen, I'm having a . . . thing.' *In for six, out for eight.* 'Can you ring me? About room three.' I pressed the hash key and the automated voice came on, telling me my options. To rerecord your message, press two. To delete your message, press three. I firmly pressed three and hung up, tears pouring down my cheeks.

Robbie had come in so quietly I hadn't noticed. When I turned, he was sitting on the bed, his arms open.

'Tell me, Jane,' he said. 'Whatever it is, it can't be all that bad.'

I lay down on the bed and looked up at the cobwebs.

I took a breath in. 'Just get ready for the Jane you probably don't remember from school,' I said.

The day had started like Saturdays normally did when I was in sixth form. The weather was good that spring, and we'd sat in the bandstand all afternoon, smoking joints and swigging from one-litre bottles of Coke stuffed with magic mushrooms. Then Ed Millet had turned up with some acid and we'd all gobbled it up like Pac-Man, getting confused over how much we'd all had, wanting to have exactly the same amount as one another, so we could feel exactly the same effects at the same time. Another quarter, another half. We smoked cigars, because it was my eighteenth birthday, even though they tasted disgusting. I found some ferns in the shape of a lion, complete with paws. We said it was a birthday lion, one which only appears on birthdays, and I shook hands with it for ages. Then we worked out it was always someone's birthday, so it must be there all year round. We spent ages working it out. We were very pleased with ourselves. Then Megan, Ruth and Sarah said I was going on an adventure with them. I was going to be blindfolded, and I wasn't allowed to ask any questions.

Robbie nodded as I told him all this, looking at me intently.

'It wasn't weird for them to blindfold me,' I said. 'We were those kinds of angsty teenagers – Ouija boards, blood sisters, horror-film nights. We liked feeling edgy.'

In the back of the car, with the blindfold on, I started to see multicoloured spirals in the blackness, all spinning. I told the others, and they said they could see them, too. I asked them to keep describing theirs to me, which they did, and that's how I got through the journey without worrying about where we were going. We were all in it together, even if I was the only one blindfolded. When the car stopped and I was led over grass and rocks, I worked out that soldiers moved their arms back and forth and kept them straight because that was the most efficient way of walking, so we all walked like soldiers – at least they said that's what they were doing.

I didn't realise we were in The Arch, even though I knew it so well by then. We went up some stairs like soldiers, which took ages. They led me along again, and then we stopped. They said, 'Don't take your blindfold off until it's finished.' They sat me down on a soft surface, and then I heard the door shut.

I sat up and asked Robbie to get me some water, and once he had returned with it, I carried on. 'I sat there like a child, waiting,' I said. 'Then the tape started playing.'

'A cassette tape?' he asked.

I nodded. I'd often wondered how long the recording on the tape actually was, where it was now. Megan said she didn't know. She just wanted to forget everything about that night.

Throughout the whole thing, I never realised it was a tape. The noises felt like they were coming from inside the room, some of them from inside my own head. The first noise was a screeching, like something being dragged across a hard surface. I giggled, expecting the others to join in, but there was no laughter from anyone else. I put my hands in front of me and called their names, then I realised I could be alone. The next sound was horses' hooves, getting louder and louder. In my head, I connected them with the lion. The horses were here to save me. I felt all right again. My friends wouldn't put me in danger. Next was the sound of a record being played backwards, then whispers. *Jane, where are you? Don't worry, you're home. Are you? Jane?* This was the worst bit so far. *Jane? Are you you? Who are you?* I thought I could be saying this to myself out loud, but I couldn't work out why my friends were letting me torture myself like this.

I whispered back to it to please stop, that I knew who I was. I thought that if I spoke in the way it spoke, it would stop. When that didn't work, I visualised a young girl in a green-and-white gingham dress who would be my saviour, and I felt amazing for a moment, but then her mouth went droopy and joined in with the whispering. *Jane? Are you here? Are you there?* I was screaming by then. 'Please! Can I take the blindfold off?' Silence, then the sound of a clock ticking, louder and louder, then rustling, more screeching.

Even though they'd told me not to, I ripped off the blindfold, sweating and trembling, and blinked around me in the dim light. I was sitting on a bed, a bare mattress. Heavy velvet curtains were drawn across the window. I could make out an old wardrobe with its doors closed, a grubby pink carpet, a bare light bulb above me, and . . . what was that hanging on the wall? I crept closer in fear. Was it a dead animal? A rat? A fox? As I inched my way towards it, more whispers came, but by then I was more scared of what was in the room with me. *Are you everywhere?* Sheets of sweat broke out on my skin as I reached whatever it was, hanging there limply. It was a filthy Babygro, on a coat hanger on a single nail in the wall. I ran to the door, but I couldn't get out. I frantically pulled and pushed at it. 'Let me out!' I shouted, sobbing hysterically. 'Please!' I waited, but no one came. And that was when the banging from inside the wardrobe started.

'Do you want to take a break?' said Robbie. 'I've read about flashbacks, and—'

I shook my head. 'This isn't a flashback. I'm just telling you what happened. It feels right.' This was the first time I'd told anyone except Jonathan what had happened. Mum and Dad had got some details out of me on the night, but I'd been too upset and out of it to really talk – and they'd left the subject on the proviso I never re-entered The Arch or saw that group of friends again. 'That's why you shouldn't trust too easily,' Dad had said at the time. 'People let you down without meaning to when drugs are involved. The drugs always win.'

'Who was in the wardrobe?' Robbie asked. 'One of your mates?'

I shook my head. If it had been, it would have all been so much better. I told him how I'd stayed near the door of the room, breathing shallowly, not wanting to know what was inside the wardrobe, praying out loud that someone would come and let me out of the room. How I didn't want to scream again, because that had been what alerted whatever was in there to my presence. I stood with my back against the wall, not taking my eyes off the wooden doors of the wardrobe. The whole thing suddenly started to shake violently, as whoever was inside rained blows down onto the insides of the doors. I huddled down into a ball, rocking. The whispers went on. It felt like they were coming out of every surface in the room, like the room knew something I didn't. *Everyone* knew something I didn't. I'd trusted the mates I loved most in the world, and now, what was happening to me? And what was going to happen?

As I told Robbie about it, I could see it all so clearly. The doors of the wardrobe had burst open and out shot a man, wild-eyed, naked. He looked absolutely out of it. 'Shit! I thought there was someone locked in there with me!' he screamed at me. 'But it was my fucking arm! I've got a dead arm, you know, like a dead leg? I fell asleep on it. I thought it was someone else's fucking arm! Jesus!'

I screamed so much, I bet you could hear it from the road. Had they planted this man here as part of the surprise? I started to throw things at him, anything I could find in the room. Tiles. Bricks. A little table. I ripped the Babygro off the wall and threw that at him, too.

'Stop it, you crazy bitch!' he shouted. 'What the fuck!' Then I heard the door being opened, and Megan and the others ran in, and we all stumbled out into the gardens as fast as we could.

'They'd actually bought balloons and cake, and champagne – real champagne,' I said as Robbie held my hands, shaking his head slowly from side to side. This was the most he'd ever concentrated on me. I lay my head on his chest. 'We didn't end up drinking any. They'd made the tape the day before, when we didn't realise we'd end up getting so off our heads. They thought the whole thing would be funny, that I'd like the danger of it, then they'd burst in and rescue me. They got carried away. When I was sobbing hysterically and banging on the door to be let out, they thought I was laughing hysterically. None of us knew who the wardrobe guy was. There were always different groups here. He was older than us, I think.'

'It sounds like a bit of a trigger for an already anxious person,' Robbie said gently. 'A perfect storm.'

'Yeah,' I nodded. 'Someone else might have been able to weather it. It definitely set something off in me. Checking the door's locked and stuff like that. It's become symbolic, I suppose. It's like, if your mates can let you down like that, so dramatically – even if it was just a massive misjudgement – can you really trust anyone? At eighteen, your mates are your world.'

'So you've not been in that room since?'

'I hadn't even been in The Arch since, until I moved in here!' I said. 'At first, I just couldn't, and then the years went by and I hadn't, and I started to think something bad might happen if I did. Why rock the boat?'

Of course I saw that group of friends again, despite my parents' protestations – we were all in sixth form together, after all - but it was never the same again, even with Megan. Sarah and Ruth, who'd stayed in the area, I hadn't seen for decades. Megan and I, although ostensibly 'best friends from school' in London, still bore the scars of that night deep down.

I brought my head up to look at him. 'Please don't think this is all I am,' I said. 'I'm a laugh, too. I'm fucking great.'

'People are made of layers and layers of complexity,' he whispered. 'I know you're a laugh. So now you've come into the building, don't you think you can try and go into room three? See that it's just a room?'

'No bloody way!' I laughed. 'That's for another lifetime.'

I breathed. I could breathe again. We sat like that for a while, and then he laid me gently into bed. That night he stayed all night.

Chapter Thirty-Four

'What do we want?'

'A centre for the people!'

'When do we want it?'

'Now!'

Our shouts rang out across the valley. At first, I'd felt self-conscious doing the chanting, but that had soon dissipated with the sheer force of the crowd's passion. I was surprised by the number of people who'd turned up: community groups from all over Derbyshire, the Socialist Workers Party, schoolkids by the dozen, not to mention numerous Foley people I half recognised from my childhood: a tattooed couple banging massive gongs; a local craft group who'd knitted their own banner; babies, grandparents and oh so many guitars. Fenella was there, too, and she'd even given me a wry nod. I guessed she'd be doing some poetry later, at the afterparty.

Robbie helmed the march, his loudhailer in hand and his banner held aloft, leading us up the hill from the bandstand, where we'd all assembled. The traffic was brought to a standstill and the drivers peered at us, some beeping in solidarity, some openly annoyed. Two police officers marched on the fringes, one chatty, the other ready for trouble.

Despite the fatigue from walking up the hill, I felt completely exhilarated once we got going, joining in with a song Foley Joe had written about how the heart of the community must beat. We'd tried to catch Gareth on his lunch break on the high street, but someone must have tipped him off, because there was no sign of him and his prawn mayo sandwich at Boots.

We gathered in the car park of the council offices and Robbie shouted up to Gareth's window, 'Rapunzel, Rapunzel, let down your golden hair!' We all joined in with gusto, waving our placards and stamping our feet. 'Come on, Gareth! You can't run away now!'

'Jane!' I heard from behind me. I turned to see Mum and Dad, their winter coats buttoned up to their necks like dolls in their Sunday best. Mum was clutching some bell-ringing newsletters in a Perspex folder.

'What?' I shrugged.

'What are you doing?' said Mum. 'You shouldn't be standing out here in the cold, with these . . . people—'

'The baby could come anytime now, Jane,' Dad added. 'It's January! Did you get our Christmas card? Are you still taking your vitamins every day?'

'I'm *living*!' I shouted at the two of them. 'I'm *living*! Why not join me?' I turned back towards the council offices and pumped my fist in the air. 'Rapunzel, Rapunzel, let down your golden hair!' I didn't look back over my shoulder again for a long while, and when I did, they'd gone.

Gareth finally came down. A jeer went up as he opened the doors along with a security guard, who looked like it was his first day in the job. Robbie and I wound our way to the front of the crowd.

You could see the security guard's white socks, and one of his shoelaces was undone. 'Erm, not today thank you, folks!' he cried in a high-pitched voice before Gareth moved him aside and addressed us.

Gareth was smartly dressed and had silky blond hair in a ponytail at the base of his neck. He clutched a piece of A4 paper, which he read from.

'OK, OK!' he shouted, gesturing for us all to be quiet.

Robbie turned and shushed us all.

'OK, well, hello, everyone,' said Gareth. He cleared his throat. 'I know why you're here. Let me just summarise everything as it stands. As you know, Simon Sinclair, aka the developer, applied to turn The Archibald Hotel into flats, and so far he's had two hearings, which haven't gone his way.'

We all cheered.

'This is his third attempt. He's made some changes to the floor plan, and we've taken into account the various concerns of the community in terms of green space and carbon emissions—' continued Gareth.

'Have you bollocks!' shouted someone from the back.

'And we feel they've been addressed, on the whole—'

'Have they bollocks!' came another voice, then laughter.

'Look!' shouted Gareth, scrunching up the piece of paper and putting it in his pocket. 'I'm not *not* on your side – that's why I'm out here talking to you. But we all know he'll just keep trying to find ways round obstacles. We've let you live there for months, treating the place—'

'Like a hotel?' I shouted, to more laughter. Robbie gave my arm a squeeze.

'You've got to accept – this is a tourist hotspot, and a desirable place for commuters to Derby and Nottingham, and there's not enough housing. Simon's addressed the concerns from the last hearing, and we've got less of a reason to block the purchase. People with disposable incomes buying properties here is so good for us locally – come on, come on, you've got to all see that . . .'

Before I knew it, I was grabbing Robbie's loudhailer from him, drowning out Gareth's final words. At first it wasn't turned on. Robbie flicked the switch for me, his eyes sparkling with apprehension, willing me on.

'We're here,' I told Gareth, 'not because we want to be.' People quietened down behind me. 'We're here, not because we *ought* to be. We're here because we *need* to be!' A loud cheer came from behind me. I didn't know what to say next, but I kept talking as if I did. I told him that this town needed to support its most vulnerable or it would lose its identity. I told him our mission statement: to *provide*. To provide support, guidance, food, at no cost to the council. As well as the volunteers who would run the needle exchange – who were already on board – Robbie would provide advice on everything from medical matters to benefits and housing issues. Bramwell would teach carpentry and foraging. Wendy would teach art, Nell yoga. I would teach creative writing, I found myself saying.

'And I'm teaching drystone walling!' shouted Foley Joe.

'And together,' I said, 'we're creating somewhere you can come when you're not on the greatest terms with life, when you're struggling with addiction, when you've been kicked out of your accommodation, or when you just fancy a cup of tea. Gareth, you must know people in Foley who are in difficult situations. How could you sleep at night knowing that they needed somewhere to go, and you denied it to them? Why are they worth less? You don't *want* to give us The Arch. You don't *dream* of giving us The Arch. But you *need* to give us The Arch! March for The Arch! March for The Arch!'

'March for The Arch!' came the chant behind me, from everyone.

I turned round, tears in my eyes. Robbie hugged me savagely before grabbing the loudhailer. I glimpsed Stuart towards the back of the crowd and he gave me a thumbs-up. I'd missed him.

'We're self-sufficient, Gareth, like Jane just said!' added Robbie. 'As well as our money from fundraising, we've had an offer from a charitable trust, we've got the full support of Women's Aid and today it's been confirmed that a private donor's going to put in fifty grand.'

We cheered like our hearts were going to leap from our chests. How could Gareth ever say no?

Chapter Thirty-Five

'Here comes the scum,' sang Foley Joe that evening, on a stage set up in the main hall. The Arch was packed full of people from the march, eating bowls of Bramwell's chilli, necking beers, nipping out into the frost to smoke and chat, to go over the day's events, to talk about what skills they could bring in, suggesting people they knew who could help or benefit. The word was that Gareth was having a rethink, talking to the developer, trying to figure out a way we could have our Arch. A woman was doing face-painting in the corner. She could only do lizards, but no one minded.

I sat with Kelly on the green leather sofa while the boys kicked pine cones up and over the swing seat in the garden, jostling the fairy lights so that they danced in the dark. People kept asking me when the baby was due. Kelly had started shouting, 'It's due in three weeks, all right?' whenever anyone so much as cast a look our way. She leant her head on my shoulder. 'What's going on with you and Robbie, then?' she said. 'Sorry it's taken me so long to ask. I've been a bit tangled up with Waggy. Becca said Robbie said you were "very, very brilliant".'

I smiled. My eyes found Robbie's in the busy throng of people. He was talking animatedly to Stuart and a few others, rubbing his hands together and smiling. 'I know my head's all over the place because I'm basically about to have a baby,' I said. 'But – I really think he makes me into a better person.'

'So you didn't do that speech earlier to try and get in his knickers, then?' she asked. 'You really meant it all?'

I grinned. 'I dunno,' I said. 'Bit of both.'

Bramwell joined us, handing Kelly a couple of whittled wooden dogs. 'For your lads,' he said. He turned to me. 'I was talking to Robbie just now,' he said. 'Have you ever noticed how I don't like room three either?'

'What do you mean?' I said.

'Well,' he said, 'I know that dude you were so scared of in the wardrobe. He was pretty scared by you, too, duck. He had most of the nineties stolen away by this and that, but he does have a hazy memory of a girl in a silver top with peroxide hair throwing a table at him. I know him quite well actually. He makes dogs out of wood.'

I threw my arms around him. 'I'm sorry,' I said. 'Oh shit, Bramwell, I'm so sorry for throwing tiles and bricks and a Babygro at you.'

'I'm so sorry, too, duck,' he replied. 'The fucking nineties, eh?'

'And now,' said Robbie into the mic, 'I'm really excited to welcome to the stage someone I mentioned earlier, who's pledged a really, really substantial donation to us. She wants to say a few words about why she's got involved with

The Arch, so please all welcome the woman of the moment: Sadie Chambers.'

I froze. My heart stopped in my chest. Sadie strolled onto the stage to applause, head dipped, smiling shyly, hands in mammoth cardigan pockets, playing the North London bohemian: the one who doesn't notice if she's wearing a ring from a cracker or from Tiffany's because she only wants to hold someone's hand and *talk*. Who prides herself in tearing through the bullshit to the nub of things because she *cares*. I felt sick.

'How do you use one of these things?' she giggled as she reached the mic, tapping it. 'Check, one, two. Check, one, two, three, four.'

'More like cheque for fifty K!' shouted Robbie.

Everyone clapped and cheered again. A woman near me was crying with joy, her child clasped in front of her, both their faces painted like lizards.

'I just want to say hello,' said Sadie. 'Because you'll probably see me around once everything's set in motion, and I believe it will be. I wouldn't be here if I didn't. Robbie, Nell, Wendy and Bramwell's work over the past year has been inspirational. What I'm doing is nothing compared to what they've put into this: canvassing, leafleting, organising meetings, pestering people on high until they listen. This area means a lot to me. It's beautiful, and so are all of you, and you deserve more as a community.' People whooped and clapped. She hadn't looked at me yet, but I knew she knew where I was. 'All my life I've tried to give to other people, and I know how it feels when hurdles are put in the way.'

She glanced at me now, of course, fleetingly.

'I don't want you to think of me as someone different,' she went on. 'I know I'm from London, but I've got connections to Foley and will have even more soon, when my first grandchild's born here!' An *awwww* went up from the crowd. 'And there it is!' She pointed to my belly. Everyone looked at me. 'Lovely Jane, who's been living here, too, helping out.'

My mouth felt like it was stuffed with cotton wool. I could feel my heart pulsing rapidly in my throat. I wanted a trapdoor to open and whisk me away, or for someone to reveal that this was all a big joke. I couldn't look up.

'What. The. *Fuck?!*' hissed Kelly in my ear.

'So I've got multiple reasons now to spend time in this amazing community,' she said.

I forced myself to clap along with the others, my smile like rigor mortis, my cheeks bright red.

'Do come and find me if you want to chat – oh, and my son Andrew's a lawyer, so I've roped him in to help with the legal element of us getting things to go our way. I'll be as excited as you are to see what the next step is in this glorious project!'

As she walked offstage, I bolted for the staircase, but she was at my shoulder before I'd even put one foot on the first step. I could see Robbie weaving his way across to us, shaking his head in disbelief.

'Not here,' I said to her over my shoulder. 'Outside.'

She completely ignored this. 'Darling! I thought that would be a nice surprise!' she said loudly, as if I was finding it all amusing, throwing her arms around my belly from behind and gently squeezing.

I jerked around.

'Darling!' she said again, kissing my cheek and rubbing my arms. I took a step away from her.

'Why couldn't you make the march, Sadie?' I asked her. 'Lunch at Claridge's?'

'Pardon, darling?' she said, her head close to mine. It was still just me and her.

'Where were you earlier, when we were putting in the real work?' I said, more loudly. 'It's pretty easy for you to give us fifty grand. You've probably got that in change around the house.'

'Jonathan's very ill,' she said gravely. 'That's why I couldn't come earlier.'

'What . . . what do you mean?'

'He's got migraine-associated vertigo. It's awful. Head-aches, feeling seasick. He's seeing a specialist in Kent. I took him to the appointment today. It's stress-related, of course. And then I drove straight up here with him and Bryan. They're at The Folly. Jonathan's desperate to see you.'

Robbie had reached us, and Kelly. I'd lost my chance to escape. But any escape would only have been temporary anyway. I was nothing more than a fly in her web: a web she hadn't even had to spin. She'd just come along – the money spider – and taken over. Was there a way I could persuade the others to turn down her offer? But what did that make me?

'My head's about to explode here!' said Robbie. 'Sadie, why didn't you say anything?'

'I've been a little bit naughty, darling – I never said it was Jane. A little surprise for you all! I wanted to wait until I was sure I could get you the money. Isn't it lovely? All these connections.' She did a big mock shiver. 'Connections, connections!'

'Well, yeah, that's what this place is about!' said Robbie. He looked at me enquiringly: *Are you OK?*

Wendy, Nell and Bramwell joined us excitedly, clustering in a small circle around me. I wished someone would come on and play some loud music, even Foley Joe again. But the stage was bare.

'Oh, did you all like the turkey?' beamed Sadie. 'Guilty!' The others gasped their gratitude. 'I had it delivered. My way of saying Happy Christmas before saying hello in person.'

'I'm going to go and lie down, I think,' I said. 'I'm not feeling great.'

'You rest while you can, Jane,' she said. 'You'll have plenty to contribute once the baby's born. We'll all help with childcare, I'm sure.'

Everyone nodded, smiling, willing, even Nell.

'You could lead classes on copywriting, couldn't you?' continued Sadie. 'All those ads you've written? Time to give something back!'

'Did you say ads?' said Nell. 'I thought you wrote instructions for barbecues.'

'Oh, that's modest of her!' replied Sadie. 'More like selling the barbecues, and the burgers, and the firelighters!'

I felt like my legs were going to give way.

'Did you see that one for the mobile phone company a few years ago? The one where the girl gets dropped off for her first year at uni? Realises she doesn't have change for the payphone but her mum's put a new phone at the bottom of her bag? And what about the one for McDonald's?

You know, where the two little boys fight over the chips and then realise they're on two for one? It was on television all the time. That was all Jane and Jonathan, wasn't it, darling?'

'I remember that one,' said Nell slowly.

I couldn't bear to look at any of them, especially Robbie, who'd already helped thousands of people all over the world for free, for – what? For love. For the love of it, while I'd blindly licked the arses of people I knew deep down were shafting each and every one of their workers.

I turned and ran for the stairs, feeling everyone's eyes on me. *Fifty steps until I can be in my room, alone.*

'Jane!' called Sadie as I put my foot on the third step. *Forty-seven steps.* I turned and caught a glimpse of Robbie's face. I couldn't bear it. 'Before you dash, I've got a letter for you from Andrew, in solicitor mode. Standard, really, in these sorts of circumstances, but anyway – got to tick the boxes and all that.'

Chapter Thirty-Six

Somehow, I got myself into my room with the door locked. I found myself in bed, shivering and sweating, shooting pains in my belly, hunched over the brown envelope with shaking hands. I ripped it open. Paperclipped to a thick wad of typed papers was a handwritten note on Jonathan's parents' letterheaded notepaper.

Darling Jane,

As I write this, I'm remembering the late stages of pregnancy with both boys – I expect you're doing a lot of sitting and eating! I do hope everyone's looking after you at The Arch. I'm sure they are.

By now you will have found out that I'm the mysterious 'donor'. I suspect you may think I'm doing it for all the wrong reasons, but I really do want to make a difference to some lives. Since I stopped work when I was pregnant, I've flitted from thing to thing, even when the boys were away at school and I had more time. I wish I'd seen more of them when they were growing up, and I don't want to make the same mistake with my first (only? Hope not!) grandchild! So now I can kill two birds with

*one stone. I desperately hope that, in time, you will grow
to trust us again.*

*I want to make you an offer. Once we've all calmed
down and you're back in London, we're happy to pay for
nannies round the clock, with you, Jonathan and the baby
living in the annexe. We've had the little room there decorated as a nursery in lemon – it's gorgeous! The nannies
we had for the boys when they were young were like part
of the family in the end – we even ate with them on Sun-
days. You won't possibly be able to imagine what life's like
with a newborn, but woman to woman – it's hell.*

*Speaking of which, we've all been dreadfully worried
about how you'll cope. Even for the strongest of us, the
hormones released after birth, the pain and drudgery of
breastfeeding, should you choose to, can topple us over into
a bad place. Bryan and I have discussed your mental-
health history (things you've told me over the years), and
we feel that you may be in danger of being one of the
topplers, as it were.*

*I beg of you to think of the child, not yourself. It's not
your fault you suffer from this thing, but do bear in mind
that you would put medical professionals in an impossible
position should anything go wrong during the birth if you
refused to do what they asked.*

*In this envelope is a draft agreement regarding access
to the child, which Andrew's drawn up if you don't feel
ready to reconcile with Jonathan yet. If you want to get a
solicitor to look over it, that's fine. It's not official until the
baby's born, but I didn't want this to come as a shock.*

*Give me (or, even better, Jonathan) a text or call when
you've had a chance to look through everything and we*

can discuss the next steps.
  Much love to you and bump,
  Sadie xxx

I frantically scanned the legal letter, most of which I didn't
understand, but from what I could glean, they weren't at
all reluctant to start legal proceedings for access, as soon
as the baby had been born. I rocked back and forth on the
bed, cradling my belly. How could I have been so stupid as
to think they were backing off? This was her way of invei-
gling her family into my future, striking at the heart of my
refuge at The Arch. Now I realised why she'd been so quiet
since I'd moved in here, why the hampers had stopped. She
must have been planning this for ages, discussing it with
Jonathan and the others, maybe even Mum and Dad.

There was a soft knocking at the door, and Robbie's voice
calling my name. I opened the door, let him in, locked it
behind him and fell into his arms.

'I'm sorry,' I sobbed. 'I'm sorry I lied about my job. I just
thought – when I first saw you, in the bookshop, I felt like
it'd sound so pathetic alongside what you do. But, honestly,
I don't want to go back to that world. Since I've been here,
I've felt for the first time that I belong somewhere. And
now, fucking Sadie – she's—'

'Jane!' he said, holding me. 'You don't need to worry
about your past. Nell's mum's on the board of HSBC! It's
what you're doing now that matters.'

'My God,' I said, relief flooding through me like honey.
'I thought you'd all hate me.'

'Of course not,' he replied. 'You're here because you want
to be, right? We all know you. Anyway, did you think I

wouldn't google you at some point? I didn't tell the others about your job because I thought you must have your reasons for not wanting us to know. It's fine. You're part of the family, love.'

'There's other stuff you don't know about me,' I said. 'It's not so bad at the moment, but – I'm a bit of a worrier. I know you know that, from how room three affected me, but you don't know how much I check things. That things are off and closed. And my health. I worry. Like, if I get a headache, I automatically think I've got a brain tumour, and google it loads until I convince myself it's true. I know I could be so happy if I could just stop worrying. It's been quite hard, actually, stopping myself from asking you about everything, with you being a doctor. But it's been really good for me not to.'

'OCD,' he said. 'Inflated sense of responsibility.'

'It's not OCD,' I said. 'I'm just a bit of a worrier. But since I've been here, it's got so much better.' It really was true. Checking had always been incorporated into my day, like brushing my teeth. But the past month since I'd arrived at The Arch was the first period in living memory when I'd been able to go to bed without first checking the gas, the windows, the hairdryer, the TV, that the door was locked. 'It's like being set free,' I continued. 'And it's all thanks to you. Because I feel looked after. Like I'm in a nest. A secret club. I could never have even set foot in this building again if it wasn't for you. And it's made me realise I really can do it. I can have this baby on my own, without help from Jonathan and his family, or mine, as long as I'm here. But now she's stepped in and . . . she's just going to ruin it all.'

He tried to speak but I didn't let him.

'And I know you'll accept her money,' I said. 'How could you not? She's made sure it's so much that you can't say no. But maybe in the years to come, we can make it back, and pay her back, then she'll be gone. You've changed me. You're the first guy who's ever made me into a better person, rather than a worse one. You're the first person from Foley I've told about room three.'

He nodded. 'I'm very honoured to hear that.'

'And I know you can't . . . I know it'd be weird for us to *do* anything, y'know, other than kiss, while I'm' – I pointed to the bump – 'but I know you could be a great, sort of, dad to it. I love you, Robbie.' The words spilled from my mouth like glitter and landed between us. Fuck it. 'I do.'

He walked to the window, stretching his shoulders out, making wide circles with his arms. 'I love you, too, Janey. We all do!'

I joined him and put my arms round his waist. 'Robbie,' I said, 'I don't love *them*. I love *you*.'

'Listen,' he said gently, 'when was the last time you ate? You must rest. You've not got long to go now. We all want the best for you and the baby.'

Fear prickled the back of my neck. 'Why are you talking to me like that? Like I'm an inpatient at a mental hospital?'

'Of course I'm not!' he laughed. 'Don't be paranoid. I really don't want you to get worked up. It's been a long day, for all of us.'

I heard Fenella's voice faintly from downstairs, doing one of her poems, spitting out the consonants like pips, but it sounded like a different language, so many worlds away from where I was. The room whirled.

'Are you saying . . .' I paused. 'So what's been happening? You kissed me on the moors, or did I dream that? You've held me almost every night and stroked my back and told me everything'll be OK. I assumed . . . well, I . . . so what was all that? Just another part of your service to the community?'

He ran his hands over his face, sitting on the end of the bed and facing away from me. 'No, no, of course it wasn't,' he said. 'I've loved it. I *do* love it. But can't we just . . . kind of, see what happens, rather than planning anything out? I don't know where I'm going to be in a year, ten years, even in a month. Certainly not living here, assuming we win – we wouldn't be allowed to sleep here once it was a social enterprise. I might need to go back to Uganda to set up another project, and even at the moment, I'm so preoccupied with The Arch that . . . how do *I* know what I'll want in the future? There's loads of people downstairs I really need to talk to. Gareth's just turned up – is there any way we can talk about this later? Or tomorrow? I know it's been a shock for you to find out about Sadie, but—'

It was as if the whole room was my heart hammering. 'So, right,' I said. 'All those times you were holding me—'

'It felt totally right!' he replied. 'We shared some amazing moments, and that's what I still want! We talked about Jonathan, about your parents, about how you and Amanda compete, how you've ended up such good mates with Kelly—'

'And you told me virtually nothing about yourself,' I said, realising. 'I don't know how many relationships you've had. I don't even know if you're gay!'

'I wanted you to feel good,' he smiled. 'You're a glorious person!'

'What does that mean, though?' I asked. 'You don't want anything to happen really?'

'I don't know!' he said. 'And I haven't really ever had a proper girlfriend, since you're asking. I did have a French girlfriend for a while, but we lived in different countries most of the time, and when Xav was born, I couldn't—'

'Xav? Who's fucking Xav?'

'Xavier, my baby,' he replied. 'Well, actually, he's seven now. He lives in France, but he should be visiting soon with his mother. I see him whenever I can. I can see now that I probably should have told you that, but my head's been in The Arch. I thought I *was* doing a kind of service, I guess, thinking about it, and maybe – yeah, probably that was the wrong thing to do. But I'm not sorry for kissing you, because it was lovely.'

He turned and smiled at me.

'Sorry,' he went on. 'Maybe we shouldn't have kissed. I'm . . . I never know where I'm going to be. So it's probably better for me to be on my own, or with someone who doesn't know where they're going to be either. I thought we were on the same page. We're all so tactile here. You didn't think Bramwell massaging your feet meant anything, did you?'

'Of course I fucking didn't,' I snapped. 'You know you're talking shit.'

'I always let people down in the end,' he said. 'You deserve better.'

He sighed deeply.

'You draw people to protect you. Your eyes – even when you laugh, there's a sadness at the back of them.'

'Great, cheers, fuck you,' I said. 'Best chat-up line ever. Not that you were ever trying to chat me up.' I dropped down onto the bed. We sat only a half metre away from each other, but I knew I would never touch him again.

'Look, love,' he said slowly. 'You're pregnant with another man's baby, who by all accounts really, *really* fucked up, but I think you're probably going to end up getting back together. He and I had a really good chat in the van the night of Monica's party, after you ran off—'

'What the fuck!'

'And – look, please listen. You're so stubborn. Just listen. And when you told me about room three, it all made sense – you know, you having problems trusting people after they let you down, and I know he really did, but he was going through so much—'

'Wow,' I said. 'Wow. Do you go to Nell's room, too, and tell her facts about herself? And Wendy's? Bramwell's?' I laughed – a hollow, bitter cackle.

'I don't know what to say to you,' he began. 'But I'm sorry if you feel like I've—'

I got him out of the room, locked the door. He banged on it a few times – 'Jane, we're all worried about you' – and I waited until I heard his footsteps recede, heard him talking to someone else, more footsteps on the stairs. More knocks, and more voices calling my name – Kelly's, Bramwell's, Monica's, Sadie's. They must have gone round to get Monica. She'd be loving all this. She would have told them all about how anxious I was, too weak and selfish to bring myself to go into a hospital, somewhere kids go with broken arms, to have my baby.

What was wrong with me? Why couldn't I just be

normal? How could I have been so stupid? Of course Robbie could see how mad I was, even though I'd tried to hide it. I could have got him to fall in love with me if I was normal. Sadie was right. I *was* going to topple. She'd said in her letter that medical professionals might be put in an 'impossible position'. Surely that meant I'd be sedated, or maybe even sectioned. That was what I deserved. I could barely look after myself. How could I be so stupid and arrogant to think I could also care for a baby? How could I have thought that Robbie and The Arch would be my salvation?

Music bled up from downstairs. Nell's voice sang the opening line of 'Baby, It's Cold Outside'. I heard Bramwell start to sing the next line. I lay on my back and gazed blindly up at the cracks and cobwebs on the ceiling, wondering how I could ever have dismissed them as part of the 'character' of The Arch, and not seen them for what they blatantly were: indicators that the ceiling might fall in, or that spiders might crawl into my mouth while I slept. I'd probably been swallowing one a night since I got here, to this so-called safe haven, where I could supposedly be whoever I wanted to be and bring up my baby amid love and care. It didn't matter that Sadie had come to ruin it all: it was a mirage all along anyway.

I thought of room three, only down the hall, which I still couldn't walk past without closing my eyes. The smell of my own sweat that day, how everything had gone into slow motion because I was so scared, the terrible realisation that although I was screaming, nobody was coming. Even though I knew now that it had only been Bramwell in the wardrobe, it made no difference: room three said everything anyone needed to know about Jane Wildgoose. Everything I trusted in would eventually let me down, including my own mind.

It became darker, and I heard the gathering thinning out downstairs. I stripped lengths of skin off my fingers until beads of blood lay glistening. I licked it all off and then worried that me swallowing blood would harm the baby. I realised I'd hardly drunk all day so mainlined nearly a litre of water from a bottle I filled in the sink, then had to pee in the sink less than half an hour later. I wasn't going to leave this room.

Many more people came and went outside the door in this time – my parents, Robbie again, Wendy, telling me that as my doula she should be by my side, shouting that I needed to eat something, to think of the baby and open the door. I ignored it all. Robbie would have told them all by now that I was in love with him, that he'd had to let me down gently. I couldn't bear the idea of them pitying me. Someone pushed some toast and peanut butter wrapped in tin foil through the gap under the door, but I threw it out of the window, even though I was starving – someone might have poisoned it in the hope I would be driven out of the room when I became ill from eating it, like when boiling water is poured on an ants' nest.

I must have dozed off briefly, then woke with my heart hammering. My mind skittered over worries as if perusing a menu at a restaurant: because everyone was preoccupied with me, the gas would be left on and we'd all die; because of the rare burger at The Sphere, the baby would have an even rarer syndrome I'd read about online, which might not be discovered until it was a teenager. In fact, how much had the baby moved today? My breathing shallow as I gripped my belly, I tried to remember when the last kick had been. I'd been so preoccupied all day. Wouldn't I have noticed the absence of kicks? Maybe not. How could I have let this slip, my only job at this point in time?

I jumped up and down, drank more water, totting up the minutes in fear. Finally, as the sun rose, I ate some chocolate I found at the bottom of my bag and the baby kicked. 'OK,' I said to myself out loud. 'OK. Have a sit down and a breathe, Jane. Just give yourself a breather.'

As I flopped onto the bed, I felt hot liquid gush from between my legs onto the duvet.

'Ah,' I said. *'Here's* the boiling water.'

Chapter Thirty-Seven

Wendy held my hand tightly as the midwives unpacked all their instruments and, for want of a better surface, laid them out on a cloth on top of the cardboard box I used as a bedside table. Wendy was the only one from The Arch I'd allowed into my room, and I wouldn't let go of her hand.

'There are about thirty people downstairs!' the older midwife, Alison, said to us all in disbelief. She'd done some of my pregnancy check-ups at the surgery. 'All very eager to help. Half of them comatose. You know them all, Jane, do you?' I shook my head.

'A birthing pool's on its way,' said Wendy to them, brightly. She almost sang it. 'Our friend's gone to get one in the van. It's going to be set up in the room across the hall.' She pressed play on some ambient music, which filled the room, and asked the midwives if she could turn off the main light as she'd prepared a 'lava lamp show'. In a minute, they said. They needed the normal light on to examine me.

'Well, your waters have definitely broken and you're four centimetres dilated,' said the other midwife, Vicki, withdrawing the speculum. 'You've probably still got a little while to go, so try and relax as much as you can. Why don't you go for a walk? Those gardens look lovely and big.'

'No,' I said, pulling my leggings back up. 'I can't leave this room.'

'Who's told you that?' asked Alison.

'Me!' I said. I felt alarm begin to rise in me. 'I've started to get cramps. Is that normal? Is everything all right?'

'You can't be asking that every time you're examined!' said Alison. She forced a smile. 'You're in the early stages, Jane. You're going on holiday, and you've not even packed your bags into the boot yet. We're all here with you. So try and chill. If there are any serious problems, we'll get you straight into hospital.'

'No, you won't,' shot Wendy.

'Won't we?' said Alison. She had dark hair tied into a bun, and never stopped moving: even when she wasn't bustling about with equipment, she was adjusting her sleeves, her watch, her collar.

'She's got a fear of hospitals,' Wendy said. 'It's in her notes. That's why she needs a home birth. Apparently, they said everything would be done to—'

'I know Jane doesn't like hospitals,' said Alison. 'I've spoken to her about this before. But I was always under the impression that the home birth was a preference. Are you saying you won't go in, even in an emergency?'

'I can't go in, under any circumstance,' I replied. 'Everyone said this would be OK.'

Vicki returned from the sink and opened my maternity notes. 'It's a waiting game now,' she said. 'We like labour to start within twenty-four hours of your waters breaking, or we have to look at inducing, so let's all cross our fingers that baby gets things going naturally.' She smiled.

'Do you mean induce me here, or in hospital?' I asked, panicking.

'Jane, calm down, and just go moment to moment,' said Alison, taking my notes from Vicki. 'And please get any ideas about what your birth's going to be like out of your head. You're thirty-seven weeks today, so already it's not what you were expecting, coming three weeks early. The more of a firm plan you have in your head, the more disappointed you'll be. I'm only saying this so you'll not give yourself a hard time if it doesn't go how you thought it would. It breaks my heart when mothers do that.'

'She's going to have it here,' Wendy said. 'She's going to have it here, and it's going to be in a pool.'

'Breathe,' whispered Wendy. 'All you have to do is breathe.' Excited voices bubbled outside my bedroom door, including Mum's. I heard Kelly saying she'd brought a bag of premature baby clothes, and some nappies. I heard the van pull up outside, then fierce knocking and Bramwell's voice: 'I've got a pool, duck. I'll set it up in Nell's room.' Alison marched out of the room, firmly shutting the door behind her.

'I can't do this,' I said, thrashing my head from side to side. 'I can't do it. I'm too hot. I can't breathe.'

Wendy reached into her pocket and handed me a Werther's Original. I put it in my mouth and sucked, waiting for calm to come. It didn't. Sweat broke out on my brow and arms and prickled my legs. They hadn't taken me not going into hospital seriously. Even Vicki, who was nice, hadn't said it definitely wouldn't happen.

Images rushed through my head. Me, in a labour ward with hard floors swarming with MRSA; medical staff bustling about, measuring, injecting, making me push for days onto starchy white sheets with nothing coming out except blood, refusing my screams for pain relief; them injecting anaesthetic for a caesarean and it not working but me being unable to tell them; my guts being cut out of me along with the baby; my screams, Wendy's, too, then the doctors' as they realise I'm haemorrhaging to death and the baby can't be saved either.

'Oh God,' I chanted, trying to gulp in air. *In for six, out for . . . what was it?* 'Oh God oh God oh God oh God. Get me in the pool. Everything'll be all right when I'm in the pool.'

'Well, three problems there,' said Alison, re-entering the room. 'The upstairs floor in this building won't hold the volume of water a birthing pool requires, you've not even started contracting yet, and anyway, he's brought you a bloody paddling pool.'

'I have to get in a pool!' I shouted. 'I have to!'

Suddenly Mum and Sadie ran in through the open door. Mum's stress rash was unprecedented. 'Do you need a birthing pool?' she gasped. 'We've got one at home, in the piano room. We hired it weeks ago, just in case. Dad's filling it up now.'

'No!' I howled.

'How far away is it?' asked Alison, starting to pack away her instruments.

'Stoney Walk,' replied Mum. 'The Old Vicarage.'

Bramwell cheerfully popped his head round the door frame, clutching a tiny grimy paddling pool covered with bright pink fish. 'Want me to carry on blowing this up, duck?' he asked.

'No!' everyone shouted.

'I can't go to Mum and Dad's,' I moaned, clinging to Wendy. 'I can't.'

'Well, make a decision,' said Alison. 'Where do you hate more – Mum and Dad's, or hospital? Tick tock.'

Chapter Thirty-Eight

Somehow, I managed to calm down a bit on the five-minute drive in the van with Wendy. I put my hand on top of hers on the gearstick so I had contact with her at all times. I now had a deep on-and-off pain in my belly, like the worst period cramps I could imagine. I remembered the talk with Becca and Kelly about how bad the pain would get. I didn't see how it could get much worse than this.

I wasn't prepared for the number of people at Mum and Dad's. Wendy and I opened the door to find a greeting party of Mum, Jonathan, Sadie, Bryan and Monica. Everyone was shouting different things. Did I need water? Tea? Mulled wine? Lemon drizzle cake?

'Is the baby OK? And are you OK?' asked Jonathan, running towards me waving the hypnobirthing CD.

'I think so, and I don't know,' I said, then he looked so overwhelmed I gave him a double thumbs-up.

Wendy pulled me through them all to the piano room, where Dad was pouring the last of the water into the birthing pool with the big saucepan they used to cook bolognese.

He was red-faced and panting, his shirt and trousers saturated with water. Alison and Vicki were laughing hysterically.

'Deserves a bloody medal, your dad,' said Alison. 'He didn't know there was a tube to fill it up with. He's done it all with a saucepan.'

Dad stood back and gave me a rueful grin, then looked down, like a child who'd forgotten his only line in the nativity. I waddled towards him and he enveloped me in his soaking arms.

Mum opened the door breathlessly, and told us all that she and Sadie were preparing a three-course meal for everybody, and did they want the lemon juice already on their smoked salmon, or would they rather squeeze it on themselves? Alison and Vicki dissolved into laughter again, and Wendy took Mum aside and told her the best thing she could do would be to get me a cup of tea and a cheese sandwich, get Dad upstairs and into some dry clothes, and keep everyone out of the room.

The pain had ramped up and was now coming in waves. I accepted some paracetamol the midwives offered after grilling them about its safety. I lay down on a sheet on the chaise longue, and Vicki got out her machine to monitor the baby's heartbeat. 'You're moving on nicely now,' she said. 'Baby might even come today.'

'What?' I said. 'You mean, it might *not* come today?'

'It's eight at night, lovie,' she smiled. 'Everyone loses track of time in labour. Your waters broke at about eight this morning. It was probably all that marching around yesterday that got things moving. So I think it will probably come tomorrow. I was joking about it being today.'

Wendy passed my bikini out of the bag she'd packed for me. 'We'll get you into that pool yet,' she said. 'You can only control what you can control.'

I asked her to get Mum.

Mum came in holding a tray with four different plates of food on it, all for me. 'Sadie made the lemon drizzle cake,' she whispered. 'So you don't have to eat it if you don't want to. She doesn't put enough sugar in it anyway.'

I pulled her down towards me. 'I'm scared, Mum,' I said. 'It hurts so much.'

She stroked my face. She was shaking. 'Darling, it's going to be OK. We're all just so excited,' she said. Then, 'I've never told you this, but because giving birth to Amanda had been so traumatic, when I had you I just crossed my legs and thought, *Well, if I don't ever uncross them, the baby can't come out.* But, believe me, when the time comes, you don't have a choice. Imagine, I suppose, a demon in your body that's fighting to get out. It's going to get out! So there's nothing to worry about.'

'That's helped, Mum, thanks,' I said. 'I'll think of my baby as a demon.'

She leapt to the piano and started to play Rachmaninov, her hands sweeping up and down the keys, her body bending at the waist. 'This'll speed things along!' she said, on the verge of hysteria. 'Demon, are you listening? Come out, come out, wherever you are!'

Wendy clapped her hands. 'I'm not sure this is helping. Could you perhaps go and make some more food for Jane?'

'Don't know any Michael Bublé, do you?' said Vicki, as Mum clambered down from the piano stool.

*

Mum gone, Bryan materialised with a tray of mulled wine. 'Your mother says you're feeling scared,' he said. 'It's fine for you to have one of these. Surgeon's honour.'

The midwives tutted him away and the tray was placed on the floor until the smell started to make me retch, and Wendy put it at the bottom of the stairs outside the door, where moments later I heard a brief commotion as Sadie knocked it over, coming down from the toilet.

'That's the first time you've smiled since you got here,' said Wendy, squeezing my hand.

The sky was black and I could see stars through a tiny gap in the curtains.

'I think I'm having contractions now,' I said. 'It's killing. Can't I get in the pool?' In the mayhem since I'd got here, I hadn't even managed to get in yet.

'We just need to listen to baby's heartbeat for a bit longer before you can get in,' explained Alison. 'How do you feel about some gas and air?'

I remembered Kelly's story about having gas and air and seeing inside her own body.

'No,' I replied.

'Breathe,' said Wendy. 'Breathe. Now, do you think you want the placenta made into tablets, like we talked about?'

'Yep,' I said. 'Aaaargh, fuck, this hurts now.'

'I've found someone who'll do it at this short notice, but the placenta needs to go in a fridge as soon as the baby's born, till she can come and collect it.'

'Mum'll be fine with that,' I panted. 'God, I am really hurting now, guys. Please!'

'Well, I can tell you now that you won't be putting it in

a hospital fridge,' said Alison. 'That's nice for a midwife who's just come off her shift, isn't it? Reaches for her tuna-mayo sandwich and gets a placenta in a Sainsbury's bag?'

'What do you mean, hospital fridge!' I shouted.

Wendy came and stroked my head. She brought her face down next to mine and spoke to me softly. 'I won't let it happen,' she said. 'You can always refuse to go in. It's your right. We can do free birthing. That'd just be me and you. You're in control, OK? Not anyone in this house, including Jonathan. Until you decide, we'll take the lead from Alison and Vicki, but you can make them go whenever you want. You know your own body more than anyone.'

'No, I don't!' I cried. 'I'm scared of my body and I'm scared of my brain! Sadie'll section me if I don't go in!'

'I don't think she can do that, can she?' Wendy asked the midwives.

'It's very unlikely,' said Alison. 'I think possibly they could section the mother, but only if a psychiatrist said she wasn't fit to make a decision—'

'I'm not!' I shouted. 'I mean, I am, I am!'

'Should I get Monica?' asked Wendy. 'Maybe if you have a chat to her about your fears—'

'No!' I shouted. 'That's literally the only thing that would make all this worse!'

The explosions of pain got closer and closer together, until I accepted the gas and air, which only made me feel even more sick.

'Can I get in the pool now?' I begged.

They said that sorry, I couldn't, as they needed to keep listening to the baby's heartbeat.

Sadie popped her head round the door like she was appearing in a children's TV programme.

'Just wanted to say that I love you!'

'Not now!' called Wendy.

The door closed softly.

Wendy got her phone out. 'Everyone back at The Arch wants to know what's happening.'

'Tell them it fucking hurts!' I wailed.

Mum came back in, carrying an entire trifle in a glass dish. 'Would this help?' she asked falteringly.

'I'm not sure trifle's the thing at the moment,' said Vicki.

'At least there's room for the placenta now I've taken it out of the fridge,' said Mum. 'Jonathan's been listening outside the door the whole time. He won't leave his post, like Greyfriars Bobby. We're all too nervous to eat!'

'Get Dad,' I shouted.

I clasped his hand. 'They're talking about me going into hospital.'

'You can do it,' he replied. 'You've done it before.'

'Yeah, about a trillion times when I was a kid! That's the problem!'

'I'm sorry, Janey,' he said. 'I just always wanted to make sure, to be a hundred per cent sure. I'm so sorry if it was me that made you hate them so much. But you're stronger than me. Look how you've got through this pregnancy.' He smiled. 'Want some trifle?'

'No thanks, Dad,' I said, tears filling my eyes.

*

Vicki and Alison convened in the corner, near Dad's stamp collections, and I could tell it wasn't good. Alison came and took the baby's heartbeat again, bustled about near my nether regions a bit and then re-joined Vicki, who was looking through my notes.

'Jane,' Alison said, coming back over. 'We're going to tell you what's happening, and we don't want you to panic, then we're going to tell you what we strongly recommend you do.'

I nodded helplessly like a child, feeling I would never get past this moment.

'Baby's heartbeat's a bit irregular for our liking, and there's meconium in your waters. It could mean baby's getting distressed, and we need an obstetrician to take a look at you as soon as possible.'

'How soon can they get here?' I asked.

'Obstetricians don't come out to home births,' Vicki said gently. Alison took my hand. Vicki made a call on her mobile in the corner and I heard the words 'ambulance' and 'paramedics on standby'.

'I can't go to hospital to have it,' I sobbed. 'You don't understand. I'm ... there's something wrong with my brain. It's not a logical thing, it's not to do with how much I love the baby, because I do, I really do. I just can't do it.'

'You must do what's right for you,' said Wendy.

Vicki and even Alison stood motionless. The only movement in the room was Wendy stroking my hair in long, deep strokes, from the crown of my head to the nape of my neck.

'It's up to you,' she whispered. 'It's up to you.'

'Fuck!' I screamed. 'Fuck!'

With those primal screams, everyone suddenly thought they had a right to barge in. I twisted in agony with every contraction, on all fours, squeezing my eyes shut, unable to concentrate on anything except gripping the edge of the chaise longue with the whole of my upper-body strength. Every time I opened my eyes there was a different person in front of me. They had a tiny window to try and convince me to go into hospital, like a horrific speed-dating show, until the next contraction came, and I was transported into a world of pain that shut down all my senses.

Mum was first, panicked, begging me to do it, saying I'd regret it forever if something went wrong. Dad did his calm voice, the one I knew he used when he told companies they had to file for bankruptcy, telling me he was proud of how far I'd come. Bryan gave me dry facts about hospitals: how clean they were, how they were highly trained experts. Monica talked psychobabble, stuff about vulnerability that I didn't understand, then Sadie was next. She said she hadn't thought through the big reveal that she was the donor and was sorry, that she couldn't wait to meet her grandchild, that she knew I was capable of going into hospital.

An even stronger contraction took hold of my body, contorting it like a lamp post after a car crash; my lower half felt like white-hot, twisting metal and the pain was breathtaking. I was screaming words like I was speaking in tongues. When it lifted, I felt like I'd been washed up on a shore – disorientated, calmer, but knowing it was only a brief respite until the next wave. I suddenly yearned for Kelly.

When I opened my eyes, there was Jonathan. The last one.

'You've not got long,' I said, 'till the next contraction.'

'I think the next one'll kill you, actually,' he said.

'Do you?' I asked. Everyone looked at him in horror.

'Oh, yeah,' he said. 'Loads of women have died from contractions. And if you make it into hospital, you won't get out.'

I nodded.

'You'll fall off the stretcher as you get out of the ambulance,' he said. 'If you don't fall, they'll drop you. You know like when magicians pull the tablecloth out from under all the stuff? It'll be like that, but the stuff'll be you, and there won't be a table to land on, there'll just be the ground, with old dressings on it, and you'll get an infection from one and die.'

'Or maybe the ambulance guys'll slip on a dressing?' I said.

'Oh yeah,' he said, taking my hands. 'They'll slip on the dressings, and they'll die, too. They'll slip and die first, in a big heap, then you'll land on top like a cherry, and die. And it'll be all your fault. Our fault, for getting pregnant. So—'

I could feel another contraction coming and started to brace myself. For a brief moment, just before I went into my other world, his eyes were wild with fright.

When it had ended, he was still gripping my hands. 'I can't do it, can I?' I gasped.

'No way!' he said. 'It'll definitely kill you. So just stay here. Put on the telly.' He was squeezing my hands so tight his knuckles were white, flecked with pink.

'Can I?' I said.

'I've told you,' he replied. 'You'll die, we'll play "The

Birdie Song" at your funeral and, y'know, we'll be sad for two or three months, but we'll all live.'

He clutched the fucking hypnobirthing CD in his other hand. I punched it to the corner of the room.

'Can I?' I whispered.

'I don't know, Jane,' he said, shaking his head. The tears fell as if from a sprinkler from each side of his face. 'I don't know.'

Spring

Chapter Thirty-Nine

Mum and Sadie hurried from group to group, carrying plates of flapjacks stacked like Jenga pieces. The garden was packed full of guests, spilling out of the marquee onto the grass, chinking glasses in the lemony sunlight. They marvelled and waved at Julia, who stayed tight in my arms like the ball in a hip socket, her mouth clamped over my aching nipple, her curls like tiny shells beneath my fingers, her white dress with its intricately embroidered yoke already covered in milk and baby sick.

'You and Amanda wore it. It's not up for discussion,' Mum had said. 'I accept you're not going to get married, so do this little thing for me.'

I remembered to swap the hair bobble to my other wrist, so I knew which breast to feed Julia from after her nap. People were still arriving en masse from the church, taking glasses of prosecco from Amanda and Dad. Dad, who sang 'Frère Jacques' to Julia every night, while Mum sterilised the breast pump and made me yet another round of toast while I grabbed any sleep I could.

I didn't recognise everyone: were some of them just people from the street who fancied a free sandwich? I spied

Stuart and Monica – holding hands – then Bramwell, Nell and Wendy.

The bell-ringers arrived in a raucous clump. I owed them thanks for the fact that they'd rung the chorus of the Beatles' 'Julia' as we'd all exited the church, the peals echoing all over the valley. My London mates followed, Megan giving me a big wave. I blew her a kiss. She was having dinner with me later. I couldn't wait – especially as she'd left her monster child Art back in London with her husband.

I scanned the garden for Kelly. I was so eager to tell her about the birth, and every time I'd seen her it had been impossible – there had been too many people around, or I'd been too tired. I felt like I needed hours. I now understood why birth stories were an 'are you sitting comfortably? Well, I'm still not' situation, far too significant to be hurried. There were details that were too big and too small to be anything other than felt. There were elements I couldn't remember, like what had happened to my placenta in the end, and who'd been holding my hand out of Jonathan and Wendy when Julia was finally born; and there were elements that were crystal clear, like me trying to take one faltering step from the chaise longue, failing, then succeeding. Then another step, and another, towards the door of the piano room, and them all applauding as I hobbled down the drive and into the waiting ambulance. I remembered telling Vicki and Alison, when they came to visit Julia and me on the ward, about how I still hadn't finished Sharon Osbourne's autobiography. Vicki had informed me with a broad smile that I had no hope of that happening now, that I'd be lucky to even wash my hair again.

Jonathan raced over with a white muslin. 'Sorry it took so long. I was looking in the wrong bloody bag. It's not too late, is it?'

'Yeah,' I replied. 'When someone needs a muslin, it's *because* it's too late!'

'Sorry,' he said. 'Sorry.'

'Hey, it's OK,' I said.

'What do you need?' he stuttered. 'I can get her blanket.'

'She doesn't need anything,' I said, looking down at her sleeping face. 'She's got a blanket. You can just hold her if you want.'

He took her gently and started to rock her in his arms, walking.

'You don't need to rock her,' I said. 'She's asleep. Just sit down.'

He ran his thumb over her head, then stopped over her fontanelle. 'It's pulsating again,' he said. 'I definitely think we should mention it to the health visitor.'

'Do you think I haven't asked about that?' I laughed. 'It's completely normal, so shut up and have a nice afternoon. Don't give me anything else to bloody worry about.'

He sat down, cradling Julia in his arms.

'I think about her all the time when I'm in London,' he said. 'I just can't stop – it's like, well, it's like when we first met. Worse, actually. I mean, better.'

'I know,' I said.

'Can I come up more?' he asked.

'Let's keep it at weekends,' I said. Then he looked too sad, so I added, 'For the *moment*. I'll be in my own flat at some point, if I can ever prise Julia from Dad's grip.'

'My mum's put Dad's files back in the little room in the

annexe, by the way,' he said. 'She knows we won't be living there. She gets it.'

We looked at Julia's face.

'Oh, Monica's asking if you want to come back for therapy, now the baby's been born,' he said. 'I said I didn't know.'

'No!' I said. 'I'm starting CBT soon. On the NHS. With someone Mum doesn't bell-ring with. Turns out Doctor Lingard knew better than me that I needed to go on the waiting list. Well, she did once she'd met Monica.'

Nell and Bramwell came over in high spirits, with a glass of prosecco for me. 'Stuart's up for us lot doing some fundraising for the bookshop,' said Nell. 'Getting new customers in.'

'Then Nell asked your mum if there was anything vegan,' Bramwell said, 'and she offered us some coriander straight from the earth!'

I stood up. 'Actually,' I said, grabbing my bag, 'could you keep her for a little while, Jonathan? She'll sleep for ages now she's had a feed.'

'Me?' he said. 'But—'

'You'll be fine!' I called, running down the drive. 'I won't be long.'

The Arch already looked different. The banners were gone from the outside, the door had been painted a deep blue, and Sadie's donation had started to be put to good use: there was a smart new sign outside. *The Arch: A Community Resource Centre.* The future of The Arch had remained precarious until the day Andrew had thought to search for the will of the original owner, who – it turned out – had left the building to the council only on the condition that it be used 'for the good of the community'. Since the council didn't provide the services The Arch would, it was all systems go.

Robbie had promised to 'pop in' to the christening, but we all knew he wouldn't be able to drag himself away. There he was, pacing each room to measure it, jotting things down on a clipboard. The door was open, and Foley Joe was packing a box, his back to me. A dark-haired boy of about seven or eight ran down the stairs towards Robbie.

'There's a praying woman in the garden!' I heard him say.

'He means the statue,' laughed a blonde woman, following the boy into the room.

They spoke with French accents. The boy ran and hid behind a cardboard box. *I see you*, mimed Robbie, chuckling, and the boy jumped out, squealing. Then Robbie was back in his own world, mapping out where everything would go, his hands dancing like a conductor's. Xavier hid again, but Robbie didn't see, and soon his mother scooped him up and carried him into the kitchen.

As I made my way round to the fire escape, I got a text from Kelly: *You better hurry up with this birth story babe. Jonathan won't tell me anything. Becca reckons four stitches, I reckon eighteen.* I smiled and jogged up the black metal staircase. This was the first time I'd been away from Julia since she was born. I heard Robbie's and Foley Joe's distant voices from the main hall as I walked along the upstairs corridor, the creaky floorboards exactly as I remembered them.

Beams of sunlight streamed onto the landing as I turned

the doorknob to room three. The bed and the wardrobe were in exactly the same places, but the bed was covered with one of Wendy's crocheted blankets, and the dirty Babygro on the wall had gone, of course, as had the tiles, the bricks and the table. I walked in even steps to the wardrobe and opened it slowly, breathing deeply. Inside, it was completely empty, apart from a scrap of white paper right at the back, folded in half. I picked it up with shaking hands and opened it. *Well done, duck. Bramwell.*

I put it carefully in my pocket and looked at my watch. Julia would be awake soon for her next feed. I closed the door to the wardrobe, lay down on Wendy's blanket, and opened the penultimate page of Sharon Osbourne's auto-biography.

Acknowledgements

First of all, a massive thank you to my editor, Lettice Franklin, whose insight, patience and humour are second to none, and who made me feel like I had a wise pal by my side throughout the writing process. Thank you also to Alan Samson, Georgia Goodall, Alainna Hadjigeorgiou, Folayemi Adebayo and all at Orion who have worked on this book. Thanks also to Holly Kyte for copy-editing, Jade Craddock for proofreading and Holly Ovenden for the cover design.

Thank you to my agent, Robert Kirby, who is always wise, honest and entertaining. Your support means a lot to me. Thank you to all at United Agents who have supported me throughout the writing process and, as always, to Amanda Emery.

On the research side, thanks to John Robins for answering my many texts about Kelly vaping, normally within thirty seconds of me sending them. Thank you to Jenny Fleming at JAA Architects, who gave me lots of time and answers about the position of The Arch and the developer, and to Laura Mucha and Pete Farnham for the help with planning permission and land law. Thanks to Mark Steel,

Lyndsay Rowan and Josie Long for their information about squats and organising protests, and a heartfelt thank you to Carl Chapple, who spent hours telling me about his experience in social enterprises. Thanks to Beth Holden for the help with the legal side of The Arch, and a big thank you to Neelo Shravat for the information about family law.

Thank you to Steve and Sue – Steve for the information about the Post Office and both of you for always being there for our family. Thanks to Liz Brown, Jemma Ashman and all my friends who had home births and gave me the details of how they work, and to Nia Kelly and Kate Barton for their very thoughtful help around the scan and birth chapters. Thank you to Jo Brand, and her mum, for the information around custody and social services. Thank you to Paul Burke for the help with the advertising element, and to Lou Yates for the gardening information. Thank you to Carol Scott and Ruth Steadman for help with Jane's struggles. Thank you to Xand van Tulleken, Carys Nathoo and Mike Wozniak for advice and help with the medical elements.

Thank you to Henry Widdicombe, who gave me kind permission to use his story from the Hay Festival for Jonathan.

Thank you so much to Sian Harries, Will Smith, Chris Neill and Daniel Kitson for reading various drafts and giving incredibly valuable feedback, and to Jeany Spark for lending me her computer when I spilt camomile tea on my Mac and thought I was going to explode with stress. For thoughts on early incarnations, thank you to Kate Grey, Callie Suttie, Viv Suttie, Maisie Bourke, Joel Morris and Jason Hazeley.

Thank you to Jonathan, Justine, Karen and all at Bookseller Crow for your ongoing support, to J.B. Morrison, and to Scarthin Books in Cromford, which inspired the layout and atmosphere of the bookshop in the novel – but is far busier and a wonderful place to spend time! Thank you to Mel and Jon – working on the very final draft at that desk in your peaceful apartment was the reason I got to the end, along with cake.

For talking elements of the story through with me, thank you to Polly Sullivan, Anne Richardson, Zoe Kingston, Jane Watkins and Annabelle Fish.

Thank you to my mum, dad and sister. And most of all, thank you from the bottom of my heart to my family – Elis, Beti and Steffan – for giving me the space and time to write this.

About the Author

Isy Suttie is a comedian, actress and writer. She has written for the *Guardian*, the *Observer*, the *New Statesman*, *Red* and *Glamour*. She appears regularly on BBC Radio 4, where her show *Pearl and Dave* won a Gold Sony Award in 2013. Her TV credits include Dobby in *Peep Show* and Esther in *Shameless*, plus appearances on *8 Out of 10 Cats*, *Would I Lie To You?* and *Q.I.* A three-time British Comedy Award nominee, her short stories have appeared in *A Love Letter To Europe* and *Dead Funny: Encore*. Her memoir, *The Actual One*, was published by Orion in 2015.

Help us make the next generation of readers

We – both author and publisher – hope you enjoyed this book. We believe that you can become a reader at any time in your life, but we'd love your help to give the next generation a head start.

Did you know that 9 per cent of children don't have a book of their own in their home, rising to 13 per cent in disadvantaged families*? We'd like to try to change that by asking you to consider the role you could play in helping to build readers of the future.

We'd love you to think of sharing, borrowing, reading, buying or talking about a book with a child in your life and spreading the love of reading. We want to make sure the next generation continue to have access to books, wherever they come from.

And if you would like to consider donating to charities that help fund literacy projects, find out more at **www.literacytrust.org.uk** and **www.booktrust.org.uk**.

THANK YOU

*As reported by the National Literacy Trust